C.J. CHERRYH

CYTEEN

"Unmistakable weight and ambition . . . readers will find much to enjoy in this striking and pleasant surprise from Cherryh."

—*Publishers Weekly*

"At once a psychological novel, a murder mystery, and an examination of power on the grand scale, encompassing light-years and outsize lifetimes [that] only hint at the richness of CYTEEN. Cherryh goes deep into political and scientific conflicts . . . examines the differing natures of born-men and azi, deals with the subtle shadings of love, desire, kinship."

—*Locus*

"Complex and thoughtful. Churning with political intrigue and heavyweight powerbrokering, thick with knotty conspiracies and plot."

—*Kirkus Reviews*

"A multi-dimensional epic . . . one of the best science fiction novels of the year."

—*Other Realms*

"A massive, multi-faceted novel that tackles a variety of ethical, social, and political issues. . . . Cherryh's world building is ambitious and her main characterizations are well individualized . . . ultimately fascinating in concept and detail. Decidedly a major work."

—*Booklist*

"A future as detailed as that of Herbert's *Dune*, with dozens of complex characters . . . all the paranoid tension of a spy thriller . . . and the plot sheds new light on several of Cherryh's important earlier novels."

—*Newsday*

Also by C.J. Cherryh

Cyteen: The Betrayal
Cyteen: The Vindication*

Published by
POPULAR LIBRARY   **forthcoming*

C.J. CHERRYH
CYTEEN:
THE REBIRTH

POPULAR LIBRARY

An Imprint of Warner Books, Inc.

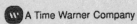 A Time Warner Company

POPULAR LIBRARY EDITION

Copyright © 1988 by C.J. Cherryh
All rights reserved.

Popular Library®, the fanciful P design, and Questar® are registered trademarks of Warner Books, Inc.

Cover illustration by Don Maitz
Book design by H. Roberts

This work is volume one in a trilogy first published in hardcover in one volume entitled CYTEEN.

Popular Library books are published by
Warner Books, Inc.
666 Fifth Avenue
New York, N.Y. 10103

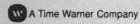 A Time Warner Company

Printed in the United States of America

Originally published in hardcover by Warner Books.
First Printed in Paperback: March, 1989

10 9 8 7 6 5 4 3

CYTEEN:
THE REBIRTH

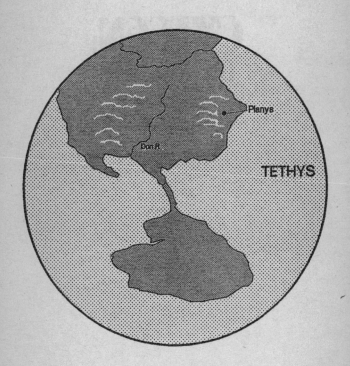

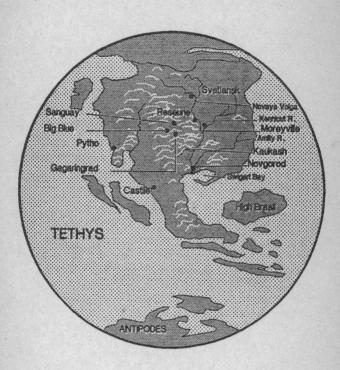

Verbal Text from:
A QUESTION OF UNION
Union Civics Series: #3

Reseune Educational Publications: 9799-8734-3
approved for 80+

Union, as conceived in the Constitution of 2301 and developed through the addition and amalgamation of station and world governments thereafter, was structured from the beginning as a federal system affording maximum independence to the local level. To understand Union, therefore, one must start with the establishment of a typical local government, which may be any system approved by a majority of qualified naturally born inhabitants. Note: inhabitants, not citizens. The only segments of the population disenfranchised for such elections are minors and azi, who are not counted as residents for purposes of an Initial Ballot of Choice, although azi may later be enfranchised by the local government.

An Initial Ballot of Choice is the normal civil procedure by which any polity becomes a candidate for representation in Union. The Ballot establishes the representative local Constitutional Congress, which will either validate an existing governmental structure as representing the will of the electorate, or create an entirely new structure which may then be ratified by the general Initial Electorate. Second of the duties of the Constitutional Congress after the election is to assign citizen numbers and register legal voters, i.e., all voters qualified by age and citizen numbers to cast their ballots for the Council of Nine and for the General Council of Union. Third and final duty of the Congress is the reporting of the census and the voter rolls to the Union Bureau of Citizens.

Subsequent Ballots of Choice and subsequent Congresses can be held on a majority vote of the local electorate, or by order of the Supreme Court of Union after due process of law. In such a re-polling of the local electorate, all native-born residents and emigrated or immigrated residents are eligible in that vote, including azi who hold modified citizen status.

Within Union, the Council of Nine represents the nine occupational electorates of Union, across all Union citizen rolls. Within those occupational electorates, votes are weighted according to registered level of expertise: i.e., most voters in, say, the Science electorate are factored at one, but a lab tech with a certain number of years' experience may merit a two; while a scientist of high professional rating may merit as high as ten, depending on professional credentials achieved for this purpose—a considerable difference, since the factors are applied in a formula and each increment is considerable. An individual can always appeal his ranking to peer review, but most advances are virtually set with the job and experience.

When a seat on the Council of Nine falls vacant, the Secretary of the Bureau regulated by that seat will assume the position of proxy until that electorate selects a replacement; or the outgoing Councillor may appoint a different proxy.

Members of the Nine can be challenged for election at any time by the filing of an opposition candidate with sufficient signatures of the Bureau on a supporting petition.

Recently the rise of rival political parties has tended to make the vacancy of a seat the occasion of a partisan contention, and a challenge to a seat almost inevitably partisan. This has rendered the position of Secretary potentially more vulnerable, and increases the importance of the internal Bureau support structure and the administrative professionals which are necessary for smooth operation through changes in upper-tier administration.

The Councillor sets policy in a Bureau. The Secretary, who is appointed, frames guidelines and issues administrative orders. The various department heads implement the or-

ders and report up the chain through the Secretary to the Councillor and through the Councillor to the Council of Nine.

The Council of Nine can initiate and vote on bills, particularly as touches the budget of the Bureaus, and national policy toward outsiders, but a unanimous vote by the delegation of any local unit can veto a law which applies only to that unit to the exclusion of others, which then will require a two-thirds majority in the General Council and a majority of the Council of Nine to override. The principle of local rule thus takes precedence over all but the most unanimous vote in Union.

A simple majority of the Nine is sufficient to pass a bill into law, unless overridden by a simple vote of the General Council of Union, which consists of one ambassador and a certain number of representatives from each world or station in the Union, according to population.

The Council of Nine presides in the General Council: the Council of Worlds (meaning the General Council without the Nine) can initiate and pass bills with a simple majority, until overridden by a vote of the Nine.

The Council of Worlds presently has seventy-six members, including the Representatives of Cyteen. When the Nine are present, i.e., when it is a General Council, the Representatives of Cyteen originally might observe but might not, until 2377, speak or vote, which was the concession granted by Cyteen as the seat of government, to run until the population of Union doubled that of Cyteen—a figure reached in the census of that year.

Certain entities within Union constitute non-represented units: these are Union Administrative Territories, which do not vote in local elections, and which are subject to their own internal regulations, having the same sovereignty as any planet or station within Union.

An Administrative Territory is immune to local law, is taxed only at the Union level, and maintains its own police force, its own legal system, and its own administrative rules which have the force of law on its own citizens. An Administrative Territory is under the oversight of the Bureau within which its principal activity falls; and is subject to Bureau intervention under certain carefully drawn rules, which fall *within the Territorial charter and which may differ from Territory to Territory.*

No discussion of the units of Union government could be complete without a mention of the unique nature of Cyteen, which has the largest concentration of population, which constitutes the largest section of any given electorate, which is also the site of Union government—over which, of course, Cyteen has no jurisdictional rights; and which is the site of three very powerful Administrative Territories.

Certain people argue that there is too much Union government on Cyteen, and that it cannibalizes local rights. Certain others say that Cyteen has far too much influence in Union, and point out that Cyteen has always held more than one seat of the Nine. Certain others, mostly Cyteeners, say that the whole planet is likely to become a government reserve, and that the amount of influence Cyteen has in Union is only fair, considering that Cyteen has become the support of the whole government, which means that Union is so powerful and the influence of the Nine so great on the planet, that everyone in Union has a say in how Cyteen is run.

Another point of contention is the use of Cyteen resources both by Union at large and by Administrative Territories, which pay no local tax and which are not within Cyteen authority. The Territories point out that their economic return to the Cyteen economy is greater than the resources they absorb; and that indeed, Cyteen's viability as a planet has been largely due to the economic strength of the several Territories on Cyteen. . . .

CHAPTER
I

The small jet touched down at Planys airfield and rolled to the front of the little terminal, and Justin unbuckled his safety belt, moving in the same sense of unreality that had been with him since the plane left the ground at Reseune.

He had thought until that very moment that some agency would stop him, that the game was giving him permission to travel and then maneuvering him or Jordan into some situation that would cancel it.

He was still scared. There were other possibilities he could think of, more than a psych of either one of them—like the chance of Reseune creating a situation they could use to harm Jordan or worsen his conditions. He tried to put thoughts like that in the back of his mind, where they only warned him to be careful; like the thoughts that armored him against the sudden recall, the sudden reversal of the travel permit, even this far into the matter.

One had to live like that. Or go crazy.

He picked up his briefcase and his bag from the locker while his Security escort were coming forward—it was the plane that shuttled back and forth between Reseune and Planys at need, a corporate plane with the Infinite Man symbol on its tail, not the red and white emblem of RESEUNEAIR, which carried passengers and freight over most of the continent and a few points overseas. Reseune Labs owned this one, even if it was a RESEUNEAIR crew that flew it; and the fact that this plane was, like *RESEUNE ONE*, private—kept its cargoes and its passenger lists from the scrutiny of the Bureau of Transportation.

A long, long flight from Reseune, over a lonely ocean. A plane with an airlock and a suction filter in the lock, and the need for D-suits and masks before they could go out there. He took his out of the locker, white, thin plastic, hotter than hell to wear, because the generic fits-everyone sort had no circulating system, just a couple of bands you put around your chest and shoulders to keep the thing from inflating like a balloon and robbing you of the air the helmet gave you.

The co-pilot took him in hand and checked his seals, collar, wrists, ankles and front, then patted him on the shoulder, pointing to the airlock. The generic suits had no com either, and you shouted or you signed.

So he picked up his baggage, likewise sealed in a plastic carry-bag, and looked to see if Security was going to let him out there.

No. One was going to lock through with him. That was how closely they were watching him.

So he went into the airlock and waited through the cycle, and went out down the ladder with the Security guard at his back, down where the ground crews, in custom-fitted D-suits, were attending the plane.

There was very little green in Planys. Precip towers did their best to keep the plants alive, but it was still raw and new here, still mostly red rock and blue scrub and woolwood. Ankyloderms were the predominant phylum of wildlife on this continent, as platytheres were in the other, in the unbridged isolation that had given Cyteen two virtually independent ecologies—except, always, woolwood and a few other windborne pests that propagated from virtually any fiber that got anywhere there was dirt and moisture.

Flora reinforced with absorbed silicates and poisonous with metals and alkaloids, generating an airborne profusion of fibers carcinogenic in Terran respiratory systems even in minute doses: the plants would kill you either in minutes or in years, depending on whether you were fool enough to eat a leaf or just unlucky enough to get an unguarded breath of air. The carbon monoxide in the air was enough to do the job on its own. But the only way to get killed by the fauna was to stand in its path, and the only way it ever died, the old joke ran, was when two of equal size met head to head and starved to death.

It was easy to forget what Cyteen was until you touched the outback.

And there was so profound a sense of desolation about this place. You looked away from the airport and the buildings, and it was Cyteen, that was all, raw and deadly.

Jordan lived in this place.

There was no taking the suits off until they got to Planys Annex, and the garage, and another airlock, where you had to brush each other off with some violence while powerful suction fans made the cheap suits rattle and flutter. You had to lift and stretch the elastic straps to get any fiber out of them, then endure a hosing down in special detergent, lock through, strip the suits and step up onto a grating without touching the outside surfaces—while the decontamination crew saw to your baggage.

Damn, he thought, anxious until the second door was shut and he and his escort were in a hall that looked more like a storm-tunnel at home—gray concrete, completely gray.

It was better on the upper floor: green-painted concrete, decent lighting. No windows . . . there was probably no window in all of Planys. A small concession to decor in a few green plastic hanging plants, cheap framed prints on the walls.

Building A, it said occasionally, brown stencil letters a meter high, obscured here and there by the hanging pictures. Doors were brown-painted metal. There was, anomaly, an office with curtained hallward windows. That was the one that said, in a small engraved-plastic sign: Dr. Jordan Warrick, Administrator, Educational Division.

A guard opened that door for him. He walked in, saw Paul at the desk, Paul, who looked—like Paul, that was all: he was dyeing his hair—who got up and took his hand and hugged him.

Then he knew it was real. "Go on in," Paul said into his ear, patting him on the shoulder. "He knows you're here."

He went to the door, opened it and went in. Jordan met him there with open arms. For a long, long while they just held on to each other without saying a word. He wept. Jordan did.

"Good to see you," Jordan said finally. "Damn, you've grown."

"You're looking good," Justin said, at arms' length, trying not to see the lines around the eyes and the mouth. Jordan felt thinner, but he was still fit and hard—perhaps, Justin thought, Jordan had done what he had done, from the day Denys had called him into his office and told him he had gotten a travel permit—run lap upon lap in the gym, determined not to have his father see him out of shape.

"I wish Grant could have come."

"So did he." It was hard to keep his composure. He got it back. And did not add that there was reason to worry, that Grant was more scared than Grant wanted to let on, being left alone at Reseune—azi, and legally under Reseune's authority. "Maybe some other trip."

This trip *had* to work. They *had* to make it as smooth and easy as possible, to get others in future. He had an idea every paper in his briefcase was going to be gone over again by every means Security had here; and that when he got back to Reseune they were going to do it all again, and strip-search him the way they had before he boarded the plane, very, very thoroughly. But he was here. He had the rest of the day and till noon tomorrow. Every minute he spent with Jordan, two high-clearance Security agents would be sitting in the same room; but that was all right, right as the cameras and the bugs that invaded every moment of his life and left nothing private.

So he walked over to the conference table with Jordan, he sat down as Paul came in and joined them, he said: "I brought my work. They'll get my briefcase up here in a bit. I'm really anxious for you to have a look at some of it."

It's a waste of time, Yanni had said, in Yanni's inimitable way, when he had begged Yanni to give him a clearance to bring his latest design with him. And then cleared it by that afternoon. *This'll cost you,* the note Yanni sent him had said. *You'll pay me in overtime.*

"How have things been going?" Jordan asked him, asking him more than that with the anxiousness in his eyes, the way a son and a psych student could read and Security and voice-stress analyzers might possibly miss.

Is there some condition to this I don't know about?

"Hell," he said, and laughed, letting the tension go, "too damn well. *Too* damn well, all year. Last year was hell. I imagine you picked that up. I couldn't do anything right, everything I touched fell apart—"

A lot of problems I can't mention.

"—but it's like all of a sudden something sorted itself out. For one thing, they took me off real-time work. I felt guilty about that—which is probably a good indicator how bad it was; I was taking too long, I was too tired to think straight, just no good at it, that's all, and too tied up in it to turn it loose. Yanni thought I could break through, you know, some of my problems that way, I know damn well what he was trying to do; then he R&R'd me into production again. Until for some reason he had a change of heart and shoved me back into R&D, on a long, long lead-time. Where I do just fine, thanks."

They had talked so long in time-lag he found himself doing it again, condensing everything into packets, with a little worry about Security objecting in every sentence. But here he had more freedom. They promised him that. There was no outside eavesdropping to worry about and they could talk about anything—that offered no hint of escape plans or hidden messages to be smuggled outside Reseune.

Jordan knew about the Project. Both Projects, Ari and Rubin.

"I'm glad," Jordan said. "I'm glad. How's Grant's work?"

"He never was in trouble. You know Grant." And then he realized how far back that question had to go.

All those years. Grant in hospital. Himself in Security's hands. Jordan being whisked away to testify in Novgorod before they shipped him out to Planys.

His hand shook, on the table in front of him, shook as he carried it to his mouth and tried to steady himself.

"Grant—came out of it all right. Stable as ever. He's fine. He really is. I don't know what I'd have done without him. Have you been all right?"

"Hell at first. But it's a small staff, a close staff. They can come and go, of course, and they know my condition here, but it's a real difference—a real difference."

O God, be careful. Anything you say, anything you admit to needing, they can use. Watch what you say.

". . . We take care of each other here. We carry each other's loads, sometimes. I think it's all that desert out there. You either go crazy and they ship you out, or you get seduced by the tranquillity here. Even Security's kind of reasonable. —Aren't you, Jim?"

One guard had settled in, taken a chair in the corner. The man laughed and leaned back, ankles crossed.

Not azi. CIT.

"Most times," Jim the guard said.

"It's home," Jordan said. "It's gotten to be home. You have to understand the mentality out here. Our news and a lot of our music comes in from the station. We're real good on current events. Our clothes, our books, our entertainment tapes, all of that—get flown in when they get around to it, and books and tapes don't get into the library here until Security vets the addition. So there's a lot of staff silliness—you have to amuse yourself somehow; and the big new E-tape is *Echoes*. Which ought to tell you something."

Three years since that tape had come out. "Damn, I could have brought you a dozen."

"Listen, anything you can do for library here will be appreciated. I've complained. Everyone on staff has complained. The garrison snags everything. *Military* priority. And they do the luggage searches. I couldn't warn you. I hope to hell you haven't got anything in your overnight kit that's in short supply here, because they've got a censored number of soldiers over at the base really desperate for censored, censored, and censored. Not to mention toilet paper. So we're not the only ones."

He laughed, because Jordan laughed and Paul laughed, and Jim-the-guard laughed, because it was desperately, bleakly funny to think of, when there was so much that was not at all funny in this isolation; because it was so much relief to know Planys finally, not as a totally barren exile, but as a place where humanness and humor were valuable.

They talked and argued theory till they were hoarse. They went to the lab and Jordan introduced him to the staffers he had never met, always with Jim and his azi partner Enny at left and right of them. They had a drink with Lel Schwartz and Milos Carnath-Morley, neither one of whom he had seen since he was seventeen; and had dinner with Jordan and Paul—and Jim and Enny.

He had no intention of sleeping. Neither did Jordan or Paul. They had allotted him a certain number of hours to stay and he could sleep on the plane, that was all.

Jim and Enny traded off with two others at 2000 of the clock. By that time Jordan and Paul were both arguing ideas with him, criticizing his structures, telling him where he was wrong and teaching him more about sociological psych integrations than he had learned from all Yanni's books.

"Oh, God," he said, toward 0400 in the morning, in a break when they were all three hoarse and still talking, "if we could consult together—if you were there or I was here—"

"You're retracing a lot of old territory," Jordan told him, "but I don't call it a dead end. I *don't know*, you understand, and I don't say that too often, pardon my arrogance. I think it's worth chasing—not that I think you'll get where you're going, but I'm just curious."

"You're my father. Yanni says I'm crazy."

"Then Ari was."

He looked sharply at Jordan. And his gut knotted up just hearing Jordan name the dead without rancor.

"She told me," Jordan said, "when I suggested she'd rigged the Aptitudes—politely, of course—that it was your essay question cinched it. I thought that was her usual kind of snide answer. I'm not so sure, now, having seen where you've taken it. Did she help you with this?"

"Not this one. The first—" Few, he almost said. Till she died. Till she was killed. Murdered. He shuddered away from the remembrance. "You didn't take me seriously, then."

"Son, it was pretty bright for a youngster. Ari evidently saw something I didn't. Now so does Yanni."

"Yanni?"

"He wrote me a long letter. A long letter. He told me what you were working on. Said you were crazy, but you were getting somewhere. That you were getting integrations on deep-sets that he could see, and that he'd run them through Sociology's computers and gotten nothing—indeterminate, insufficient data, field too wide. That sort of thing. Sociology hates like hell to have its computers give answers like that; you can imagine how nervous it makes them."

Jordan started back to the table with the tea, and sat down. Justin dropped into his chair, shivering from too little sleep, too late hours. And leaned on his folded arms and listened, that was all.

"Ariane Emory helped map those sociology programs," Jordan said. "So did I. So did Olga Emory and James Carnath and a dozen others. You've at least handed them something that exceeds their projective range, that the computer's averaging can't handle. It's what I said. *I don't know* is a disturbing projection—when it comes from the machines that hold the whole social paradigm. Sociology, I think, is less interested in what you've done than in the fact that your designs refuse projection: Sociology's computers are very sensitive to negatives. That's what they're programmed to turn up."

He knew that.

"And there's either no negative in the run or it can't find it. It carried it through thirty generations and kept getting an *I don't know*. That may be why Administration sent you here. Maybe Reseune is suddenly interested. I am. They have to wonder if I'd lie—or lie to myself—because I'm your father. . . ."

Justin opened his mouth and stopped. So did Jordan stop, waiting on him; and there were the guards, there was every likelihood that they were being taped for later study by Security. And maybe by Administration.

So he did not say: *They can't let me succeed. They don't want me to call their Project into question by being anything like a success.* He clamped his mouth shut.

Jordan seemed to sense the danger. He went on quietly,

precisely: "And I would lie, of course. I have plenty of motives. But my colleagues at Reseune wouldn't: they know there's something in this, Yanni says so, the Sociology computers say so, and they certainly don't have ulterior motives."

They could lock me away like you, couldn't they? What doesn't get out, doesn't breach Security. No matter what it contradicts.

Except—except I said it to Denys: if I go missing from Reseune, there are questions.

"I don't know if there's a hope in hell of getting you transferred to Planys," Jordan said. "But I'll ask you the question first: do you *want* to transfer?"

He froze then, remembering the landscape outside, the desolation that closed about him with a gut-deep panic.

He hated it. For all its advantages of freedom and relief from the pressure of Reseune, Planys afflicted him with a profound terror.

He saw the disappointment on Jordan's face. "You've answered me," Jordan said.

"No, I haven't. —Look, I've got a problem with this place. But it's something I could overcome. You did."

"Say I had a limited choice. Your choice is real. That's what you can't overcome. No. I understand. Your feelings may change with time. But let's not add that to the problems. We're certainly going to have Yanni in the loop. No way they're going to let us send anything anywhere without someone checking it for content. We'll just work on it—as we can, when we can. They're curious right now, I'm sure. They aren't so locked on their Project they can't see the potential in an unrelated idea. And that, son, is both a plus and a minus. You see how concerned they are for my well-being."

"Ser," the guard said.

"Sorry," Jordan said, and sighed, staring at Justin for a long while with somber emotions playing freely across his face.

Not free here, not as free as seems on the surface.

Succeed and gain protection; and absolutely protected, become an absolute prisoner.

He felt a lump in his throat, part grief, part panic. For a terrible moment he wanted to leave, now, quickly, before the dawn. But that was foolishness. He and Jordan had so little time. That was why they stayed awake and drove themselves over the edge, into too much honesty.

Dammit, he left a kid, and I'm not sure how he sees me. As a man? Or just as someone grown? Maybe not even someone he knows very well. I know him and he knows so little what I am now.

Damn them for that.

There's no way to recover it. We can't even say the things to each other that would let us know each other. Emotions are the thing we can't give away to our jailers.

He looked away, he looked at Paul, sitting silent at the table, and thought that their life must be like his with Grant—a pressured frustration of things they dared not say.

It's no different from Reseune, here, he thought. *Not for Jordan. Not really, no matter what the appearance they put on it. He can't talk. He doesn't dare.*

Nothing, for us, is different from Reseune.

———————————— ii ————————————

"Working late?" the Security guard asked, stopping in the doorway, and Grant's heart jumped and kept up a frantic beat as he looked up from his desk.

"Yes," he said.

"Ser Warrick's out today?"

"Yes."

"Is he sick?"

"No."

Where Justin was fell under Administrative need-to-know. That was one of the conditions. There were things he could not say, and the silence was irritating to a born-man. The man stared at him a moment, grunted and frowned and continued on his rounds.

Grant let go his breath, but the tension persisted, the downside of an adrenaline rush, fear that had only grown from the time Justin had told him he was going to Planys.

Justin was going—alone, because that was one of the conditions Administration imposed. He had brushed off Justin's worry about him and refused to discuss it, because Justin would go under whatever conditions, Justin had to go: Grant had no question about it.

But he was afraid, continually, a fear that grew more acute when he saw the plane leave the ground and when he walked back into Reseune alone.

It was partly ordinary anxiety, he told himself: he relied on Justin; they had not been apart since the incidents around Ari's death, and separation naturally brought back bad memories.

But he was not legally Justin's ward. He was Reseune's; and as long as Justin was not there to obstruct Administration and to use Jordan's leverage to protect him, he had no protection and no rights. Justin was at risk, traveling completely in the hands of Reseune Security—which might arrange an incident; but much more likely that they might take an azi down to the labs where they could question him or, the thing he most feared, run tape on him.

There was no good in panic, he told himself, since there was nothing, absolutely nothing he could do about it, nowhere he could hide and nothing he could do, ultimately, to stop them if that was what they intended.

But the first night that he had been alone with all the small lonely sounds of a very large apartment and no knowledge what was happening on the other side of the world, he had shot himself with one of the adrenaline doses they kept, along with knock-out doses of trank, in the clinical interview room; and taken kat on top of it.

Then he had sat down crosslegged at the side of his bed, and dived down into the innermost partitions he had made in himself, altering things step by step in a concentration that slicked his skin with sweat and left him dizzy and weak.

He had not been sure that he could do it; he was not sure when he exited the haze of the drug and the effort, that the combination of adrenaline and cataphoric would serve, but his heart was going like a hammer and he was able to do very little more after that than fall face down on the bed and count the beats of his heart, hoping he had not killed himself.

Fool was the word for a designer who got into his own sets and started moving them around.

Not much different, though, from what the test-unit azi did, when they organized their own mental compartmentalizations and controlled the extent to which they integrated new tape. It was a question of knowing one's own mental map, very, very thoroughly.

He turned off the computer, turned off the lights and locked the office door on his way out, walking the deserted hall to go back to that empty apartment and wait through another night.

Azi responses, dim and primal, said go to another Supervisor. Find help. Take a pill. Accept no stress in deep levels.

Of course doing the first was extremely foolish: he was not at all tempted. But taking a pill and sleeping through the night under sedation was very, very tempting. If he sedated himself deeply enough he could get through the night and go meet Justin's plane in the morning: it was only reasonable, perhaps even advisable, since the trank itself would present a problem to anyone who came after him, and if they were going to try anything at the last moment—

No, it was a very simple matter to delay a plane. They could always get more time, if they suddenly decided they needed it.

Mostly, he decided, he did not trank himself because he felt there was some benefit in getting through this without it; and that thought, perhaps, did not come from the logical underside of his mind—except that he saw value in endocrine-learning, which the constantly reasonable, sheltered, take-a-tape-and-feel-good way did not let happen. If it were an azi world everything would be black and white and very, very clear. It was the grays of flux-thinking that made bornmen. Shaded responses in shaded values, acquired under endocrine instability.

He did not enjoy pain. But he saw value in the by-product.

He also saw value in having the trank in his pocket, a double dose loaded in a hypospray, because if they tried to take him anywhere, he could give them a real medical emergency to worry about.

iii

Nelly, Ari reflected, was still having her troubles.

"We have to be careful with her," Ari said to Florian and

Catlin, in a council in Florian and Catlin's room, while Nelly was in the dining room helping Seely clean up.

"Yes, sera," Florian said earnestly; Catlin said nothing, which was normal: Catlin always let Florian talk if she agreed. Which was not to say Catlin was shy. She was just that way.

And Nelly had taken severe exception to Catlin showing Ari how to do an over-the-shoulder throw in the living room.

"You'll hurt yourself!" Nelly had cried. "Florian, Catlin, you should have better sense!"

Actually, it was Florian who was the one with the complaint coming, since Florian was the one on the floor. He was being the Enemy. Florian was all right: he could land and come right back up again, but Catlin wasn't teaching her what to do next, just first, and Florian was lying down being patient while Catlin was showing her how to make sure he wouldn't get up.

Nelly had heard the thump, that was all, and come flying in after Florian was down in the middle of the rug. Catlin was demonstrating how to break somebody's neck, but she was doing it real slow. If Catlin was really doing it and pulling it, she was so fast you could hardly see what she did. Catlin and Florian had showed her how to fall down and roll right up again. It was marvelous what they could do.

Sometimes they played Ambush, when they had the suite to themselves. You turned out the lights and had to find your way through.

She was *always* the one who was Got. That was all right. She was getting harder to Get and she was learning things all the time. It was a lot more fun than Amy Carnath.

Florian showed her a whole lot of things about computers and how to set Traps and do real nasty things with a Minder, like blow somebody up if you had a bomb, but they kept those down in the Military section. She knew about voice-prints and how the Minder knew who you were, and how handprint locks were linked into the House computer, along with retina-scans and all sorts of things; and how to make the electric locks open without a keycard.

Florian found out a lot of things, real fast. He said the House residential locks were all a special kind that was real hard to get past. He said that uncle Denys' apartment had a lot of interesting stuff, like really *special* special locks, that were tied in somewhere Florian couldn't trace, but he thought it was Security: he said he could try to find out, but he could get in trouble and they were Olders and he would do it only if she wanted.

He wouldn't tell her that until they were outside, because he and Catlin had found out other things.

Like the Minder could listen to you.

It was a special kind, Florian had told her: it could hear anything and see anything, and it was specially quiet, so you never knew; and specially shielded, with the tape functions somewhere outside the apartment. The lenses and the pickups could be small as pinheads, the lenses could be fish-eyed and the pickups could be all kinds, motion detection and sound. "They can put one of those in the walls," Florian said, "and it's so tiny and so transparent you can't see it unless you go over the walls with a bright light sort of sideways, or if you've got equipment, which is the best, but they have real good focus. Then they can digitalize and you can get it a lot tighter than that. Same with the audio. They can run a voice-stress on you. If they want something they can get it. That's if they want to. It's a lot of work. Most Minders are real simple and you can get into them. The ones in the House are all the complicated kind, all security, all built-ins, and it's really hard to spot all the pickups if they set them into the cement between stones and stuff.''

That had made her feel real upset. "Even in the *bathroom*?'' she had asked.

Florian had nodded. "Especially, because if you're setting up surveillance, they're going to try to go places they don't think they'll have a bug.''

She had gone to uncle Denys then, and asked, worried:

"Uncle Denys, is there a bug in my bathroom?''

And uncle Denys had said: "Who told you that?''

"Is there?''

"It's for Security,'' uncle Denys had said. "Don't worry about it. They don't turn them on unless they have to.''

"I don't want it in my bathroom!''

"Well, you're not a thief, either, dear, are you? And if you were, the alarm would go off in Security and the Minder would watch and listen. Don't worry.''

"Yes, ser," she said; and had Florian go over the whole bathroom till he found the lenses and the pickups and put a dab of clay over them. Except the one in the wall-speaker. So she hung a towel over it, and Nelly kept moving it, but she always put it back.

Florian found the ones in the bedroom too, but uncle Denys called her in and told her Security had found the bathroom pickups dead in a regular test they ran, and he would let her cover up the bathroom ones, but the rest were apartment Security, and she had better not mess with them.

So they hadn't.

That wasn't the only Security, either. Catlin said Seely was Security. So was Abban, Giraud's azi. She could tell. Florian said he thought so too.

Catlin taught her things too: how to stand so still nobody could hear you, and where all the spots were that you ought to hit for if somebody attacked you.

So uncle Denys didn't need to worry so much about security all the time, and didn't need to worry about her being in the halls. And when maman's letter came—it had to come, soon; she had the months figured out—then she could take care of herself going to Fargone.

She was a lot more scared of going where there were strangers than she had ever been, since she had begun to understand there were a lot of people outside Reseune who wanted to break into places and steal and a lot who would kill you or grab you and steal *you*; but at least it was a scared that knew how to spot somebody being wrong; and she was learning how to handle nasty people more than by getting Hold of them and Working them.

She would really like to do it to Amy Carnath.

But that was where you stopped thinking about like-to and knew how wide that would go, all over the place, and Amy would really be dead, which meant something you couldn't take back and you couldn't Work and you couldn't get Hold of.

You got a lot more by Working people, if you had the time.

That was something she showed Florian and Catlin a little about. But not too much. First, they were azi, and you couldn't push them and it was hard to show them without *doing* it; and, second, she didn't want them learning how to do it at her.

For one thing she had to be best at it. She was their Super.

For another, they made her scared sometimes; sometimes she really wanted them, and sometimes she wished she didn't have them, because they made her mad and they made her laugh and they made her think sometimes, in the middle of the night, that she shouldn't like them that much, because maman might not let them come.

She didn't know why she thought that, but it hurt a lot, and she hated it when people made her scared; and she hated it when people made her hurt.

"We shouldn't get in trouble," she said to Florian and Catlin, when they were in the room after Nelly had scolded them; and finally, because it was on her mind, sneaked up on what she had been wanting to tell them for a long time, but it was hard to put words on it and it made her stomach upset. "I know a lot of people who aren't here anymore. You get in trouble and they get Disappeared."

"What's that?" Florian asked.

"They just aren't here anymore."

"Dead?" Catlin asked.

Her heart jumped. She shook her head, hard. "Just Disappeared. Out to Fargone or somewhere." The next was hard to talk about. She warned them with her face to be real quiet or she would be mad, because it wasn't Nelly she was going to talk about. "My maman and her azi got Disappeared. She didn't want to. Uncle Denys said she had real important business out on Fargone. Maybe that's so. Maybe it isn't. Maybe it's what they tell you because you're a kid. A lot of kids got Disappeared, too. That's why I'm real careful. You've got to be careful."

"If anybody Disappears us," Catlin said, "we'll come back."

That was like Catlin. Catlin *would*, too, Ari thought, or at least Catlin and Florian would do a lot of damage.

"My maman is real smart," she said, "and Ollie is real strong, and I'm not sure they just grab you. I think maybe they Work you, you know, they psych you."

"Who's our Enemy?" Florian asked.

It was the way they thought. Her heart beat hard. She had

never, ever talked about it with anyone. She had never, ever thought about it the way the azi did, without being in the middle of it. Things suddenly made sense when you thought the way they did, straight and plain, without worrying. And when you thought: what if it *could* be an Enemy? She sat trying to think about who could do things like grab people and psych people and Disappear strong grown-up people without them being able to do anything about it.

She dragged Florian real close and whispered right into his ear between her two hands, the way you had to do if you really wanted something to be secret, because of the Minder—and if they were talking about an Enemy, you didn't know where you were safe. "I think it might be Giraud. But he's not a regular Enemy. He can give you orders. He can give Security orders."

Florian looked real upset. Catlin elbowed him and he leaned over and whispered in Catlin's ear the same way.

Then Catlin looked scared, and Catlin didn't do that.

She pulled Catlin close and whispered: "That's the only one I know could have Got my maman."

Catlin whispered in her ear: "Then you have to Get him first."

"He might not be it!" she whispered.

She sat and she thought, while Catlin passed it to Florian. Florian said something back, and then leaned forward and said to her:

"We shouldn't be talking about this now."

She looked at Florian, upset.

"An Older is real dangerous," Florian said. And in the faintest whisper of all: "Please, sera. Tomorrow. Outside."

They understood her, then. They believed her, not just because they were azi. What she said made sense to them. She tucked up her legs in her arms and felt shaky and stupid and mad at herself; and at the same time thought she had not put a lot of things together because she hadn't had any way of making it make sense. She had thought things just happened because they happened, because they had always happened and the world was that way. But that was stupid. It wasn't just things that happened, people made things happen, and Florian and Catlin knew that the way she should have known it if it hadn't always been there, all the time.

What's unusual? was a game they played. Florian or Catlin would say: What's unusual in the living room? And they timed how long it took you to find it. Once or twice she beat Catlin and once she beat Florian at finding it; a couple of times she set things up they had to give on. She wasn't stupid about things like that. But she felt that way about this.

The stupid part was thinking things had to be the way they were.

The stupid part was that she had thought when maman went away, that someone had made her go, but then she had just fitted everything together so that wasn't so important—if maman had had to go without her, it was because she was too young and it was too dangerous. And *that* was what she had been looking at, when the Something Unusual was sitting right in plain sight beside it.

The stupid part now was the way she still didn't want to think all the way to the end of it, about how if there was an enemy and he Got maman, she didn't really know whether maman was all right; and she was scared.

She remembered arguing with uncle Denys about the party last year. And her not wanting Giraud to come; and uncle Denys said: *That's not nice, Ari. He's my brother.*

That was scary too.

That was scary, because uncle Giraud might get uncle Denys to do things. Uncle Giraud had Security; and they might get into her letters. They might just stop the letters going to maman at all.

And that tore up *everything*.

Stupid. Stupid.

She felt sick all over. And she couldn't ask uncle Denys what was true. Denys would say: *He's my brother.*

---

iv

Giraud poured more water and drank, tracking on the reports, bored while the tutors argued over the relative merits of two essays, one out of archives, one current.

Denys, Peterson, Edwards, Ivanov, and Morley: all of them around a table, discussing the implications of vocabulary choice in eight-year-olds. It was not Giraud's field. It was, God help them, Peterson's.

"The verbal development," Peterson said, in the stultifying murmur that was Peterson in full display, "is point seven off, the significant anomaly in the Gonner Developmentals. . . ."

"I don't think there's any cause for worry," Denys said. "The difference is Jane and Olga, not Ari and Ari."

"Of course there is some argument that the Gonner battery is weighted away from concept. Hermann Poling maintained in his article in—"

It went on. Giraud drew small squares on his notepaper. Peterson did good work. Ask him a question, he had a prerecorded lecture. Teacher's disease. Colleagues and strangers got the same as his juvenile subjects.

"In sum," Giraud said, finally, when the water was at half in his glass, and his paper was full of squares. "In sum, in brief, then, you believe the difference was Olga."

"The Poling article—"

"Yes. Of course. And you don't think corrective tape is necessary."

"The other scores indicate a very substantial correspondence—"

"What John means—" Edwards said, "is that she's understanding everything, she knows the words, but so much of her development was precocious, she had an internal vocabulary worked out that for her is a kind of shorthand."

"There may be a downside effect to insisting on a shift of vocabulary," Denys said. "Possibly it *doesn't* describe what she's seeing. She simply prefers slang and her own internal jargon, which I haven't tried to discourage. She does know the words, the tests prove that. Also, I'm not certain we're seeing the whole picture. I rather well think she's resisting some of the exams."

"Why?"

"Jane," Denys said. "The child hasn't forgotten. I hoped the letters would taper off with time. I hoped that the azi could make a difference in that."

"You don't think," Edwards said, "that the way that was handled—tended to make her cling to that stage; I mean, a subconscious emphasis on that stage of her life, a clinging to those memories, a refusal—as it were, to leave that stage, a kind of waiting.''

"That's an interesting theory," Giraud said, leaning forward on his arms. "Is there any particular reason?"

"The number of times she says: 'My maman said—' The tone of voice.''

"I want a voice-stress on that," Denys said.

"No problem," Giraud said. "It's certainly worth pursuing. Does she reference other people?"

"No," Edwards said.

"Not family members. Not friends. Not the azi."

"Nelly. 'Nelly says.' When it regards something about home. Sometimes 'my uncle Denys doesn't mind' this or that. . . . She doesn't respect Nelly's opinions, she doesn't respect much Nelly says, but she evidences a desire not to upset her. 'Uncle Denys' is a much more respectful reference, but more that she uses the name as currency. She's quite willing to remind you that 'my uncle Denys' takes an interest in things." Edwards cleared his throat. "Quite to the point, she hints her influence with 'uncle Denys' can get me a nicer office.''

Denys snorted in surprise, and laughed then, to Edwards' relief. "Like the party invitation?"

"Much the same thing."

"What about Ollie?" Giraud asked.

"Quite rarely. Almost never. I'm being precise now. I'd say she used to mention Ollie right after Jane left. Now—I don't think I've heard that name in a long time. Maybe more than a year.''

"Interesting. Justin Warrick?"

"She never mentions him. I did, if you recall. She was quite anxious to quit the subject. That name never comes up.''

"Worth the time on the computers to run a name search," Denys said.

On all those tapes. On years of tapes. Giraud let his breath flow out and nodded. More personnel. More time on the computers.

Dammit, there was pressure outside. A lot of pressure. They were prepared to go public finally, to break the story; and they had an anomaly; they had a child far less serious than the first Ari, far more capricious and more restrained in temper. The azi had not helped. There was a little more seriousness to the child lately, a little gain in vocabulary: Florian and Catlin were better at essay than she was, but the hard edge was not there, maman was still *with* Ari in a very persistent sense, and the Warrick affair, Yanni's sudden revelation that young Justin had handed them something that stymied the Sociology computers—

Give it to Jordan, Denys had suggested. Send *him* to Jordan. The Warricks are far less likely to cause trouble with the Project if they're busy, and you know Jordan would work on the damned thing, no matter what it was, if it gave him a chance to see his son.

Which was trouble with Defense: they were jealous of Warrick's time. There was a chance Defense would take official interest in Justin Warrick: there was no way to run him past their noses unnoticed, and in the way of Defense, Defense wanted anything that might seem to be important, or useful, or suddenly anomalous.

Damn, and damn.

Ari wanted him, Yanni had said. *And, dammit, there's something there.*

There was the paradox of the Project: how wide the replication had to be. How many individuals, essential to each other? Thank God the first Ari's society had been extremely limited in terms of personal contacts—but it had been much more open in terms of news-services and public contact from a very early age.

"We've got to go ahead," Giraud said. "Dammit, we've got to take her public, for a whole host of reasons, Lu's out of patience and we're running out of time! We can't be wrong, there's no way we can afford to be wrong."

No one said anything. It was too evident what the stakes were.

"The triggers are all there," Petros said. "Not all of them have been invoked. I think a little more pressure. Academic will do. Put it on her. Frustrate her. Give her things she's bound to fail in. Accelerate the program."

That had consistently been Petros' advice.

"She hasn't met intellectual frustration," Denys said, "—yet."

"We don't want her bloody bored with school, either," Giraud snapped. "Maybe it *is* an option. What do the computers say lately, when they're not running Warrick's school projects?"

"Do we run it again?" Peterson asked. "I don't think there's going to be a significant change. I just don't believe you can discount the results we have. Accelerating the program when there's an anomaly in question—"

Petros leaned forward, jaw jutting. "Allowing the program to stagnate while the anomaly proliferates is your answer, is it?"

"Dr. Ivanov, allow me to make my point—"

"I *know* your damn point, we *know* your damn point, doctor."

Giraud poured another glass of water.

"Enough on it," he said. "Enough. We run the damn tests. We take the computer time. We get our answers. Let's have the query in tomorrow, can we do that?"

Mostly, he thought, the voice-stress was the best lead. All those lesson-sessions to scan.

The Project ate computer time at an enormous rate. And the variances kept proliferating.

So did the demands of the Council investigating committee, that wanted to get into documents containing more and more details of Science Bureau involvement in the Gehenna project, because Alliance was asking hard questions, wanting more and more information on the Gehenna colonists, and linking it to the betterment of Alliance-Union relations.

The Centrists and the Abolitionists wanted the whole archives opened. Giraud's intelligence reported Mikhail Corain was gathering evidence, planning to call for a Council bill of Discovery to open the entire Emory archives, charging that there were other covert projects, other timebombs waiting, and that the national security took precedence over Reseune's sovereignty: that Reseune had no right to the notes and papers which Ariane Emory had accrued while serving as Councillor for Science, that those became Union property on her death, and that a bill of Discovery was necessary to find out what was Reseune's and what of Emory's papers belonged to Union archives.

There were timebombs, for certain. The essential one was

aged eight, and exposing her to the vitriol and the hostility in Novgorod—making her the center of controversy—

Everything came down to that critical point. They had to go public.

Before they ended up with a Discovery bill opening all Ari's future secrets into public view, where a precocious eight-year-old could access them out of sequence.

V

In mornings it was always lessons, and Ari took hers with Dr. Edwards in his office or in the study lab, but it was not just mornings now, it was after lunch in the library and the tape-lab, so there was a lot of follow-up and Dr. Edwards asked her questions and gave her tests.

Catlin and Florian had lessons every day too, their own kind, down in the Town at a place they called Green Barracks; and one day a week they had to stay in Green Barracks overnight. That was when they did a Room or did special drill. But most times they were able to meet her at the library or the lab and walk her home.

They did this day, both of them very proper and solemn in their black uniforms, but more solemn than usual, when they walked down to the doors and out to the crosswalk.

"This is as safe as we can find to talk," Catlin said.

"But you don't know," Florian said. "There's equipment that can hear you this far if they want to. You can't say they won't, you can just keep changing places so if they're not really expecting you to say something they want right then they won't bother. Set-up is a lot of work if your Subject moves around a lot."

"If they didn't hear us last night, I don't think they would be onto us," Ari said. She knew how to be nice enough not to get in trouble without being too nice and making people think she was up to something. But she didn't say that. She walked with them along toward the fishpond. She had brought food in her pocket. "What were you going to tell me?"

"It's this," said Catlin. "You should hit your Enemy first if you can. But you have to be sure, first thing, *who* it is.

Then how many, where are they, what have they got? That's the next thing you have to find out.''

"When your Enemy is an Older," Florian said, "it's real hard to know that, because they know so much more."

"If he's not expecting it," Catlin said, "anybody can be Got."

"But if we try and miss," Florian said, "they *will* try to Disappear us. So we're not sure, sera. I think we could Get them. For real. I could steal some stuff that would. They put it in Supply, and they're real careless. They ought to fix that. But I can get it. And we could kill the Enemy, just it's real dangerous. You get one chance with an Older. Usually just one.''

"But if you don't know where his partners are," Catlin said, "they'll Get you. It depends on how much that's worth."

That made a lot of things she was thinking fall into place. Click. She walked along with her hands in her pockets and said: "And if you don't know all those things, it's more than getting caught; it's not knowing what one to grab next. There's things that run all over Reseune, there's what his partners are going to do, there's who's friends and who's not, and who's going to take Hold of things, and we can't do that.''

"I don't know," Florian said. "You'd have to know those things, sera, we wouldn't. I know we could Get one, maybe two, if we split up, or if we could get the targets together. That's the main ones. But it's not near all the ones that would be after us."

They reached the fishpond. Ari knelt down at the edge of the water and took the bag of fish-food out of her pocket. Catlin and Florian squatted beside her. "Here," she said, passing them the bag to get their own, and then tossed a bit into the water for the white one that came up, from under the lilies. White-and-red was almost as fast. She watched the rings go out from the food, and from the strike, and the lilies swaying. "He's not easy," she said finally. "We can't Get everything. There are too many hook-ups. Connections. He's important; he's got a lot of people, not just in Reseune, and what he's got—Security, for one thing. I don't know what else. So even if he was gone—'' It was strange and upsetting to be talking about killing somebody. It didn't feel real. But it was. Florian and Catlin really could do it. She was not sure that made her feel safer, but it made her feel less like things were closing in on her. "—We'd still be in trouble.

"Also," she said, "they could Get my maman and Ollie. For real." They didn't understand that part, she thought, because they had never had a maman, but they looked at her like they took it very seriously. "I'm afraid they could have. They're at Fargone. I sent letters. They should have got there by now. Now I'm not sure—" Dammit, she was going to snivel. She saw Florian and Catlin look at her all distressed. "—I'm not sure," she said in a rush, hard and mad, "they ever got sent."

They didn't understand, for sure. She tried to think of what she had left out they had to know.

"If there is an Enemy," she said, "I don't know what they want. Sometimes I thought maman left me here because it was too dangerous to go with her. Sometimes I thought she left me here because they made her. But I don't know why, and I don't know why she didn't tell me."

The azi didn't say anything for a minute. Then Florian said: "I don't think I'd try to say. I don't think Catlin can. It's CIT. I don't understand CITs."

"CITs have connections," she said. It was like telling them how to Work someone. She felt uneasy telling them. She explained, making a hook out of two fingers to hook together. "To other CITs. Like you to Catlin and Catlin to you and both of you to me. Sometimes not real strong. Sometimes real, real strong. That's the first thing. CITs do things *for* each other, sometimes because it feels good, sometimes because they're Working each other. And sometimes they do things to Get each other. A lot of times it's to protect themselves, sometimes their connections: connections are a lot more in danger, sometimes, if you don't let your Enemy be sure where *your* connections are, and whether some of them are to people he's connected to. Like building-sticks."

Wide, attentive stares. Anxious stares. Even from Catlin.

"So you can Work somebody to make them do something if you want to, if you tell him you'll hurt him or hurt somebody he's connected to. Like if somebody was going to hurt me, you'd react." While she was saying it she thought: *So it's maman they must want something out of, because maman's important. If that's true she's all right. They're Working her with me.*

It couldn't be the other way. They haven't told me they'd hurt maman.

Could that be?

But they're Olders, like Florian says, and they always know more and they don't tell you everything you need.

"That's one way to Work people," she said. "There's others. Like finding out what they want and almost doing it and then not, if they don't make you happy. But maman wouldn't leave me just for something she wanted."

Would she?

Is there anything she would want more than me?

Ollie?

"There's ways to Get someone that way," she said, "instead of just Working them. You get them to get in trouble. It's not real hard. Except you have to know—"

What can get Giraud in trouble?

What could I get instead if I could Work him like that?

"—you have to know the same things: who are they, how many are there, what have they got? It's the same thing. But you can find out by Working them a *little* and then watching what they do."

Their eyes never left her. They were learning, that was what, they were paying attention the way azi could, and they would never ask questions until she was done.

"Me," she said, thinking carefully about how much she was giving away, "I don't give anybody anything I don't have to. They take Nelly in and they ask her stuff and she'll tell them right off. I can't Work that. I wish I could. But if they try to take you, I'll Work them good. It's easier. Uncle Denys said you're mine. So if Security tells you to go to hospital, you go right to me first. That's an order. All right?"

"Yes, sera." One movement, one nod at the same time.

"But," Florian said, "we're not like Nelly. Nobody but you can give us orders. They'd have to go to you first and you have to tell us. That's the Rule, because otherwise we're supposed to Get them."

She had not known that. She had never even suspected that. It made her feel a lot better in one way, and feel threatened in another. Like everything had always been a lot more serious than she had thought. And they had always known. "If you come to me, I'll tell them no. But they're stronger than you are."

"That's so," Catlin said. "But that's the Rule. And they know it. Nobody else's orders."

She drew a long breath. "Even if uncle Denys is a Super."

"Not for us," Catlin said. "You told us mind him. And Nelly. We'll do that. But if it's any big thing we come to you."

"You come to me first after this, if it's anything more than a 'pick that up.' You don't go anywhere they tell you and you don't go with anybody they tell you, until after you tell me."

"Good. If you tell us that, that's the Rule."

"You be sneaky about it. Don't fight. Just get away."

"That's smart. That's real good, sera."

"And you don't ever, ever tell on me, no matter who asks. You lie if you have to. You be real smooth and then you come and tell me what they asked."

"Yes, sera." Both of them nodded, definitely.

"Then I'll tell you a big secret. I never tell anybody everything. Like on my exam this morning. I could have put down more. But I won't. You don't let anybody but me know what you really know."

"Is that a Rule?"

"That's a big Rule. There's a boy named Sam: I used to play with him. He's the one that gave me the bug. He's not real smart, but everybody likes Sam—and I figured out it's easier to *be* Sam most of the time. That way I can get a lot of people to be nicer: that way even stupid people can understand everything I need them to if I'm going to Work them. But they can't know you're not like that, you can't let them find out from anybody. So you do it all the time. I learned that from Sam and uncle Denys. He does it. He's smart, he always uses little words, and he's real good at getting points on people. That's one thing you do. You don't want them to know you're doing it unless that's part of the Working. And we don't. So here's what we do. We start being real nice to Giraud. But not right off. The first thing we do is shake him up. Then we let him yell, then we act like he yelled too much, then we get him to do something nice to make up for it. Then he won't be surprised when we start being nice, because he thinks he's Working *us*. That's how you Work an Older.''

"That's sneaky," Catlin said, and actually grinned.

"I'll tell you another secret. I've been counting What's Unusuals. It's Unusual that people Disappear. It's Unusual that maman didn't tell me she was going or even say goodbye. It's Unusual Nelly goes to the hospital all the time. It's Unusual a CIT kid has two azi to Super. It's Unusual I have to get my blood tested every few days. It's Unusual I go to adult parties and other kids don't. It's Unusual I'm so smart. It's Unusual you're on a job when you're still kids. I'm still counting the Unusuals. I think there's a lot of them. A whole lot. I want you to think and tell me all the ones you know. And tell what you can do to find out stuff without getting caught.''

---

vi

The plane touched and braked and rolled toward the terminal, and Grant gave a sigh of profoundest relief, watching it from the windows.

There was still a lot to wait through: there was a Decon procedure for anything coming in from the other hemisphere, not just the passengers having to go through Decontamination, but the luggage had to be treated and searched, and the plane itself had to be hosed down and fumigated.

That was starting when Grant left the windows and walked over to the Decon section and stationed himself outside the white doors, hands locked between his knees, flexing and clenching—nervous tic, that. You have a lot of tension, a Supervisor would tell him, who saw it.

A Supervisor could say that about any CIT anytime, Grant reckoned. Flux-thinking bred it. Azi-mindset said: there's not enough data to solve the problem, and the sane and sensible azi filed it and blanked out to rest or worked on another problem. A CIT threw himself at a data-insufficient problem over and over, exploring the flux in his perceptions and shades of value in his opinions, and touching off his endocrine system, which in turn brought up his flux-capable learning—which hyped the integrative processes in the flux. He was doing too much of it lately for his liking. He hated the stress level CITs lived at.

And here he was sitting here worrying about four and five problems at once, simply because he had become an adrenaline addict.

The white doors opened. Part of the crew came out. They ignored him and walked on down the hall.

Then the doors opened again, and Justin came through. Grant got up, caught the relief and the delight in Justin's expression and went and hugged him because Justin offered him open arms.

"Are you all right?" Grant asked.

"I'm fine. Jordan's fine." Justin pulled him out of the way of more people coming out the doors, and walked with him behind them. "Got to pick up my briefcase and my bag," he said, and they walked to Baggage, where it was waiting, fogged, irradiated, and, Grant reckoned, searched and scanned, case and light travel bag alike.

"I'll carry them," Grant said.

"I've got them." Justin gathered everything up and they walked to the doors, to the waiting bus that would take them up to the House.

"Was it a good trip?" Grant said, when they were where no eavesdropper could likely pick it up, going out the doors into the dark.

"It was," Justin said, and gave the bags to the azi baggage handler.

Security was in the bus, ordinary passengers like themselves, from this point. They sat down, last aboard. The driver shut the doors and Justin slumped in the seat as the bus pulled out of the lighted portico of the terminal and headed up toward the house.

"I got to talk to Jordan. We stayed up all night. Just talking. We both wished you were there."

"So do I."

"It's a lot better there than I thought it was. A lot worse in some ways and a lot better. There's a good staff. Really fine people. He's getting along a lot better than I thought he would. And Paul is fine. Both of them." Justin was a little hoarse. Exhausted. He leaned his head on the seat-back and said: "He's going to look at my projects. He says at least there's something there that the computers aren't handling. That he's interested and he's not just saying that to get me there. There's a good chance I can go back before the year's out. Maybe you too. Or you instead. He'd really like to see you."

"I'm glad," Grant said.

There was not much they could say, in detail. He *was* glad. Glad when they pulled up in the portico of the House, checked in through the front door, and Justin doggedly, stubbornly, insisted to carry his own baggage, tired as he was.

"You don't carry my bags," Justin snapped at him, hoarsely.

Because Justin hated him playing servant in public, even when he was trying to do him an ordinary favor.

But Justin let him take them and put them over against the wall when they were inside, in their own apartment, and Justin took his coat off and fell onto the couch with a sigh. "It was good," he said. "All the way. It's hard to believe I was there. Or that I'm back. It's so damned different."

"Whiskey?"

"A little one. I slept on the plane. I'm out, already."

Grant smiled at him, Justin half-nodding with time-lag. He went and fixed the whiskey, never mind now that he was playing servant. He made two of them.

"How's it been here?" Justin asked, and there was a small upset at Grant's stomach.

"Fine," he said. "Just fine." The upset was more when he brought the drink and gave it into Justin's hand.

Justin took it. His hand shook when he drank a sip of it, and Justin looked up at him with the most terrible, weary look. And smiled with the same expression as he lifted the glass in a wry toast. There was no way for either of them to know, of course, whether the other had been tampered with.

But that was all right: there was nothing either of them could do about it, if Security had done anything. There was nothing, Grant thought, worth the fight for either of them if that was the case.

Grant lifted his glass the same way, and drank.

Then he went to the bedroom and pulled a note out from under Justin's pillow. He brought it back to him.

If I'm showing this to you, it said, *I'm in my right mind. If I didn't, and you just found it, I'm not. Be warned.*

Justin looked at him in frightened surmise. And then in earnest question.

Grant smiled at him, wadded up the note, and sat down to drink his whiskey.

---

vii

It wasn't hard at all to get out the kitchen way. They didn't go together. Catlin and Florian went first because they were Security and the kitchen staff wouldn't know they shouldn't: Security went everywhere.

Then Ari went in. She Worked her way through, made herself a pest to the azi who was mixing up batter, and got a taste, then went over to the azi chopping up onions and said it made her cry. So she went out onto the kitchen steps and dived right off and down, and ran fast to get down the hill, where the hump was Florian and Catlin told her about.

She slid down on her back and rolled over and grinned as they looked at her, lying on their stomachs too.

"Come on," Catlin said then. She was being Team Leader. She was the best at sneaking.

So they followed her, slithered down to the back of the pump building where she stripped off her blouse and her pants and put on the ones Florian gave her, azi-black. Getting shoes that fit was harder, so she had bought some black boots on uncle Denys' card that worked all right if nobody looked close. And she was wearing those. Florian got her card off her blouse and taped a black band across the bottom and a mark like the azi triangle in the CIT blank.

"Do I look right?" she said when she had clipped the card on.

"Face," Catlin said. So she made an azi face, very stiff and formal.

"That's good," Catlin said.

And Catlin slithered over, looked around the corner of the pump building, then got up and walked out. They followed Catlin as far as the road, and then they just walked together like they belonged there.

It was going to take them a while to miss her up at the House, Ari thought, and then Security was going to get real upset.

Meanwhile she had never seen the Town except from the House, and she wished they could walk faster, because she wanted to see as much as she could before they got caught.

Or before she decided to go back, somewhere around dark. It was going to be fun at the same time as it was not going to be: it was going to be a lot of trouble, but she really hoped they could sneak back up and get her clothes, and just sneak back in by the kitchen, when everyone was really in a panic. But that might look too smart, and that might make them watch her too close.

It was better to be Sam, and get caught.

That way she would say she made her azi do it, and that would work, because they had to take her orders, and everybody knew that. So they wouldn't get in any trouble. She would. And that was what she wanted.

She just wanted to have a little fun before they caught her.

_____ viii _____

The problem was running, the computer working timeshare on a Beta-class design and going slow this morning, because Yanni Schwartz had the integrative set running: everyone else got a lower priority. So Justin leaned back, got up, poured himself a cup of coffee, and filled Grant's empty cup, Grant working away at his terminal in that kind of fixed concentration that was not going to lose that chain of thought if the ceiling fell around him.

Grant reached over without even looking away from the screen, picked up the coffee cup and took a sip.

Someone arrived in the door, brusque, abrupt, and more than one. Justin's ears had already registered that as he looked around, saw Security black, and had a man in his office, two others behind him.

Muscles tightened, gut tightened in panic.

"You're wanted in Security," the man said.

"What for?"

"No questions. Just come with us."

He thought of the hot coffee in his hands, and Grant *had* noticed, Grant was getting up from his chair, as another Security guard moved in behind the first.

"Let's go straighten this out," Justin said calmly, and put the cup down.

"Let me shut down," Grant said.

"Now!" the officer said.

"My program—"

"Grant," Justin said, articulate, he did not know how. It was happening, the thing he had been expecting for a long, long time; and he thought of doing them all the damage he could. But it could be something he could talk his way out of. Whatever it was. And there was, whatever else, enough force at Reseune Administration's disposal to take care of two essentially sedentary tape-designers, however well-exercised.

The only thing he could hope for was to keep the situation calm, the way he had mapped it out in his mind years ago. He kept his hands in sight, he got himself and Grant peacefully out the door, he walked with the Security guards without complaint, to take the lift down to the basement storm-tunnel.

The lift door opened, they walked out as the guards directed. "Hands on the wall," the officer said.

"Grant," he said, catching Grant by the arm, feeling the tension. "It's all right. We'll sort it out."

He turned to the wall himself, waited while two of them searched Grant for weapons and put on the handcuffs, then took his own turn. "I don't suppose," he said calmly as he could with his face against the wall and his arms pulled behind him, "you people know what this is about."

"Come along," the officer said, and faced him about again.

No information. After that at least the guards were less worried.

Keep to the script. Cooperate. Stay calm and give absolutely no trouble.

Through a locked door into a Security zone, lonelier and lonelier in the concrete corridors. He had never seen this part of Reseune's storm-tunnels in all his life, and he hoped to hell they *were* going to Security.

Another locked door, and a lift, with the designation

SECURITY 10N on the opposing wall: he was overwhelmingly glad to see that sign.

Up, then, with extraordinary abruptness. The doors opened on a hall he did know, the back section of Security, a hall that figured in his nightmares.

"This is familiar," he said lightly, to Grant; and suddenly the guards were pulling Grant off toward one of the side rooms and himself off down the hall, toward an interview room he remembered.

"Don't we get checked in?" he asked, fighting down the panic, walking with them on legs suddenly gone shaky. "I hate to complain, but you're violating procedures all the way through this."

Neither of them spoke to him. They took him into the room, made him sit down in a hard chair facing the interview desk, and stayed there, grim and silent, behind him.

Someone else came in behind him. He turned his head and twisted to see who it was. Giraud.

"Thank God," Justin said, half meaning it. "I'm glad to see somebody who knows the answers around here. *What* in hell's going on, do you mind?"

Giraud walked on to the desk and sat down on the corner of it. Positional intimidation. Moderate friendliness. "You tell me."

"Look, Giraud, I'm not in any position to know a thing. I'm working in my office, these fellows come in and haul me over here, and I haven't even seen the check-in desk. What's going on here?"

"Where did you go for lunch?"

"I skipped lunch. We both did. We worked right through. Come on, Giraud, what does lunch have to do with anything?"

"Ari's missing."

"What do you mean missing?" His heart started doubling its beats, hammering in his chest. "Like—late from lunch? Or *missing*?"

"Maybe you know. Maybe you know all about it. Maybe you lured her outside. Maybe she just went with a friend."

"God. No."

"Something Jordan and you set up?"

"No. Absolutely not. My God, Giraud, *ask the guards at*

Planys, there wasn't a time we weren't watched. Not a moment.''

"That they remember, no."

It *had* reached to Jordan. He stared at Giraud, having trouble breathing.

"We're going over your apartment," Giraud said calmly. "Never mind your rights, son, we're not being recorded. I'll tell you what we've found. Ari went out the kitchen door, all right. We found her clothes at the back of the pump station."

"My God." Justin shook his head. "No. I don't know anything."

"That's a wide shore down there," Giraud said. "Easy for someone to land and get in. Is that what happened? You get the girl out to a meeting, where you don't show up, but someone else does?"

"No. No. No such thing. She's probably playing a damn *prank*, Giraud, it's a damn kid escapade—didn't you ever dodge out of the House when you were a kid?"

"We're searching the shore. We've got patrols up. You understand, we're covering all the routes."

"I wouldn't hurt that kid! I wouldn't do it, Giraud."

Giraud stared at him, face flushed, with a terrible, terrible restraint. "You'll understand we're not going to take your word."

"I understand that. Dammit, I want the kid found as much as you do."

"I doubt that."

"I'll consent. Giraud, I'll give you a consent, just for God's sake let Grant be with me."

Giraud got up.

"Giraud, does it cost you anything? Let him be here. Is that so much? *Giraud, for God's sake, let him be here!*"

Giraud left in silence. "Bring the other one," Giraud told someone in the hall.

Justin leaned against the chair arm, broken out in cold sweat, not seeing the floor, seeing Ari's apartment, seeing it in flashes that wiped out here and now. Hearing the opening of doors, the shouts in distance, the echoes of footsteps coming his way. Grant, he hoped. He hoped to God it was Grant first, and not the tech with the hypo.

Olders passed them on the sidewalk and Ari kept on being azi, did just what Florian and Catlin did, made the little bow, and kept going.

They were not the only kids. There were youngers who bowed to them, solemn and earnest. And one group hardly more than babies following an Older leader in red, the youngers all in blue, all solemnly holding each other's hands.

"This is Blue," Florian said as they walked along past the string of youngers. "Mostly youngers here. I was in that building right over there when I was a Five."

They took the walk between the buildings, going farther and farther from the road that ran through the Town.

They had already seen Green Barracks, outside, because it would be hard to get out without questions, Catlin said; and they had seen the training field; and the Industry section, and they walked up and looked in the door of the thread mill; and the cloth mill; and the metal shop; and the flour mill.

The next sign on the walk was green, and then white in green. It was real easy to find a place in the town: she knew how to do it now. She knew the color sequence, and how the Town was laid out in sections, and how you could say, like they were now, red-to-white-to-brown-to-green, and you just remembered the string. That meant you went *to* red from where you were, and then you looked for red with a white square, and so on.

The next was a huge building, bigger than the mills, and they had come to the very end of the Town: fields were next, with fences that went all the way to the North Cliffs and the precip towers.

So they stood right at the edge, and looked out through the fences, where azi worked and weeded with the sniffer-pigs.

"Are there platytheres out there?" Ari asked. "Have you ever seen one?"

"I haven't," Florian said. "But they're out there." He pointed to where the cliffs touched the river. "That's where they come from. They've put concrete there. Deep. That stops them so far."

She looked all along the fence to the river, and looked

along the other way, toward the big barn. There were big animals there, in a pen, far away. "What are those?"

"Cows. They feed them there. Come on. I know something better."

"Florian," Catlin said. "That's risky."

"What's risky?" Ari said.

Florian knew a side door to the barn. It was dark inside with light coming from open doors at the middle and down at the far end. The air was strange, almost good and not quite bad, like nothing she had ever smelled. The floor was dirt, and feed-bins, Florian called them, lined either wall. Then there were stalls. There was a goat in one.

Ari went to the rail and looked at it up close. She had seen goats and pigs up by the House, but never up close, because she was not supposed to go out on the grounds. It was white and brown. Its odd eyes looked at her, and she stared back with the strangest feeling it was thinking about her, it was alive and thinking, the way not even an AI could.

"Come on," Catlin whispered. "Come on, they'll see us."

She hurried with Catlin and Florian, ducked under a railing when Florian did, and followed him through a door and through a dark place and out another door into the daylight, blinking with the change.

There was a pen in front of them, and a big animal that jangled tape-memory, tapes of Earth, story-tapes of a long time ago.

"He's Horse," Florian said, and stepped up and stood on the bottom rail.

So did she. She leaned her elbows on the top rail as Catlin stepped up beside her, and just stared with her heart thumping.

He snorted and threw his head, making his mane toss. That was what you called it. A mane. He had hooves, but not like the pigs and the goats. He had a white diamond on his forehead.

"Wait," Florian said, and dived off the rail and went back in. He came back out with a bucket, and Horse's ears came up, Horse came right over and put his head over to the rail to eat out of the bucket.

Ari climbed a rail higher and put out her hand and stroked his fur. He smelled strong, and he felt dusty and very solid. Solid like Ollie. Solid and warm, like nothing in her life since Ollie.

"Has he got a saddle and a bridle?" she asked.

"What's that?" Florian asked.

"So you can ride him."

Florian looked puzzled, while Horse battered away with his head in the bucket Florian was holding. "Ride him, sera?"

"Work him close to the corner."

Florian did, so that Horse was very close to the rail. She climbed up to the last, and she put her leg out and just pushed off and landed on Horse's back.

Horse moved, real sudden, and she grabbed the mane to steer with. He felt—wonderful. Really strong, and warm.

And all of a sudden he gave a kind of a bounce and ducked his head and bounced again, really hard, so she flew off, up into the air and down again like she didn't weigh anything, the sky and the fence whirling until it was just ground.

Bang.

She was on her face, mostly. It hurt and it didn't hurt, like part of her was numb and all her bones were shaken up.

Then Catlin's voice: "Don't touch her! Careful!"

"I'm all right," she said, tasting blood and dust, but it was hard to talk, her breath was mostly gone and her stomach hurt. She moved her leg and tried to get up on her arm, and then it really hurt.

"Look out, look out, sera, don't!" Florian's knee was right in her face, and that was good, because the pain took her breath and she fell right onto his leg instead of facedown in the dirt. "Catlin, get help! Get Andy! Fast!"

"I think I needed a saddle," she said, thinking about it, trying not to snivel or to throw up, because she hurt all through her bones, worse than she had ever hurt, and her shoulder and her stomach were worst. There was still dust in her mouth. She thought her lip was cut. "Help me up," she told Florian, because lying that way hurt her back.

"No, sera, please, don't move, your arm's broken."

She tried to move on her own, to get a look at what a broken arm looked like. But she was hurting worse and worse, and she thought she would throw up if she tried.

"What did Horse do?" she asked Florian. She could not figure that.

"He just flipped his hind legs up and you flew off. I don't think he meant to, I really don't, he isn't mean."

There were people running. She heard them, she tried to move and see them, but Florian was in the way until they were all around, azi voices, quiet and concerned, telling her the meds were coming, warning her not to move.

She wished she could get up. It was embarrassing to be lying in the dirt with everyone hovering over her and her not able to see them.

She figured Giraud was going to yell, all right; that part would work real well.

She just wished the meds would hurry.

X

Grant sat with his back braced against the padded wall, with a cramp in his folded legs gone all the way to pain under Justin's weight, but he was not about to move, not about to move even his hands, one on Justin's shoulder, one on Justin's forehead, that kept him stable and secure. No movement in the cell, no sound, while the drug slowly ebbed away.

Security would not leave them unattended. There were two guards in the soundproofed, glass-walled end of this recovery cell. Rules, they said, did not permit anyone but a physician with a detainee in recovery. But Giraud had not regarded any of the rules this far. He did whatever he wanted; and permission was easy for him, an afterthought.

Justin was awake, but he was still in that de-toxing limbo where the least sensation, the least sound magnified itself and echoed. Grant kept physical contact with him, talked to him now and again to reassure him.

"Justin. It's Grant. I'm here. How are you doing?"

"All right." Justin's eyes half-opened.

"Are you clearer now?"

A little larger breath. "I'm doing all right. I'm still pretty open."

"I've got you. Nothing's going on. I've been here all the time."

"Good," Justin murmured, and his eyes drifted shut again.

Beyond that Grant did not attempt to go. Giraud had limited the questioning to the visit with Jordan and the possibility of Justin's involvement in Ari's disappearance. To reassure Justin there would be no more questions would be dangerous. There might be. To encourage him to talk, when they were likely being taped—was very dangerous, tranked as he was.

Giraud had asked: "How do you feel about young Ari?"

And Justin had said, with all his thresholds flat: "Sorry for her."

There was motion in the glass-walled booth. Grant looked up, saw Denys Nye in the room with the guards, saw them exchange words, saw the guards come and open the door into the recovery cell to let Denys in.

Grant gave Denys a hard look, locked his arms across Justin, and bent close to his ear: "Justin. Ser Denys is here, easy, I have you, I won't leave."

Justin was aware. His eyes opened.

Denys walked very quietly for so large a man. He came close and stopped, leaning near, speaking very softly. "They've found Ari. She's all right."

Justin's chest moved in a gasp after air. "Is that true?" he asked. "Grant, is he telling the truth?"

Grant glared at Denys, at a round, worried face, and gave up a little of his anger. "I think he may be." He tightened his arms again so Justin could feel his presence.

"It's true," Denys said and leaned closer, keeping his voice very, very quiet. "Justin, I'm terribly sorry. Truly I am. We'll make this up to you."

Justin's heart was hammering under his hand. "Easy," Grant said, his own heart racing while he sorted Denys' words for content. And then because he had never felt so much unadulterated anger in his entire life. "How are you going to do that, ser?" he said to Denys softly, so softly. "The child is safe. What about the rest of Reseune's resources? You're *fools*, ser. You've risked a mind whose limits you don't even know, you've persecuted him all his life, and you treat him as if he were the perpetrator of every harm in Reseune—when he's never, *never*, in his entire life—done harm to any human being, when Yanni Schwartz could tell you they took him *off* real-time because he couldn't stand people suffering. Where's Reseune's vast expertise in psychology, when it can't tell that he isn't capable of harming *anyone*, not even the people who make his life *hell*?''

"Grant," Justin murmured, "Grant, —''

Denys' brow furrowed. "No," he said in a hushed voice, "I know, I know, I'm sorry is too little, and far too late. Grant is quite right. You're going home now, you're going home. Please. Believe me. We did find Ari. She's in hospital, she had a fall, but everything's all right. She ran away on her own, disguised herself—it was a childish prank, absolutely nothing you had anything to do with, we know that. I won't stay here, I know I have no business here, but I felt I had to tell you Ari's all right. I believed you'd want to know that because you *don't* want any harm to her, and God knows you deserve some courtesy after this. I mean it. I'll make this up somehow, I promise that. I let too much go on for *security's* sake, and it's not going to go on happening. I promise that, too.'' He put a hand on Grant's shoulder. "Grant, there's a group of meds coming here. They'll take him the tunnel route, over to your Residency, they'll take him home, if that's what he wants. Or he can rest here till he recovers. Whatever he wants.''

"Home," Grant said. "Is that right, Justin? Do you want to go home now?''

Justin nodded faintly. "I want to go home.''

Carefully enunciated. More self-control than a moment ago. Justin's arm twitched and lifted and he laid it on his stomach, in the same careful way, return of conscious control.

"I promise you," Denys said tightly. "No more of this.''

Then Denys left, anger in the attitude of his body.

Grant hugged Justin and laid his head against Justin's, editing the tension out of his own muscles, because Justin could read that. Azi-mind. Quiet and steady.

"Was Denys here?" Justin asked.

"He just left," Grant said. "Just a little while and you're going home. I say it's true. They found Ari, it wasn't your fault, they know that. You can rest now. Wake up at your own speed. I'm not going to leave you, not even for a minute."

Justin heaved a sigh. And was quiet then.

_____ **xi** _____

Ari rode back home in the bus, just for that little distance, and she argued with uncle Denys until he let her walk from the front door herself, holding his hand, with the other arm in a sling; but after the ride, it was almost longer, she thought, than she was going to be able to make. Her knees were getting weak and she was sweating under her blouse, that they had had to cut because of the cast, even to get it on.

She was not going to be out in public in her nightgown and her robe. She was going to walk, herself. She was determined on that.

But she was terribly glad to see the inside of uncle Denys' apartment, and to see Nelly there, and Florian and Catlin, all looking worried and so glad to see her. Even Seely looked happy.

She felt like crying, she was so glad to see them. But she didn't. She said: "I want my bed." And uncle Denys got her there, with the last strength that she had, while Nelly fluttered ahead of them.

Nelly had her bed turned down. Poo-thing was there where he belonged. The pillows were fluffed up. It felt so good when she lay down.

"Let me help you out of your clothes," Nelly said.

"No," she said, "just let me rest a while, Nelly." And uncle Denys said that was a good idea.

"I want a soft drink, Nelly," she said, while uncle Denys was leaving. "I want Florian and Catlin."

So Nelly went out; and in a little while Florian and Catlin came in, very quiet, very sober, bringing her soft drink.

"We feel terrible," Florian said. And they both looked it.

They had been with her at the hospital. They had been so scared, both of them, and they had stayed with her and looked like they could jump at anybody who looked wrong. But finally they had had to go home, because she told them to, uncle Denys said she should, they were so scared and so upset, and they needed to settle down. So she woke up enough to tell them it wasn't their fault and to send them home.

I'll be there in a little while, she had said.

So she was.

Dr. Ivanov said she was lucky she had only broken her arm, and not her head. And she felt lucky about it too. She kept seeing the sky and the ground, and feeling the jolt in her bones.

Uncle Denys said she was lucky too, that Horse could have killed her, and he was awfully upset.

That was true. But she told uncle Denys it wasn't Horse's fault, he just sort of moved. "Horse is all right, isn't he?" she had asked.

"Horse is fine," uncle Denys had said. "He's just fine. You're the one we're worried about."

That was nice. People generally weren't, not in any nice way. Dr. Ivanov was kind to her, the nurses gave her soft drinks, Florian and Catlin hung around her until she sent them away. The one thing she had not gotten out of it was uncle Giraud: uncle Giraud had not come at all, but she was too tired to want him there anyway, it was all too much work.

Now Florian and Catlin were back and she was safe in her bed and she really, truly, felt just sort of—away from everything. Quiet. She was glad people were being nice, not because she couldn't Work them, but because she was so tired and it took so much, and she just wanted to lie there and not hurt awhile, after she had drunk a little of her soft drink.

"It's not your fault," she said to Florian and Catlin. "It was my idea, wasn't it?"

"We shouldn't have let you," Florian said.

"Yes, you should have," she said, frowning real quick. "You do what I tell you and that's what I told you. Isn't that so?"

"Yes," Catlin said after a moment. "That's so."

They both looked happier then.

She slept all afternoon, with her arm raised in a sling the

way Dr. Ivanov said she had to, to keep her hand from swelling. She didn't think that would work, because she always tossed around a lot, but it did: she went right off to sleep, waked up once when Nelly told her to take a pill, and went back to sleep, because it was her bed and her room, and the pills that kept her from hurting also made her very drowsy.

But Nelly woke her up for supper, and she had to eat with her left hand. Dr. Ivanov had said things about left-right dominance to her and said how she mustn't do any writing until she got out of the cast, but she could do everything else. Dr. Ivanov said she should have a Scriber to help her with her lessons, just like his, and she liked that idea.

He said that she ought to be in the cast about three weeks, because he had done a lot of special things to help it heal fast, and it was going to be good as new. He said she was going to do gym exercises after, to make her arm strong again. She agreed with that. Having a broken arm was an adventure, but she didn't want it to do anything permanent.

It was kind of interesting to have the cast and all, and to have everyone fussing over her. The way people changed when they were anxious was interesting. She thought a lot about it when she was awake.

She had her supper, things she could eat with her fingers, and she wanted Florian and Catlin to stay in her room, because she was awake now. But uncle Denys came in and said they could come in a little while, but right then he had to have a Talk with her.

"I don't want to," she said, and pouted a little, because she really hurt, and it wasn't fair of uncle Denys, uncle Denys had been nice all day, and now everybody was going to go back the other way before she was ready for it, she saw it coming.

"It won't be a long one," uncle Denys said, shutting the door, "and I'm not even going to mention about your going down to the Town."

That wasn't what she expected. So she was curious and uncomfortable at the same time, while he pulled Nelly's chair over: she was glad he wasn't going to sit on the bed, because she was just settled and he was so heavy.

"Ari," he said, leaning forward with his elbows on his knees and his face very anxious. "Ari, I want to tell you why everyone was so upset, but this isn't about the Town: it's about how important you are, and how there are people—there are people who might want to hurt you, if they got into Reseune. That's why you scared Security so bad.''

That was serious. It clicked right in with the Safety in the Halls lecture and the fact that she was the only kid she knew who had two Security azi for company. She was interested and scared, because it was like it sent out little hooks into a whole lot of things. "So who are they?"

"People who would have hurt your predecessor. Do you know why they put PR on a CIT number?"

"Because they're a Parental Replicate."

"Do you know what that means?"

She nodded, definitely. "That means they're a twin to their own maman or their papa.''

"Just any kind of twin?"

"No. Identical."

"Identical all the way down to their genesets, right?"

She nodded.

"You don't have a PR on your number. But you could have.''

That was confusing. And scary. It didn't make sense at all.

"Pay attention. Don't think about it. Let me guide you through this, Ari. Your maman, Jane Strassen, had a very good friend, who died, who died very suddenly. Reseune was going to make another one of her, which, you know, means making a baby. Jane said that she wanted that baby, she wanted to bring it up herself, for her own, because she didn't want that baby to go to anybody else. She did it for her friend, who died. And when she got that baby she loved it so much it was hers. Do you understand me, Ari?"

There was a cold lump in her throat. She was cold all over, right down to her fingers.

"Do you understand me, Ari?"

She nodded.

"Jane *is* truly your maman. That's so, nothing can change that, Ari. Your maman is whoever loves you and takes care of you and teaches you like Jane did.''

"*Why did she leave me?*"

"Because she had to do something only she could do. Because, next to the first Ari herself, Jane Strassen is the best one to do it. Also, Ari, Jane had another daughter—a grown daughter named Julia, who was terribly jealous of the time you took; and Julia had a daughter too, named Gloria Strassen, who's your age. Julia made things very hard for your maman, because Julia was being very difficult, and Julia was assigned to Fargone too. Your maman finally had to see about her other daughter, and her granddaughter, because they were terribly jealous and upset about her being your maman. She didn't want to, but that was the way it was. So she went to Fargone and she took them with her because she wasn't going to leave them here where they could be mean to you. She told me to take care of you, she told me she would come back if she could, but it's a terribly long way, Ari, and your maman's health isn't too good. She's quite old, you know, and it would be awfully dangerous for her now. So that's why your maman left, and why she knew she might not be able to come back: she'd done everything for her friend who died, to start with. And she knew she'd have to go away before you were grown. She thought it would be easy, when she started. But she really got to be your maman, and she got to love you not just because of the Ari who died, but because *you're* Ari, and you're *you*, and she loves you just because, that's all.''

Tears started rolling down her face. She didn't even know she was crying till she felt that. Then she moved the wrong arm to wipe them and had to use the other hand, which was awkward.

''She can't have you at Fargone,'' uncle Denys said, ''because, for one thing, she has Julia and Gloria there. And because you're *you*, you're Ari, and your genemother was what she was, and because you have enemies. You could grow up safe here. There were teachers to teach you and people to take care of you—not always the best; I know I'm not the best at bringing up a little girl, but I really have tried, Ari, and I go on trying. I just figure it's time I explained some things to you, because you're old enough to try to go places on your own, that's pretty plain, isn't it? You might run into people who might accidentally say the wrong thing to you, and most of all I didn't want you to hear any of this from some stranger down in the Town. A lot of people know who you are, and you're getting old enough to start asking questions—like why your name is Emory and not Strassen, to start with."

She *hated* to feel stupid. And that was a big one, a terribly, terribly big one. Of course people had different names, a lot of people had different names. She thought it was who maman picked to make her baby with.

You got into trouble, making up your mind why things were that grown-ups wouldn't tell you.

Why can't I be Strassen? she remembered asking maman.

Because you're Emory, maman had said, because, that's why. I'm Strassen. Look at Tommy Carnath. His maman is Johanna Morley. Grown-ups figure these things out.

Her stomach turned over, suddenly, and she felt sweaty and cold.

"Please," she said, "uncle Denys, I'm going to be sick. Call Nelly."

Denys did, real quick. And Nelly got her arm unhooked and got her to the bathroom, where she felt that way for a long time, but nothing happened. She only wished she could be, because she hurt inside and out.

Nelly got her a glass of fizzy stuff for her stomach, and it was awful, but she drank it. Then she felt a little better, and lay against her pillows while Nelly stroked her face and her hair a long, long time and worried about her.

Nelly was the same. Nelly was the way Nelly had always been to her. She guessed it was true maman was really still her maman, but she was not sure who *she* was anymore. She wanted to find out. Uncle Denys knew, and she wanted to ask him, but she was not sure she wanted any more yet.

Uncle Denys came back in finally, and he came and patted her shoulder, the good one. "Are you all right, sweet? Are you going to be all right?"

Maman called her that. Uncle Denys never had. Ari bit her lip till it hurt more than that did.

"Ari?"

"What other things was I going to notice?"

"That there was a very famous woman at Reseune who had the same name as you," uncle Denys said, and pulled the chair over, so Nelly got back, and took some stuff off the night-table and took it to the bath. "That you look just like her when she was a little girl, and her pictures are all through the tapes you really need to study. She was very, very smart, Ari, smarter than anyone. She wasn't your maman. You aren't her daughter. You're something a lot closer. How close we don't know yet, but you're a very extraordinary little girl, and I know Jane is very, very proud of you.''

He patted her shoulder then. Nelly had come back through and left. Now he got up again. She didn't care. She was still thinking and it was like her brains were mush.

''Ari, I'm going to have Florian and Catlin stay all night in your room, if you want. I think you'd like that, wouldn't you?''

She didn't know how she was going to tell Florian and Catlin she had been that stupid. They wouldn't stop liking her: they were her azi, and they had to like her. But they were going to be upset. They were going to be upset by her being upset. So she swiped the back of her left hand across her face and tried to stop sniveling.

''Ari?''

''Does Nelly know?''

''Nelly knows. Nelly doesn't understand, but Nelly knows, she always has.''

That made her awfully mad at Nelly.

''Nelly was your maman's, Ari. Your maman put an awfully heavy load on Nelly, telling her as much as she did, and telling Nelly she had to keep that secret. Nelly is very loyal to your maman. Of course she would.''

''Ollie knew too.''

''Ollie knew. Do you want me to send Florian and Catlin to spend the night? They can have pallets over in the corner. They won't mind at all.''

''Do they know?''

''No. Only your maman's people knew. They're yours.''

She felt better about that. At least *they* hadn't been laughing at her. ''Does Amy Carnath know?''

Uncle Denys frowned and took a second about that. ''Why does Amy Carnath knowing matter?''

''Because it *does*,'' she snapped at him.

''Ari, I'm in charge of your education. Your maman and I agreed that there are some questions I just won't answer, because they're for you to figure out. You'll be mad at me sometimes, but I'll have to stay by what I agreed with your maman. You're very, very bright. Your maman expects you to figure out some of these things yourself, just the way the first Ari would, because she knows how good you are at figuring things out. It's part of your growing up. There'll be a lot of times you'll ask me things—and I'll say, you have to figure that one, because you're the one who wants that answer. Just remember this: whatever you ask anyone—can tell them a lot. You think about that, Ari.''

He closed the door.

Ari thought about it. And thought that uncle Denys was maybe doing what maman had said; and maybe again uncle Denys wasn't. It was hard to tell, when people could be lying to you about what maman had said.

Or even about what she was.

In a little while more Florian and Catlin came in, very quiet and sober. ''Ser Denys says you have orders for us,'' Catlin said.

Ari made her face azi-like, very quiet. Her eyelashes were still wet. She figured her nose was red. They would pick all of that up, but she couldn't stop that, they had to be near her. ''I've got something to tell you first. Sit down on the bed. I've found out some answers.''

They sat down, one on a side, very carefully, so they didn't jostle her.

''First,'' she said, ''uncle Denys says I'm not from maman's geneset at all, I'm a PR of somebody else, and she was a friend of maman's. That maman has a grown-up daughter and a granddaughter maman never told me about, and Nelly and Ollie both knew all about where maman got me. But he won't tell me a whole lot else. He says *I* have to find it out.'' She made the little sign with her fingers that said one of them should come close and listen. But she couldn't make it with the right hand. So it was Florian who got up and came clear around the bed to put his ear up against her mouth. ''It might be uncle Denys Working me. I don't know. And I don't know why he would, except Giraud is his brother. Pass it to Catlin.''

He did, and Catlin's eyebrows went up and Catlin's face got very thoughtful and still when she looked at her. Catlin nodded once, with a look that meant business.

So she was not sure whether she felt stupid or not, or whether it was true at all, or whether part of it was.

Florian and Catlin could track down a lot of things, because that was what they knew how to do.

It answered a lot of the What's Unusuals, that was what scared her most, except it didn't answer all of them.

Like why the Disappeareds and what Giraud was up to.

Like why maman hadn't written *her* a letter in the first place, or what had happened to it if maman had.

There were new ones.

Like it was Unusual that they didn't just tell her the truth from the start.

Like it was Unusual maman had gone all round the thing about her name, and told her her papa was a man named James Carnath. Which was still not where she got the Emory.

It was Unusual maman had dodged around a whole lot of things that maman had not wanted to answer. She had not wanted to ask very much when she was a little kid, because she felt it make maman real uncomfortable.

And when she thought about it, she knew maman had Worked her too, she could feel it happen when she remembered it.

That was what made her want to throw up.

She was scared, scared that nothing was true, not even what uncle Denys was telling her. But she couldn't let anybody know that.

That last uncle Denys had said was something she knew: what you asked told a whole lot to somebody you might not want to trust. So uncle Denys knew that too, and warned her not to ask him things.

Like maman, only uncle Denys did it a different way, straight out: don't give things away to me because you don't know whether I'm all right or not.

If uncle Denys wanted to Work her, he was doing something real complicated, and the pain medicine made her brain all fuzzy. If that was what he was doing he was starting off by confusing her.

Or taking her Fix off what she was trying to look at.

Dammit, she thought. Dammit.

Because she was stuck in this bed and she hurt and she couldn't think at all past the trank.

_____ **xii** _____

Report to my office, the message from Yanni said, first thing that Justin read when he brought the office computer up; and he turned around and looked at Grant. "I've got to go see Yanni," he said; and Grant swung his chair around and looked at him.

No comment. There was nothing in particular to say. Grant just looked worried.

"See you," Justin said with a wry attempt at humor. "Wish you could witness this one."

"So do I," Grant said, not joking at all.

He was not up to a meeting with Yanni. But there was no choice. He shrugged, gave Grant a worried look, and walked out and down the hall, with his knees close to wobbling under him, it was still that bad and he was still that much in shock.

God, he thought, get me around this.

Somehow.

Grant had kept track, with Grant's azi-trained memory and Grant's professional understanding of subject, psychset, and what he was hearing, of everything that had gone on around him while he was answering Giraud's questions and of everything that had gone on around him in recovery, right down to the chance words and small comments of the meds that had taken him home. Playing all that back and knowing it was *all* that had gone on, was immeasurably comforting; having Grant simply *there* through the night had kept him reasonably well focused on here and now, and made him able to get up in the morning, adopt a deliberately short-sighted cheerfulness, and decide he was going to work.

I can at least get some of the damned records-keeping done, he had said to Grant, meaning the several towering mounds of their own reports that had been waiting weeks to be checked against computer files and archives and hand-stamped as Archived before being sent for the shredder. Can't think of a better day for it.

He could not cope with changes, and he reckoned on his way down the hall and up to Yanni's door that Security thought it had found something or suspected something in the interview, God knew what, and Yanni—

God knew.

"Marge," he said to Yanni's aide, "I'm here."

"Go on in," Marge said. "He's expecting you."

A flag on his log-on, that was what.

He opened the door and found Yanni at his desk. "Ser."

Yanni looked up and he braced himself. "Sit down," Yanni said very quietly.

Oh, God, he thought, gone completely off his balance. He sank into the chair and felt himself tensed up and out of control.

"Son," Yanni said, more quietly than he had ever heard Yanni speak, "how are you?"

"I'm fine," he said, two syllables, carefully managed, damn near stammered.

"I raised hell when I heard," Yanni said. "All the way to Denys' office *and* Petros *and* Giraud. I understand they let Grant stay through it."

"Yes, ser."

"Petros put that as a mandate on your charts. They better have. I'll tell you this, they *did* record it, not on the Security recorders, but it exists. You can get it if you need it. That's Giraud's promise, son. They're sane over there this morning."

He stared at Yanni with a blank, sick feeling that it had to be a lead-in, that he was being set up for something. Recorded, that was sure. Trust the man and he would come in hard and low.

"Is this another voice-stress?" he asked Yanni, to have it out and over with.

The line between Yanni's brows deepened. "No. It's not. I want to explain some things to you. Things are real difficult in Giraud's office right now. A lot of pressure. They're going to have to break the secrecy seal on this. The kid's timing was immaculate. I don't want to go into it more than that, except to tell you they've broken the news to Ari, at least as far as her not being Jane Strassen's biological daughter, and her being a replicate of somebody named Ariane Emory, who's no more than a name to her. So some of that pressure is going to be relieved real soon. She's got a broken arm and a lot of bruises. They threw the news at her while she was tranked so they could at least hold the initial reaction to the emotional level where they could halfway control it, get it settled and accepted on a gut level before she heads at the why of it with that logical function of hers, which, I don't need to tell you, is damned sharp and damned persistent. I'm telling you this because she's come your way before and she's going to be hunting information. If it happens, don't panic. Follow procedures, call Denys' office, and tell her you have to do that: that Security will get upset if you don't—which is the truth.''

He drew easier breaths, told himself it was still a trap, but at least the business assumed some definable shape, a calamity postponed to the indefinable future.

"Do you have any word,'' he asked Yanni, "how Jordan came through this?''

"I called him last night. He said he was all right, he was concerned for you. You know how it is, there's so damned much we can't do on the phone. I told him you were fine; I'd check on you; I'd call him again today.''

"Tell him I'm all right.'' He found himself with a deathgrip on the right chair arm, his fingers locked till they ached. He let go, trying to relax. "Thanks. Thanks for checking on him.''

Yanni shrugged, heaved a sigh and scowled at him. "You suspect me like hell, don't you?''

He did not answer that.

"Listen to me, son. I'll put up with a lot, but I know something about how you work, and I knew damn well you hadn't had anything to do with the kid, it was Giraud's damn bloody insistence on running another damn probe on a mind that just may be worth two or three others around this place, never mind *my* professional judgment, *Giraud* is in a bloodyminded *hurry*, to hell with procedures, to hell with the law, to hell with everything in his way.'' Yanni drew breath. "Don't get me started. What I called you in here to tell you is, Denys just put your research on budget. Not a big one, God knows, but you're going to be seeing about half the load you've been getting off the Rubin project, and you're going to get computer time over in Sociology, not much of it, but some. Call it guilt on Administration's part. Call it whatever you like. You're going to route the stuff through me to Sociology, through Sociology over to Jordan, and several times a year you're going to get some time over at Planys. That's the news. I thought it might give you something cheerful to think about. All right?"

"Yes, ser," he said after a moment, because he had to say something. The most dangerous thing in the world was to start trusting Yanni Schwartz, or believing when indicators started a downhill slide that it had been a momentary glitch.

"Go on. Take a break. Go. Get out of here."

"Yes, ser." He levered himself up out of the chair, he got himself out the door past Marge without even looking at her, and walked the hall in a kind of numb terror that somewhere Security was involved in this, that in the way they had of getting him off his guard and then hitting him hardest, he might find something had happened to Grant—it was the most immediate thing he could think of, and the worst.

But Grant was there, Grant was in the door waiting for him and worried.

"Yanni was polite," he said. The tiny, paper-piled office was a claustrophobic closeness. "Let's go get a cup of coffee." No mind that they had the makings in the office. He wanted space around him, the quiet, normal noise of human beings down in the North Wing coffee bar.

Breaking schedule, being anywhere out of the ordinary, could win them both another session with Giraud. Nothing was safe. Anything could be invaded. It was the kind of terror a deep probe left. He ought to be on trank. Hell if he wanted it.

He told Grant what Yanni had said, over coffee in the restaurant. Grant listened gravely and said: "About time. About time they came to their senses."

"You trust it?" he asked Grant. Desperately, the way he had taken Grant's word for what was real and what was not. He was terrified Grant would fail him finally, and tell him yes, believe them, trust everything. It was what it sounded like, from the one point of sanity he had.

"No," Grant said, with a little lift of his brows. "No more than yesterday. But I think *Yanni's* telling the truth. I think he's starting to suspect what you might be and what they might lose in their preoccupation with young Ari. That's the idea he may have gotten through to Denys. If it gets to Denys, it may finally get through to Giraud. No. Listen to me. I'm talking very seriously."

"Dammit, Grant, —" He felt himself ludicrously close to tears, to absolute, overloaded panic. "I'm not holding this off well. I'm too damned open, even wide awake. Don't confuse me."

"I'm going to say this and get off it, fast. *If* the word is getting up to them from Yanni, it's perfectly logical they're turning helpful. I'm not saying they're any different. I'm saying there may be some changes. For God's sake take it easy, take it quietly, don't try to figure them on past performance, don't try to figure them at all for a few days. You want me to talk to Yanni?"

"No!"

"Easy. All right. All right."

"Dammit, don't patronize me!"

"Oh, we *are* short-fused. Drink your coffee. You're doing fine, just fine, just get a grip on here, all right? Yanni's gone crazy, you're just fine, I'm just fine, Administration's totally off the edge, I don't know what's different."

He gave a sneeze of a laugh, made a furtive wipe at his eyes, and took a sip of cooling coffee.

"God, I don't know if I can last this."

"Easy, easy, easy. One day at a time. We'll cut it short today and go home, all right?"

"I want us near witnesses."

"Office, then."

"Office." He drew a slow breath, getting his pulse-rate back to normal.

And bought a holo-poster at the corner shop, on the way back, for the office wall over his desk.

Grant lifted an eyebrow, getting a look at it while he was handing the check-out his credit card.

It was a plane over the outback. FLY RESEUNEAIR, it said.

Verbal Text from:
A QUESTION OF UNION
Union Civics Series: #3

**Reseune Educational Publications: 9799-8734-3
approved for 80 +**

*In the years between 2301 and 2351, Expansion was the un-
questioned policy of Union: the colonial fervor which had led
to the establishment of the original thirteen star stations
showed no sign of abating.*

*The discovery of Cyteen's biological riches and the new
technology of jumpspace travel brought Cyteen economic
self-sufficiency and eventual political independence, not,
however, before it had reached outward and established a
number of colonies of its own. The fact that Cyteen was
founded by people seeking independence from colonial poli-
cies of the Earth Company, however, provided a philosophical base important to all Union culture—the idea of a new
form of government.*

*From the time the tensions between Cyteen and the Earth
Company they had fled, led to the Company Wars and the
Secession, we have to consider Cyteen as one planet within
the larger context of Union. Within that context, the desire
for independence and the strong belief in local autonomy;
and second, the enthusiasm for exploration, trade, and the
development of a new frontier—have been the predominant
influences. The framers of the Constitution made it a cardinal
principle that the Union government will not cross the local*

threshold, be it a station dock, a gravity well, or a string of stars declaring themselves a political unit within Union—unless there is evidence that the local government does not have the consent of the governed, or unless one unit exits its own area to impose its will on a neighbor. So there can be, and may one day be, many governments within Union, and still only one Union, which maintains what the founders called a consensus of the whole.

It was conceived as a framework able to exist around any local structure, even a non-human one, a framework infinitely adaptable to local situations, in which local rule serves as the check on Union and Union as the check on local rule.

But, in the way of secessions, Union began in conflict. The Company Wars were a severe strain on the new government, and many institutions originated as a direct response to those stresses—among them, the first political parties.

The Expansionist party may be said to have existed from the founding of Union; but as the war with the Earth Company entered its most critical phase, the Centrist movement demanded negotiation and partition of space at Mariner. The Centrists, who had a strong liberal, pacifist and Reunionist leaning in the inception of the organized party, gained in strength rapidly during the last years of the War, and ironically, lost much of that strength as the Treaty of Pell ended the War in a negotiation largely unpopular on the home front. Union became generally more pro-Expansion as enormous numbers of troops returned to the population centers and strained the systems considerably.

From that time the Centrist platform reflected in some part the growing fears that unchecked Expansion and colonization would lead to irredeemable diffusion of human cultures—and, in the belief of some, —to war between human cultures which had arisen with interests enough in common to be rivals and different enough to be enemies.

But except for social scientists such as Pavel Brust, the principal proponent of the Diffusion Theory, the larger number of Centrists were those who stood to be harmed by further colonization, such as starstations which looked to become peripheral to the direction of that expansion, due to accident *of position; and the war-years children, who saw themselves locked in a cycle of conflict which they had not chosen.*

The Centrists received a considerable boost from two events: first, the peaceful transition within the Alliance from the wartime administration of the Konstantins to that of the Dees, known to be moderates; second, the discovery of a well-developed alien region on the far side of Sol. Sol, sternly rebuffed by the alien Compact, turned back toward human space, and it became a principal tenet of the Centrist Party that a period of stability and consolidation might lead to a reunification of humanity, or at least a period of peace. To certain people troubled by the realization that they were not only not alone, but that they had alien competitors, this seemed the safest course.

In 2389 the Centrists were formally joined by the Abolitionists, who opposed the means by which existing and proposed colonies were designed, some on economic grounds and others on moral grounds ranging from philosophical to religious, denouncing practices from mindwipe to psychsurgery, and calling for an end to the production of azi. Previously the Abolitionists had lacked a public voice, and indeed, were more a cross-section of opposition to the offworld government, including the Citizens for Autonomy, who wished to break up the government and make all worlds and stations independent of central authority; the Committee Against Human Experimentation; the Religious Council; and others, including, without sanction of the official party, the radical Committee of Man, which committed various acts of kidnapping and terrorism aimed at genetics research facilities and government offices.

To those who feared Sol's influence, and those who felt the chance of alien war was minimal, the Centrist agenda seemed a dangerous course: loss of momentum and economic collapse was the Expansionist fear. And at the head of the new Expansionist movement was a coalition of various interests, prominent among whom, as scientist, philosopher and political figure, was Ariane Emory.

Her murder in 2404 touched off a furor mostly directed at the Abolitionists, but the Centrist coalition broke under the assault.

What followed was a period of retrenchment, reorganiza-

tion, and realignment, until the discovery in 2412 of the Gehenna plot and the subsequent investigations of culpability
gave the Centrists a cause and an issue. Gehenna lent sub-
stance to Centrist fears; and at the same time tarnished the
image of the Expansionist majority, not least among them
Ilya Bogdanovitch, the Chairman of the Nine; Ariane Emory
of Reseune; and admiral Azov, the controversial head of Defense, who had approved the plan.

The Centrists for the first time in 2413 gained a majority in
the Senate of Viking and in the Council of Mariner; and held
a sizable bloc of seats and appointed posts within the Senate
of Cyteen. They thus gained an unprecedented percentage of
seats in the Council of Worlds and frequently mustered four
votes of the Nine.

Although they did not hold a majority in either body, their
influence could no longer be discounted, and the swift gains
of the Centrists both worried the Expansionist majority and
made the uncommitted delegates on any given issue a pivotal
element: delegates known to be wavering were courted with
unprecedented fervor, provoking charges and counter-
charges of influence-trading and outright bribery that led to
several recall votes, none of which, however, succeeded in
unseating the incumbent.

The very fabric of Union was being tested in the jousting of
strong interest groups. Certain political theorists called into
question the wisdom of the founders who had created the
electorate system, maintaining that the system encouraged
electorates to vote their own narrow interests above that of
the nation at large.

It was the aphorism of Nasir Harad, president of the Council, on his own re-election after his Council conviction on
bribery charges, that: **"Corruption means elected officials
trading votes for their own advantage; democracy means
a bloc of voters doing the same thing. The electorates
know the difference."**

CHAPTER 2

i

An announcement came through the public address in Wing One corridors—storm alert, Justin thought, ticking away at his keyboard on a problem while Grant got up to lean out the door and see what it was.

Then: "Justin," Grant said urgently. "*Justin.*"

He shoved back and got up.

Everything in the hall had stopped, standing and listening.

"*. . . in Novgorod,*" the PA said, "*came in the form of briefs filed this morning by Reseune lawyers on behalf of Ariane Emory, a minor child, seeking a Writ of Succession and an injunction against any Discovery proceedings of the Council against Reseune. The brief argues that the child, who will be nine in five days, is the legal person of Ariane Emory by the right of Parental Identity, that no disposition of Ariane Emory's property can be taken in any cause without suit brought against the child and her guardians. The second brief seeks an injunction against the activities of the Investigatory Commission on the grounds that their inquiries invade*" *the privacy and compromise the welfare and property rights of a minor child.*

"The news hit the capital as the Commission was preparing to file a bill requiring the surrender of records from Reseune Archives pertinent to the former Councillor, on the grounds that the records may contain information on other Gehenna-style projects either planned or executed.

"Mikhail Corain, leader of the Centrist party and Councillor of Citizens, declared: 'It's an obvious maneuver. Reseune has sunk to its lowest.'

"James Morley, chief counsel for Reseune, when told of the comment, stated: 'We had no wish to bring this suit. The child's privacy and well-being have been our primary considerations, from her conception. We cannot allow her to become a victim of partisan politics. She has rights, and we believe the court will uphold the point. There's no question about her identity. A simple lab test can prove that.'

"Reseune Administration has refused comment. . . ."

---
ii

Ari thought she was crazy sometimes, because twice an hour she thought everyone was lying, and sometimes she thought they were not, that there really had been an Ari Emory before she was born.

But the evening when she could get out of bed and come in her robe to the living room with her arm still in a sling, uncle Denys said he had something to show her and Florian and Catlin; and he had a book filled with paste-in pictures and old faxes.

He had them sit at the table, himself on her left and Florian and then Catlin on her right, and he opened the book on the table, putting it mostly in front of her, a book of photos and holos, and there were papers, dim and showing their age. He showed her a picture of *her*, standing in the front portico of the House with a woman she had never seen.

"That's Ari when she was little," Uncle Denys said. "That's *her* maman. Her name was Olga Emory." There was another picture uncle Denys turned to. "This is James

Carnath. That was your papa." She knew that. It was the picture maman had once showed her.

The girl in the picture looked just exactly like her, but it was not her maman; but it was the right name for her papa. It was all wrong. It was *her* standing there. It was. But the front doors were not like that. Not quite. Not now.

She felt her stomach more and more upset. Uncle Denys turned the page and showed her pictures of old Reseune, Reseune before the House was as big, before the Town was anything but old barracks, and the fields were real small. There were big buildings missing, like the AG barn, and like a lot of the mills and half the town, and *that* Ari was walking with her maman down a Town Road that was the same road, toward a Town that was very different.

There was that Ari, sitting in her same classroom, with a different teacher, with a kind of screwed-up frown on her face while she looked at a jar that was like her saying *Ugh*, she could feel it right in her stomach and feel her own face the way it would be.

But she never had a blouse like that, and she never wore a pin like that in her hair.

She felt herself all sick inside, because it was like it was all real, maman *had* tricked her, and she was stupid like she had been afraid she was, in front of Catlin and Florian, in front of everybody. But she couldn't *not* look at these things, she couldn't do anything but sit there with her arm aching in the dumb cast and herself feeling light-headed and silly being out here in the dining room in her robe and her slippers, looking at herself in a place that was Reseune a long, long time ago.

A *long* time ago.

That Ari had been born—that long ago. Her maman's friend, uncle Denys had called her; and she had not thought when he said that, just how old maman was.

A hundred thirty-four years. No. A hundred forty-one, no, *two*, she was real close to her ninth birthday and maman was that old now.

A hundred forty-two. . . .

She was close to her ninth birthday and maman's letter *had* to come, any day now, and maybe maman would explain some of these things, maybe maman would send her all the letters maman must have written too, all at once, like hers. . . .

"There's your maman," uncle Denys said, and showed her a picture of her and a bunch of other kids all playing, and there was this pretty woman with black hair, with her maman's mouth and her maman's eyes, only *young*, with *her*, but she was about five or six. A baby. Maman had had another Ari, *first*, a long, long time ago.

It hurt to see maman so pretty and not with her at all, not really, but with that other baby. It had stopped hurting until then. And it made her throat ache.

Uncle Denys stopped and hugged her head against his shoulder gently. "I know. I know, Ari. I'm sorry."

She shoved away. She pulled the book over so it was in front of her and she looked at that picture till she could see everything about it, what her maman was wearing, what that Ari was wearing, that proved it was not something she had forgotten, it was really not her, because everything about it was old-fashioned and long-ago.

"That's your uncle Giraud," uncle Denys said, pointing to a gangly boy.

He looked like anybody. He didn't look like he was going to grow up to be nasty as Giraud was. He looked just like any kid.

She turned the page. There was that Ari with her maman, and a lot of other grown-ups.

Then there was *her* with Florian and Catlin, but it was not them, they were all in the middle of old-time Reseune.

She felt another deep chill, like when she flew off Horse and hit the ground. She felt scared, and looked at Florian and Catlin for how they saw it.

They didn't ask. They wouldn't ask. They were being proper with uncle Denys and not interrupting, but she knew they were confused and they were upset, because they had both gone completely azi, paying real close attention.

She couldn't even reach to Florian to squeeze his hand, it was the side with the cast.

"Do you recognize them?" uncle Denys asked.

"Who are they?" Ari asked, angry, terribly angry of a sudden, because it was not making sense, and she was scared, she knew Florian and Catlin were scared, everything was inside out.

"You're not the only one who's come back," Denys said very softly. "There was one other Catlin and one other Florian: they belonged to that other Ari Emory. They protected her all their lives. Do you understand me, Florian? Do you, Catlin?"

"No, ser," Florian said; and: "No, ser," Catlin said. "But it makes sense."

"Why does it make sense?" uncle Denys asked.

"We're azi," Catlin said, the most obvious thing in the world. "There could be a lot of us."

But I'm a CIT, Ari thought, upset all the way through. *Aren't I?*

"You're Alphas," uncle Denys said, "and, no, it's not ordinary with Alphas. You're too difficult to keep track of. You change so fast. But you're still a lot easier to duplicate than a CIT, you're right, because azi start with very specific tape. Teaching Ari has been—ever so much harder."

Teaching me. Teaching me—what? Why?

But she knew that. She understood all across the far and wide of it, that uncle Denys was saying what she was, and not saying it to her, but to Florian and Catlin, because it was something she could not understand as easily as her azi could.

Do you know, maman had asked her, the day she saw the babies, *the difference between a CIT and an azi?*

I only thought I did.

Denys left that page open a long time. "Ari," he said. "Do you understand me?"

She said nothing. When you were confused, it was better to let somebody else be a fool, unless you were the only one who knew the question.

And uncle Denys knew. Uncle Denys was trying to tell her what he knew, in this book, in these pictures that weren't her.

"Your maman taught you," uncle Denys said, "and now I do. You're definitely a CIT. Don't mistake that. You're *you*, Ari, you're very exactly *you*, exactly the way Florian is Florian and Catlin is Catlin, and that's hard to do. It was ever so hard to get this far. Ari was a very, very special little girl, and you're taking up everything she had, everything she could do, everything she held and owned, which is a very great deal, Ari. That you hold Florian and Catlin's contracts is all part of that, because you all belong together, you always have, and it wouldn't be right to leave them out. You own a major share of Reseune itself, you own property enough to make you very, very rich, and you've already proved to us who you are, we haven't any doubt at all. But remember that I told you Reseune has enemies. Now some of those enemies want to come in here and take things that belong to you—they don't even know there *is* an Ari, you understand. They think she died, and that was all of her, and they can just move in and take everything that belonged to her—that belongs to *you*, Ari. Do you know what a lawsuit is? Do you know what it means to sue somebody in court?"

She shook her head, muddled and scared by what uncle Denys said, getting too much, far too much from every direction.

"You know what judges are?"

"Like in a court. They get all the records and stuff. They can send you to hospital."

"A civil suit, Ari: that's different than a criminal case. They don't send you to hospital, but they can say what's so and who owns what. We've lodged a suit in the Supreme Court, in Novgorod, to keep these people from taking everything you own. They can't, you understand, if somebody *owns* it, really owns it. The only thing is, people don't know you exist. You have to show up in that court and *prove* you're really Ari and that you have a right to Ari's CIT-number."

"That's stupid!"

"How do they know you're not just some little girl all made up and telling a lie?"

"I know who I am!"

"How do you prove it to people who've never seen you?"

She sat there trying to think. She had the shivers. "You tell them."

"Then they'll say we're lying. We can send the genetic records, that can prove it, beyond any doubt. But they could say we just got that out of the lab, because of course the Ari geneset is there, isn't it, because you were born out of the lab. They could say there isn't any little girl alive, and she hasn't got any right to anything. That's what could happen.

That's why you have to go, and stand in that court, and tell the judges that's your genetic record, and you're you, Ariane Emory, and you own all that stuff these people in the Council want to take.''

She looked at her right, at Florian and Catlin, at two pale, very azi faces. And back at uncle Denys. ''Could they take Florian and Catlin?''

''If you don't exist, you can't hold a contract, can you?''

''That's *stupid*, uncle Denys! They're stupid!''

''You just have to prove that, don't you? Dear, I wish to hell I could have saved this till you felt better. But there isn't any time. These people are moving fast, and there's going to be a law passed in Council to take everything, *everything* that belongs to you, because they don't know about you. You've got to go to Novgorod and tell the judges it does belong to you and they can't do that.''

''When?''

''In a few days. A very few days. There's more to it, Ari. *Because* you've been a secret, your enemies haven't known about you either. If you go to Novgorod they will know. And you'll be in very real danger from then on. Most of them would sue you in court and try to take what you've got, *that* kind of enemy; but some of them would kill you if they could. Even if you're a little girl. They're that kind.''

''Ser,'' Catlin said, ''who?''

''A man named Rocher, for one. And a few random crazy people we don't know the names of. We wish we did. If Ari goes to Novgorod she'll have a lot of Security with her. Armed Security. They can stop that kind of thing. But you have to watch out for it, you have to watch very closely, and for God's sake, leave any maneuvering to the senior Security people, you two. Just cover Ari.''

''Do we have weapons, ser?''

''I don't think Novgorod would understand that. No. Just cover Ari. Watch around you. Keep her safe. That's all.''

Ari drew a deep breath. ''What am I supposed to do?''

''You talk to the judges. You go in front of the court, you answer their questions about when you were born, and where, and what your name and number are. Uncle Giraud will be there. Giraud knows how to argue with them.''

She went cold and clammy all over. "I don't want Giraud! I want *you* to come."

"Dear, uncle Giraud is especially good at this. He'll show them all the records, and they won't have any trouble believing you. They may take a little cell sample. That'll sting a little if they do that, but you're a brave girl, you won't mind that. You know what that's for. It proves you're not lying. Everyone in the world has seen pictures of Ari Emory—you won't have any trouble with that. But there *will* be other people to deal with. People not in the court. Newspeople. Reporters. There'll be a lot of that. But you're a little girl, and they can't be nasty, they'd better not be, or your uncle Giraud will know exactly what to do with them."

She had never thought it could be a good thing to have uncle Giraud. But uncle Denys was right, uncle Giraud would be a lot better at that.

If he wasn't *with* the Enemy in the first place. Things were getting more and more complicated.

"Florian and Catlin are going for sure?"

"Yes."

"The judges can't just take them, can they?"

"Dear, the law can do anything; but the law won't take what belongs to you. You have to prove you're *you*, that's the whole problem. That's what you're going there for, and if you don't, nothing is safe here either."

So Ari sat in a leather seat in *RESEUNE ONE*, a seat so big her feet hardly reached the floor; and Florian and Catlin sat in the two seats opposite her, taking turns looking out the windows, only she had one right beside her, with the real outback under them for as far as you could see.

They would land at Novgorod, they would land at the airport there, but before they landed they were going to see the city from the air; they would see the spaceport, and the Hall of State and the docks where all the barges went, that chugged past Reseune on the Novaya Volga. They were going to see Swigert Bay and the Ocean. The pilot kept telling them where they were and what they were looking at, which right now was the Great West Sink, which was a brown spot on the maps and a brown place from the air with a lake in the middle. She could talk back to the pilot if she pushed a button by her seat.

"We're coming up on the Kaukash Range on the right side," the pilot said.

They had let her go up front for a little while. She got to see out past the pilot and the co-pilot, when they were following the Novaya Volga.

The pilot asked if she liked flying. She said yes, and the pilot told her what a lot of the controls were, and showed her how the plane steered, and what the computers did.

That was the best thing in days. She had him show Florian and Catlin, until uncle Giraud said she had better sit down and study her papers and let the pilot fly the plane. The pilot had winked at her and said she ought to, they were spilling uncle Giraud's drinks.

She wished she had her arm out of the cast, because that was a nuisance; and gave uncle Giraud an excuse to tell her she ought to stay belted-in in her seat.

Most of all she wished they were all through the court business and the reporters, and they could get to the things uncle Denys told her they were going to get to see while they were in Novgorod. That would be fun. She was going to have her birthday in Novgorod. She wanted to prove everything and then get to that part of it.

Most of all she was worried what would happen if uncle Denys was wrong.

Or if uncle Giraud *couldn't* prove who she was.

The court couldn't make a mistake, uncle Denys said, over and over. Not with the tests they had, and the law was the law: they couldn't take what belonged to somebody without suing, and then it was going to be real hard for them to sue a little girl. Especially because Giraud had a lot of friends in the Defense Bureau, who would classify everything.

That meant Secret.

The reporters are going to be a bigger problem than the court, uncle Denys had said. *The reporters will pull up a lot of the old pictures of the first Ari. You have to expect that. They'll talk about a little girl Reseune birthed a long time ago, a PR off Estelle Bok. It didn't work right. You've beaten all that little girl's problems. If they say you're like that other little girl they're being nasty, and you answer them that you're you, and if they doubt that they can wait and see how you grow up. I've no doubt at all that you can handle that sort of thing. You don't have to be polite if reporters start being nasty, but you can get a lot more out of them if you act like a nice little kid.*

It sounded like a fight. That was what it sounded like. She figured that. It was one of the only times uncle Denys had ever talked to her about Working people, but uncle Denys was good at it, and she was sure he knew what was what.

The Enemy cheats, Catlin always said.

It worried her, about whether the Court ever did.

"Sera," Catlin had come to whisper in her ear that night when they were all going to bed, Florian and Catlin on their pallets, and herself in her own bed with her arm propped up again, "sera, who's our side in this?"

Florian was usually the one who asked all the questions. That was one of Catlin's best ever.

And Catlin waited while she thought about it, and motioned Catlin up close and whispered back: "I am. I'm your side. That's all. You never mind what anybody says, that's still the Rule. They can't say I'm anybody else, no matter what."

So Catlin and Florian relaxed.

She looked at the papers uncle Giraud had given her to study about what the reporters and the judges could ask, and wished *she* could.

---

iii

There was very little work getting done in Wing One, or likely anywhere else in Reseune on this morning, and if there was a portable vid no matter how old not checked out or rented anywhere in the House and the Labs, it was well hidden.

Justin and Grant had theirs, the office door shut—some of the junior designers were clustered together in the lounge downstairs, but the ones in some way involved with the Project sealed themselves in offices alone or with closest associates, and nothing stirred, not even for phone calls.

The cameras were the official ones in the Supreme Court,

no theatrics, just the plain, uncommentaried coverage the Supreme Court allowed.

Lawyers handed papers to clerks, and the Court proceeded to ask the clerk if there were any absences or faults in the case.

Negative.

There was a very young girl sitting with her back to the cameras, at the table beside Giraud, not fidgeting, not acting at all restless through the tedium of the opening.

Listening, Justin reckoned. Probably with that very memorable frown.

The news-services had been right on it when the plane landed, and a single news-feed from the official camera set-up at the airport reception lounge had given the news-services their first look at Ari Emory, no questions allowed, until after the ruling.

Ari had stood there with her good hand in uncle Giraud's, the other arm in a cast, wearing a pale blue and very little-girl suit, with black-uniformed Florian and Catlin very stiff and looking like kids in dress-up, overkill in mimicking elder Ari—until a piece of equipment clanked, and eyes went that way and bodies stiffened like the same muscle moved them.

"That'll send chills down backs," Justin had muttered to Grant. "Damn. That *is* them, no way anyone can doubt it. No matter what size they are."

The news-services had done archive filler after, brought up split-screen comparisons between the first and second Ari and Catlin and Florian, from old news photos; and showed a trio so much like them it was like two takes in slightly different lighting, Ari in a different suit, standing beside Geoffrey Carnath instead of Giraud Nye.

"My God, it's right down to mannerisms," he had murmured, meaning the frown on Ari's face. On both Ari-faces. The way of holding the head. "Have they *taught* her that?"

"They could have," Grant had said, unperturbed. "All those skill tapes. They could do more than penmanship, couldn't they? —But a lot of *us* develop like mannerisms."

Not in a CIT, had been his internal objection. *Damn, they've got to have done that. Skill tapes. Muscle-learning. You could get that off a damn good actress.*

Or Ari herself. No telling what kind of things Olga re-corded. —Are they going that far with the Rubin kid?

He watched that still, attentive little girl at the table, in front of the panel of judges. They had not let Florian and Catlin sit with her. Just Giraud and the team of lawyers.

"Reseune declines to turn genetic records over to the court," the Chief Justice observed. *"Is that the case?"*

"I need not remind the Court," Giraud said, rising, *"that we're dealing with a Special's geneset. . . ."*

The Justices and uncle Giraud talked back and forth and Ari listened, listened very hard, and remembered not to fidget, uncle Giraud had told her not.

They were talking about genetics, about phenotype and handprints and retinal scan. They had done all the tests but the skin sample already, when she checked in with the court ID office.

"Ariane Emory," the Chief Justice said, "would you come stand with your uncle, please?"

She got up. She didn't have to follow protocols, uncle Giraud said, the Court didn't expect her to be a lawyer. She only had to be very polite with them, because they were lawyers themselves, the ones who solved all the most difficult cases in Union, and you had to be respectful.

"Yes, ser," she said, and she gave a little bow like Giraud's, and walked up to the railing, having to look up at them. There were nine of them. Like Councillors. She had heard about the Court in her tapes. Now she was here. It was interesting.

But she wished it weren't her case.

"Do they call you Ari?" the Chief Justice asked.

"Yes, ser."

"How old are you, Ari?"

"I'm four days from nine."

"What's your CIT number, Ari?"

"CIT 201 08 0089, but it's not PR." Uncle Giraud told her that in the paper she had studied.

The Justice looked at his papers, and flipped through things, and looked up again. "Ari, you grew up at Reseune."

"Yes, ser. That's where I live."

"How did you get that cast on your arm?"

Just answer that, Giraud had said, about any question on her accident. So she said: "I fell off Horse."

"How did that happen?"

"Florian and Catlin and I sneaked out of the House and went down to the Town; and I climbed up on Horse, and he threw me over the fence."

"Is Horse a real horse?"

"He's real. The labs birthed him. He's my favorite." She felt good, just remembering that little bit before she went over the fence, and the Justice was interested, so she said: "It wasn't his fault. He's not mean. I just surprised him and he jumped. So I went off."

"Who was supposed to be watching you?"

"Security."

The Justice looked funny at that, like she had let out more than she intended; and all the Justices thought so, and some thought it was terribly funny. But that could get out of control and make somebody mad, so she decided she had better be careful.

"Do you go to school?"

"Yes, ser."

"Do you like your teachers?"

He was trying to Work her, she decided. Absolutely. She put on her nicest face. "Oh, they're fine."

"Do you do well on tests?"

"Yes," she said. "I do all right."

"Do you understand what it means to be a PR?"

There was the trap question. She wanted to look at uncle Giraud, but she figured that would tell them too much. So she looked straight up at the Justice. "That means I'm legally the same person."

"Do you know what *legally* means?"

"That means if I get certified nobody can say I'm not me and take the things that belong to me without going through the court; and I'm a minor. I'm not old enough to know what I'm going to need out of that stuff, or what I want, so it's not fair to sue me in court, either."

That got him. "Did somebody tell you to say that?"

"Would you like it if somebody called you a liar about who you are? Or if they were going to come in and take your stuff? They can tell too much about you by going through all that stuff, and that's not right to do to somebody, especially if she's a kid. They can *psych* you if they know all that stuff.''

Got him again.

"God,'' Justin said, and lifted his eyes above his hand, watching while Giraud got Ari back to her seat.

"She certainly answered that one,'' Grant said.

Mikhail Corain glared at the vid in his office and gnawed his lip till it bled.

"Damn, damn, *damn*,'' he said to his aide. "How do we deal with *that*? They've got that kid primed—''

"A kid,'' Dellarosa said, "can't take priority over national security.''

"You say it, I say it, the question is what's the Court going to hold? Those damn fossils all came in under Emory's spoils system—the head of Justice is *Emory's* old friend. Call Lu in Defense.''

"Again?''

"Again, dammit, tell him it's an emergency. He knows damn well what I want—you go over there. No, never mind, *I* will. Get a car.''

". . . *watch the hearing*,'' the note from Giraud Nye had read, simply. And Secretary Lu watched, fist under chin, his pulse elevated, his elbows on an open folio replete with pictures and test scores.

A bright-eyed little girl with a cast on her arm and a scab on her chin. That part was good for the public opinion polls.

The test scores were not as good as the first Ari's. But they were impressive enough.

Corain had had his calls in from the instant he had known about the girl. And Lu was not about to return them—not until he had seen the press conference scheduled for after the hearing, the outcome of which was, as far as he was concerned, a sure thing.

Of paramount interest were the ratings on the newsservices this evening.

Damned good bet that Giraud Nye had leaned on Catherine Lao of Information, damned good bet that Lao was leaning on the newsservices—Lao was an old and personal friend of Ari Emory.

Dammit, the old coalition seemed strangely alive, of a sudden. Old acquaintances reasserted themselves. Emory had not been a friend—entirely. But an old and cynical military man, trying to assure Union's simple survival, found himself staring at a vid-screen and thinking thoughts which had seemed, a while ago, impossible.

Fool, he told himself.

But he pulled out a piece of paper and initiated a memo for the Defense Bureau lawyers:

Military implications of the Emory files outweigh other considerations; draft an upgrading of Emory Archives from Secret to Utmost Secret and prepare to invoke the Military Secrets Act to forestall further legal action.

And to his aide: *I need a meeting with Harad. Utmost urgency.*

Barring, of course, calamity in the press conference.

---

iv

"Ari," the Chief Justice said. "Would you come up to the bar?"

It was after lunch, and the Justice called her right after he had called uncle Giraud.

So she walked up very quiet and very dignified, at least as much as she could with the cast and the sling, and the Justice gave a paper to the bailiff.

"Ari," the Justice said, "the Court is going to certify you. There's no doubt who your genemother was, and that's the only thing that's at issue in this Court today. You have title to your genemother's CIT number.

"As to the PR designation, which is a separate question, we're going to issue a temporary certification—that means your card won't have it, because Reseune is an Administrative Territory, and has the right to determine whether you're a sibling or a parental replicate—which in this case falls within Reseune's special grants of authority. This court doesn't feel there's cause to abrogate those rights on an internal matter, where there is no challenge from other relatives.

"You have title to all property and records registered and accrued to your citizen number: all contracts and liabilities, requirements of performance and other legal instruments not legally lapsed at the moment of death of your predecessor are deemed to continue, all contracts entered upon by your legal guardian in your name thereafter and until now are deemed effective, all titles held in trust in the name of Ariane Emory under that number are deemed valid and the individuals within this Writ are deemed legally identical, excepting present status as a minor under guardianship.

"Vote so registered, none dissenting. Determination made and entered effective as of this hour and date."

The gavel came down. The bailiff brought her the paper, and it was signed and sealed by the whole lot of judges. *Writ of Certification*, it said at the top. With her name: Ariane Emory.

She gave a deep breath and gave it to uncle Giraud when he asked for it.

"It's still stupid," she whispered to him.

But she was awfully glad to have it, and wished she could keep it herself, so uncle Giraud wouldn't get careless and lose it.

The reporters were *not* mean. She was real glad about that, too. She figured out in a hurry that there weren't any Enemies with them, just a lot of people with notebooks, and people with cameras; so she told Catlin and Florian: "You can relax, they're all right," and sat on the chair they let her have because she said she was tired and her arm hurt.

She could swing her feet, too. Act natural, Giraud had said. Be friendly. Don't be nasty with them: they'll put you on the news and then everybody across Union will know you're a nice little girl and nobody should file lawsuits and bring Bills of Discovery against you.

That made perfect sense.

So she sat there and they wrote down questions and passed them to the oldest reporter, questions like: "How did you break your arm?" all over again.

"Ser Nye, can you tell us what a horse is?" somebody asked next, out loud, and she thought that was funny, of course people knew what a horse was if they listened to tapes. But she was nice about it:

"I can do that," she said. "Horse is his name, besides what he is. He's about—" She reached up with her hand, and decided that wasn't high enough. "Twice that tall. And brown and black, and he kind of dances. Florian knows. Florian used to take care of him. On Earth you used to ride them, but you had a saddle and bridle. I tried it without. That's how I fell off. Bang. Right over the fence."

"That must have hurt."

She swung her feet and felt better and better: she Had them. She liked it better when they didn't write the questions. It was easier to Work them. "Just a bit. It hurts worse now, sometimes. But I get my cast off in a few weeks."

But they went back to the written ones. "Do you have a lot of friends at Reseune? Do you play with other girls and boys?"

"Oh, sometimes." Don't be nasty, Giraud had said. "Mostly with Florian and Catlin, though. They're my best friends."

"Follow-up," somebody said. "Ser Giraud, can you tell us a little more about that?"

"Ari," Giraud said. "Do you want to answer? What do you do to amuse yourself?"

"Oh, lots of things. Finding things and Starchase and building things." She swung her feet again and looked around at Florian and Catlin. "Don't we?"

"Yes," Florian said.

"Who takes care of you?" the next question said.

"Nelly. My maman left her with me. And uncle Denys. I stay with him."

"Follow-up," a woman said.

Giraud read the next question. "What's your best subject?"

"Biology. My maman taught me." Back to that. News got to Fargone. "I sent her letters. Can I say hello to my maman? Will it go to Fargone?"

Giraud didn't like that. He frowned at her. *No.*

She smiled, real nice, while all the reporters talked together.

"Can it?" she asked.

"It sure can," someone called out to her. "Who is your maman, sweet?"

"My maman is Jane Strassen. It's nearly my birthday. I'm almost nine. Hello, maman!"

Because nasty uncle Giraud couldn't stop her, because Giraud had told her everybody clear across Union would be on her side if she was a nice little girl.

"Follow-up!"

"Let's save that for the next news conference," uncle Giraud said. "We have questions already submitted, in their own order. Let's keep to the format. Please. We've granted this news conference after a very stressful day for Ari, and she's not up to free-for-all questions, please. Not today."

"Is that the Jane Strassen who's director of RESEUNESPACE?"

"Yes, it is, the Jane Strassen who's reputed in the field for work in her own right, I shouldn't neglect to mention that, in Dr. Strassen's service. We can provide you whatever material you want on her career and her credentials. But let's keep to format, now. Let's give the child a little chance to catch her breath, please. Her family life is *not* a matter of public record, nor should it be. Ask her that in a few years. Right now she's a very over-tired little girl who's got a lot of questions to get through, and I'm afraid we're not going to get to all of them if we start taking them out of order. —Ari, the next question: what do you do for hobbies?"

Uncle Giraud was Working them, of course, and they knew it. She could stop him, but that would be trouble with uncle Giraud, and she didn't want that. She had done everything she wanted. She was safe now, she knew she was, because Giraud didn't dare do a thing in front of all these people who could tell things all the way to her maman, and who could find out things.

She knew about Freedom of the Press. It was in her Civics tapes.

"What for hobbies? I study about astronomy. And I have an aquarium. Uncle Denys got me some guppies. They come all the way from Earth. You're supposed to get rid of the bad ones, and you can breed ones with pretty tails. The pond fish would eat them. But I don't do that. I just put them in another tank, because I don't like to get them eaten. They're kind of interesting. My teacher says they're throw-backs to the old kind. My uncle Denys is going to get me some more tanks and he says I can put them in the den.''

"Guppies are small fish," uncle Giraud explained.

People outside Reseune didn't get to see a lot of things, she decided.

"Guppies are easy," she said. "Anybody could raise them. They're pretty, too, and they don't eat much." She shifted in her chair. "Not like Horse."

V

There was a certain strange atmosphere in the restaurant in the North corridor—in the attitude of staff and patrons, in the fact that the modest-price eatery was jammed and taking reservations by mid-afternoon—and only the quick-witted and lucky had realized, making the afternoon calls for supper accommodations, that thoroughly extravagant *Changes* was the only restaurant that might have slots left. Five minutes more, Grant had said, smug with success, and they would have had cheese sandwiches at home.

As it was, it was cocktails, hors d'oeuvres, spiced pork roast with imported fruit, in a restaurant jammed with Wing One staff spending credit and drinking a little too much and huddling together in furtive speculations that were not quite celebration, not quite confidence, but a sense of Occasion, a sense after hanging all day on every syllable that fell from the mouth of a little girl in more danger than she possibly understood—that something had resulted, the Project that had monopolized their lives for years had unfolded unexpected wings and demonstrated—God knew what: something alchemical; or something utterly, simply human.

Strange, Justin thought, that he had felt so proprietary, so anxious—and so damned personally affected when the Project perched on a chair in front of all of Union, swung her feet like any little girl, and switched from bright chatter to pensive intelligence and back again—

Unscathed and still afloat.

The rest of the clientele in *Changes* might be startled to find the Warrick faction out to dinner, a case of the skeleton at the feast; there were looks and he was sure there was comment at Suli Schwartz's table.

"Maybe they think we're making a point," he said to Grant over the soup.

"Maybe," Grant said. "Do you care? I don't."

Justin gave a humorless laugh. "I kept thinking—"

"What?"

"I kept thinking all through that interview, God, what if she blurts out something about: 'My friend Justin Warrick.'"

"Mmmn, the child has much too much finesse for that. She knew what she was doing. Every word of it."

"You think so."

"I truly think so."

"They say those test scores aren't equal to Ari's."

"What do you think?"

Justin gazed at the vase on the table, the single red geranium cluster that shed a pleasant if strong green-plant scent. Definite, bright, alien to a gray-blue world. "I think—she's a fighter. If she weren't, they'd have driven her crazy. I don't know what she *is*, but, God, I think sometimes, —God, why in *hell* can't they declare it a success and let the kid just grow up, that's all. And then I think about the Bok-clone thing, and I think—what happens if they did that? Or what if they drive her over the edge with their damn hormones and their damn tapes—? Or what if they stop now—and she can't—"

"—Integrate the sets?" Grant asked. Azi-psych term. The point of collation, the coming-of-age in an ascending pyramid of logic structures.

It fit, in its bizarre way. It fit the concept floating in his mind. But not that. Not for a CIT, whose value-structures were, if Emory was right and Hauptmann and Poley were wrong, flux-learned and locked in matrices.

"—master the flux," he said. Straight Emory theory, contrary to the Hauptmann-Poley thesis. "Control the hormones. Instead of the other way around."

Grant picked up his wine-glass, held it up and looked at it. "One glass of this. God. Revelation. The man accepts flux-theory." And then a glance in Justin's direction, sober and straight and concerned. "You think it's working—for Emory's reasons?"

"I don't know anymore. I really don't know." The soup

changed taste on him, went coppery and for a moment unpleasant; but he took another spoonful and the feeling passed. Sanity reasserted itself, a profound regret for a little girl in a hell of a situation. "I keep thinking—if they pull the program from under her now— Where's her compass, then? When you spend your life in a whirlwind—and then the wind dies down—there's all this quiet—this terrible quiet—"

He was not talking about Ari, suddenly, and realized he was not. Grant was staring at him, worriedly, and he was caught in a cold clear moment, lamplight, Grant, the smell of geranium, in a dark void where other faces hung in separate, lamplit existence.

"When the flux stops," he said, "when it goes null—you feel like you've lost all contact with things. That nothing makes sense. Like all values going equal, none more valid than any other. And you can't move. So you devise your own pressure to make yourself move. You invent a flux-state. Even panic helps. Otherwise you go like the Bok clone, you just diffuse in all directions, and get no more input than before."

"Flow-through," Grant said. "Without a supervisor to pull you out. I've been there. Are we talking about Ari? Or are you telling me something?"

"CITs," Justin said. "CITs. We can flux-think our flux-states too, endless subdivisions. We tunnel between realities." He finished his soup and took a sip of wine. "Anything can throw you there—like a broken hologram, any piece of it the matrix evokes the flux. The taste of orange juice. After today—the smell of geraniums. You start booting up memories to recollect the hormone-shifts, because when the wind stops, and nothing is moving, you start retrieving old states to run in—am I making sense? Because when the wind stops, you haven't got anything else. Bok's clone became a musician. A fair one. Not great. But music is emotion. Emotional flux through a math system of tones and ratios. Flux and flow-through state for a brain that might have dealt with hyperspace."

"Except they never took the pressure off Bok's clone," Grant said. "She was always news, to the day she died."

"Or it was skewed, chaotic pressure, piling up confusions. *You're brilliant. You're a failure. You're failing us. Can you tell us why you're such a disappointment?* I wonder if anyone ever put any enjoyment loop into the Bok clone's deep-sets.''

"How do you do that," Grant asked, "when putting it in our eminently sensible sets—flirts with psychosis? I think you teach the subject to enjoy the adrenaline rushes. Or to produce pleasure out of the flux itself instead of retrieving it out of the data-banks.''

The waiter came and deftly removed the empty soup-bowls, added more wine to the glasses.

"I think," Justin said uncomfortably, "you've defined a masochist. Or said something.'' His mind kept jumping between his own situation, Jordan, the kid in the courtroom, the cold, green lines of his programs on the vid display, the protected, carefully stressed and de-stressed society of the Town, where the loads were calculated and a logical, humane, human-run system of operations forbade overload.

Pleasure and pain, sweet.

He reached for the wine-glass, and kept his hand steady as he sipped it, set it down again as the waiters brought the main course.

He was still thinking while he was chewing his first bite, and Grant held a long, long silence.

God, he thought, do I *need* a state of panic to think straight?

Am I going off down a tangent to lunacy, or am I onto something?

"I'm damn tempted," he said to Grant finally, "to make them a suggestion about Ari.''

"God," Grant said, and swallowed a bite in haste. "They'd hyperventilate.—You're serious. *What* would you suggest to them?''

"That they get Ari a different teacher. At least one more teacher, someone less patient than John Edwards. She isn't going to push her own limits if she has Edwards figured out, is she? She's got a whole lot of approval and damned little affection in her life. Which would *you* be more interested in, in the Edwards set-up? Edwards is a damned nice fellow—damned fine teacher, does wonders getting the students interested; but if you're Ari Emory, what are you going to work for—Edwards' full attention—or a test score?''

Grant quirked a brow, genuine bemusement. "You could be right."

"Damn, I know I'm right. What in hell was she looking for in the office?" He remembered then what he had thought of when they made the reservations, that Security could find them, Security could bug the damned geranium for all he knew. The thought came with its own little adrenaline flux. A reminder he was alive. "The kid wants attention, that's all. And they've just given her the biggest adrenaline high she's had in years. *Sailing* through the interview. *Everyone* pouring attention on her. She's happier than she's been in her poor manipulated life. How can Edwards fight *that* when she gets back? What's he got to offer, to keep her interested in her studies, against that kind of rush? They need somebody who can get *her* attention, not somebody who lets her get *his*." He shook his head and applied his knife to the roast. "Damn. It's not my problem, is it?"

"I'd strongly suggest you not get into it," Grant said. "I'd suggest you not mention it to Yanni."

"The problem is, no one wants to be the focus of her displeasure," Justin said. "No one wants to stand in that hot spot, no more than you or I do. Ari always did have a temper—the cold sort. The sort that knew how to wait. I'm not sure how far it went, I never knew her that well. But senior staff did. Didn't they?"

_____ **vi** _____

They got out of the car with Security pouring out of the other cars, and Ari stepped up on the walk leading to the glass doors, with uncle Giraud behind her and Florian and Catlin closing in tight to protect her from the crush of their Security people and the reporters.

The doors opened. She could see that, but she could not see over the shoulders around her. Sometimes they frightened her, even if it was her they had come to see and even if it was her they were trying to protect.

She was afraid they were going to step on her, that was how close it was; and she was still bruised and sore.

They had driven around and seen the docks and the Volga

where it met Swigert Bay, and they had seen the spaceport and places that Ari would have given a great deal to have gotten out to see, but uncle Giraud had said no, there were too many people and it was too hard.

Like at the hotel, where they had spent the night in a huge suite, a whole floor all to themselves; and where people had jammed up in the lobby and around their car. That had scared her. It scared her in the Hall of State when they were stopped in the doors and they started to close while she was in them; but Catlin shot out a hand and stopped them and they got through, all of them.

The Hall of State was the first thing they had really gotten to see at all, because there were all these people following them around, and all the reporters.

It was the way it looked in the tapes, it was huge and it echoed till it made you dizzy when you were looking around at it, with all the people up on the balconies looking down at them: it was real, the way the Court had been just a place in a tape, and now she knew what the room at the top of the steps was going to look like the moment uncle Giraud told her that was where the Nine met.

The noise died down. People were all talking, but they were not shouting at each other, and the Security people had put the reporters back, so they could walk and look at things.

Uncle Giraud took her and Florian and Catlin upstairs where she shook hands with Nasir Harad, the Chairman of the Nine: he was white-haired and thin and there was a lot of him that he didn't give away, she could tell that the way she could tell that there was something odd about him, the way he kept holding her hand after she had shaken his, and the way he looked at her like he wanted something.

"Uncle Giraud," she whispered when they were going through the doors into the Council Chamber, "he was *funny*, back there."

"Shush," he said, and pointed to the big half-circle desk where all the Councillors would sit if they were here.

It was funny, anyway, to be asking *Giraud* whether anybody was a friendly or not. She looked at what he was telling her, which seat was which, and where Giraud sat when he was on Council—that was Science, she knew that: they had driven past the Science Building, and Giraud said he had an office there, and one in the Hall of State, but he wasn't there a lot of the time, he had secretaries and managers to run things.

He had Security push a button that opened the wall back, and she stood there staring while the Council Chamber opened right into the big Council Hall, becoming a room to the side of the seats, with the Rostrum in front of the huge wall uncle Giraud said was made out of stone from the Volga banks, all rough and red sandstone, just like it was a riverside.

The seats all looked tiny in front of that.

"This is where the laws are made," uncle Giraud said, and his voice echoed, like every footstep. "That's where the Council President and the Chairman sit, up there on the Rostrum."

She knew that. She could tape-remember the room full, with people walking up and down the aisles. Her heart beat fast.

"This is the center of Union," uncle Giraud said. "This is where people work out their differences. This is what makes everything work."

She had never heard uncle Giraud talk like that, never heard uncle Giraud talk in that quiet voice that said these things were important. He sounded like Dr. Edwards, somehow, doing lessons for her.

He took her back outside then, where it was noisy and Security made room for them. Down the stairs then. She could see cameras set up down below.

"We're going to do a short interview," uncle Giraud told her, "and then we're going to have lunch with Chairman Harad. Is that all right?"

"What's going to be for lunch?" she asked. Food sounded good. She was not so sure about Chairman Harad.

"Councillor," an older woman said, coming up to them, and put her hand on uncle Giraud's sleeve and said: "Private. Quickly. *Please.*"

It was some kind of trouble. Ari knew it, the woman was giving it off like she was about to explode with worry, and Giraud froze up just a second and then said: "Ari. Stand here."

They talked together, and the woman's back was to them. The noise blurred everything out.

But uncle Giraud came back very fast, and he was upset. His face was all pale.

"Sera," Florian said, very fast, very soft, like he wanted her to say what to do. But she didn't know where the trouble was coming from, or what it was.

"Ari," uncle Giraud said, and took her aside, along by the wall, the huge fountain, and down to the other end where there were some offices. Security moved very fast, Florian and Catlin went with her, and nobody was following them. There was just that voice-sound, everywhere, murmuring like the water.

Security opened the doors. Security told the people inside to go into a back office and they looked confused and upset.

But: "Wait out here," uncle Giraud said to Florian and Catlin, and she looked at them, scared, uncle Giraud hurrying her into an empty office with a desk and a chair. They were going to follow her, not certain what to do, but he said: "*Out!*" and she said: "It's all right."

He shut the door on them. They were scared. Uncle Giraud was scared. And she didn't know what was going on with everyone, except he took her by the shoulders and looked at her and said:

"Ari, —Ari, there's news on the net. It's from Fargone. I want you to listen to me. It's about your maman. She's died, Ari."

She just stood there. She felt his hands on her shoulders. He hurt her right one. He was telling her something crazy, something that couldn't be about maman, it didn't make sense.

"She died some six months ago, Ari. The news is just breaking over the station net. It just got here. They're picking it up out there, on their comlinks. That woman—heard it; and told me, and I didn't want you to hear it out there, Ari. Take a breath, sweet. Ari."

He shook her. It hurt. And she couldn't breathe for a moment, couldn't, till she got a breath all at once and uncle Giraud hugged her against him and patted her back and called her sweet. Like maman.

She hit him. He hugged her so she couldn't, and just went on holding her while she cried.

"It's a damn lie!" she yelled when she got enough breath.

"No." He hugged her hard. "Sweet, your maman was very old, very old, that's all. And people die. Listen to me. I'm going to take you home. Home, understand? But you've got to walk out of here. You've got to walk out of here past all those people and get to the car, you understand me? Security's going to get the car, we're going to go straight to the airport, we're going to fly home. But the first thing you have to do is get to the car. Can you do that?"

She listened. She listened to everything. Things went past her. But she stopped crying, and he set her back by the shoulders and wiped her face with his fingers, and smoothed her hair and got her to sit down in the chair.

"Are you all right?" he asked her, very, very quiet. "Ari?"

She got another gulp of air. And stared through him. She felt him pat her shoulder, and heard him go to the door and call Catlin and Florian.

"Ari's maman has died," she heard him say. "We just found it out."

More and more people. Florian and Catlin. If all of them believed it, then it was truer and truer. All the people out there. Maman was on the news. The whole of Union knew her maman had died.

Uncle Giraud came back and got down on one knee and got his comb and very carefully began to comb her hair. She messed it up and turned her face away. *Go away.*

But he combed it again, very gentle, very patient, and patted her on the shoulder when he finished. Florian brought her a drink and she took it in her good hand. Catlin just stood there with a worried look.

Dead is dead, that was what Catlin said. Catlin didn't know what to do with a CIT who thought it was something else.

"Ari," uncle Giraud said, "let's get out of here. Let's get you to the car. All right? Take my hand. There's no one going to ask you any questions. Let's just walk to the car."

She took his hand. She got up and she walked with her hand in Giraud's out into the office and outside again, where all the people were standing, far across the hall; and the voice-sound died away into the distance. She could hear the fountain-noise for the first time. Giraud shifted hands on her, and put his right one on her shoulder, and she walked with him, with Catlin in front of her and Florian on her other side, and all the Security people. But they didn't need them. Nobody asked any questions.

They were sorry, she thought. They were sorry for her. And she hated that. She *hated* the way they looked at her.

It was a terribly long walk, until they were going through the doors and getting into the car, and Florian and Catlin piling in on the other side, while uncle Giraud got her into the back seat and sat down with her and held her.

Security closed the back doors, one of them got in and closed the doors and the car started up, fast and hard, the tunnel lights flashing past them.

"Ari," Giraud said to her on the plane, moving Florian out of his seat to sit down across the little table from her, once they were in the air. "I've got the whole story now. Your maman died in her office. She was at work. She had a heart attack. It was very fast. They couldn't even get her to hospital."

"Where are my letters?" she asked, looking straight at him, looking him right in the face.

Giraud looked at her straight too. "At Fargone. I'm sure she read them."

"Why didn't she answer me?"

Giraud took a moment. Then: "I don't know, Ari. I truly don't know. I don't know if I can ever answer that. I'll try to find out. But it takes time. Everything between here and Fargone—takes a long time."

She turned her face away from him, to the window where the outback showed hazy reds.

She had not had her maman for six months. And she had never felt it. She had gone on as if nothing had happened, as if everything was still the same. It made her ashamed. It made her mad. Terrible things could have happened besides that, and it would take that long to know about them.

"I want Ollie to come home," she said to Giraud.

"I'll see about it," Giraud said.

"Do it!"

"Ollie has a choice too," Giraud said. "Doesn't he? He's your maman's partner. He'll have taken care of your maman's business. He'll have seen that things went right. He's not a servant, sweet, he's a very good manager, and he'll be handling your maman's office and handling her affairs for her. He'd want to do that. But I'll send and ask him what he wants to do."

She swallowed at the lump in her throat. She wished Giraud would go away. She didn't know what she thought yet. She was still putting it together.

She thought of that long walk and everybody in the Hall staring at her. And she had to do that again at Reseune—everybody staring at her, everybody knowing what was going on.

It made her mad. It made her so mad it was hard to think.

But she needed to. She needed to know where people were lying to her.

And who would want to take things from her. And whether that *was* what had happened to maman.

Who are they, where are they, what have they got?

She looked at Giraud when he was not looking, just looked, a long time.

vii

The news played the clip over and over, the solemn, shaken girl in the blue suit, walking with Giraud and Florian and Catlin past the silent lines of newspeople and government workers, just the cameras running, and the quick, grim movement of Security flanking them as they passed through the hall.

Mikhail Corain watched it with his jaw clamped, watched the subsequent clips, some provided by Reseune, of Ari's childhood, of Jane Strassen's career, all interposed with the Court sequences, the interview after, and then back through the whole thing again, with interviews with the Reseune Information Bureau, with Denys Nye, with child psychologists—with solemn music and supered images and reportorial garbage making photo comparisons between the original Ariane standing solemnly at her mother's funeral, and the replicate's decorously pale, shock-stricken face in a still from the clip they played and played and played, dammit.

The whole of Cyteen was wallowing in the best damn theater Reseune could have asked for. That bitch Catherine Lao hardly had to bend any effort to key up the news-services, which had already been covering the Discovery bill—then the bombshell revelation that there was an Emory replicate filing for the right of Succession, no Bok clone, *brilliant*—then the court appearance, the interview—all points on the Expansionist side; Defense's invocation of the Military Secrets Act against the bill, a little coverage of Centrist objections, a possible gain against the tide—

Then Strassen's death, and the child getting the news, virtually on live cameras—

God, it was a circus.

A freighter docked at Cyteen Station and shot the content of its Fargone-acquired informational packet into the Cyteen data-sorters, the news-packet hit the Cyteen news-comp, the news-comp upgraded its information and scrolled it past the human watcher, and what might have been a passing-interest kind of story, the death of a Reseune administrator who was not even a known name to the average citizen, became the biggest media event since—

Since the murder at Reseune and the Warrick hearing.

The news had to be real: the data-storage of a starship—the whole system that carried news, electronic mail, publications, stockmarket data, financial records and statistics, ballots and civil records—was the entire data-flow of the last station visited, shot out of a starship's Black Box when it came to dock, as the current station's data spooled in. It was the system that kept the markets going and the whole of Union functioning: tampering with a Black Box was physically unlikely and morally unthinkable, and Fargone was six Cyteen months away, so there was no way in hell the information could have been timed for the impact it had—

God, he found himself sorting through every move he had made and every contact with Giraud Nye and Reseune he had had, wondering if there was any remotest chance he had been maneuvered into the Discovery bill at a time when Reseune was ready.

A lifetime of dealing with Emory, that was what made him have thoughts like that.

Like Strassen being murdered. Like the kind of ruthlessness that would use a kid the way they created and used this one—killing off one of their own, who was, God knew, a hundred forty-odd and already on the brink—

What was a life, to people who created and destroyed it as a matter of routine?

It was a question worth following up, quietly, by his own investigatory channels; but by everything he knew of RESEUNESPACE, existing in the same separate station as the Defense Bureau installation at Fargone with absolutely nothing to link them with Fargone Station except a twice-daily shuttle run, it was difficult to get at anything or anyone on the inside.

And the Centrist party could lose, considerably, by making the wrong move right now—by making charges that might not prove out, by going ahead with the bill that had to result in lengthy hearings and a court case involving the little girl who had turned seasoned reporters to emotional jelly and generated such a flood of inquiries the Bureau of Information had set aside special numbers for the case.

That was only the beginning. The ships that undocked from Cyteen Station this week were the start of a wave front that would go clear to Earth before it ran out of audience.

No way in hell to continue with the bill. *Anything* that involved drawn-out procedures could intersect with future events in very unpredictable ways.

While I consider the investigation ultimately necessary in the public interest, it seems inappropriate to proceed at this time. That was the sentence his speechwriters were still hammering out.

He was damned to look bad no matter what he did. He had thought of demanding an investigation into the child's welfare, and raising the issue of Reseune's creating the child precisely to shield those records.

The whole Centrist party suddenly found itself saddled with a serious position problem.

Nelly helped her take the blouse off—it fastened on the bad shoulder, and the sleeve was cut and fastened back together, so it would come on and off over the cast. She had several of the same kind, and she wore things with jackets, that she could wear draped over the shoulder on the right side.

She felt better then. She had to take a shower with a plastic bag taped and sealed around her arm, and when she came out again, Nelly helped her take the tape off and get into her pajamas.

Nelly was upset, Ari could feel it, and she knew she shouldn't let her mad get loose with Nelly, she shouldn't let it get loose with anybody.

"I'm not going to bed yet," she said when Nelly wanted to put her there, and Nelly said:

"You're supposed to."

Which made her want to hit Nelly, or to cry, both of which were stupid. So she said, very patiently: "Nelly, let me alone and go to bed. Right now."

She had been to maman's memorial service today. She had gotten through it and not cried, at least she had not made a scene like Victoria Strassen, who had sniffed and hiccuped and finally Security had walked over and talked to her. She had never met aunt Victoria. She was already mad at her. Maman would have been mad at her, even if she was maman's half sister. Herself, she had sores on the inside of her mouth where she had bitten down to keep from crying, and she didn't mind, that was all right, it was better than aunt Victoria.

I want you to think about going, uncle Denys had said. *You don't have to, understand. I'm sure your maman wouldn't mind one way or the other: you know how she felt about formal stuff—She's gone to the sun at Fargone: that's a spacer funeral, and your maman was a spacer before she lived at Reseune. But here in the House we do things a little differently: we go out in the East Garden, where all the memorials are, if the weather's such we can, or somewhere—and your maman's friends will tell a few stories about your maman, that's the way we do. I don't want you to go if it's going to upset you; but I thought you might want to hear those things,*

*and it might help you learn about your maman, who she was
when she was young, and all the things she did. If you don't
want to, don't go. If you want to go and then change your
mind, all you have to do is pull at my sleeve and you and I
will just walk out the gate and no one will think anything
about it: children don't always go to these things. Not even
all the friends do. It just depends on the person, whether they
feel they need to, you understand?*

Florian and Catlin had not gone. They were too young and
they were azi, uncle Denys said, and they didn't understand
CIT funerals.

You don't want them to have to take tape for it, uncle
Denys had said.

She was terribly, terribly glad it was over. She felt bruised
inside the way she was outside, and uncle Denys kept giving
her aspirin, and Dr. Ivanov had given her a shot he said
would make her feel a little wobbly, but it would help her get
through the services.

She wished he hadn't. She had wanted to hear some of it
clearer, and it all rolled around in her head and echoed.

It still did, but she put Nelly out the door and told Nelly
send Catlin and Florian and go to bed and take the tape Dr.
Ivanov wanted her to have.

"Yes," Nelly said, looking miserable.

Ari bit her lip again. She wanted that badly to yell at her.
Instead she went and fed her fish, and watched them chase
after the food and dodge in and out of the weeds. There were
a lot of babies. One of the big ones had had hers. And there
was her prettiest male who was in the tank with all the ugly
females, to see if the babies would be prettier. Florian could
net him out for her and put him back in his regular tank: she
was afraid of hurting him with the net, working with her left
hand.

Tomorrow. She was not in the mood to do anything with
them tonight.

Catlin and Florian came in, still in their uniforms, and
looking worried, the way they had been constantly since they
found out about maman. They didn't understand half how it
felt, she knew that, but they were hurting all the same, because she hurt.

Florian had told her he felt terribly guilty about her arm

and then her maman, and asked her if there was anything they could do.

She wished there were. But he couldn't be guilty, he just felt bad: she told him that, and asked him if he needed tape, the way she was supposed to if her azi came to her.

Uncle Denys had told her that.

"No," Florian had said, very quick, very definite. "We don't want to. What if you needed us, and we'd be in hospital? No. We don't want that."

Now:

"I want you to stay here tonight," she said when they came in.

"Yes, sera," Florian said; and: "We'll get our stuff," Catlin said, as if both of them were happy then.

She felt better when they were with her, when no one else was. It was hard to go out where there were people, like going out with no clothes on, like she was made out of glass and people would know everything inside her and find out everything she didn't want everyone to know. But she never felt that way with Florian and Catlin. They were her real friends, and they could sleep in the same room and sit around in just their pajamas together, even if Florian was a boy.

And with the door shut and with just them, she could stop having that knotted-up feeling that made her broken arm ache and made her feel sick at her stomach and tired, so tired of hurting.

"They said a lot of nice things about maman," she said when they had gotten their pallets made in the corner and gotten into their pajamas and settled down on the end of her bed.

A lot of the staff had really been maman's friends. A lot of them were really sorry and really missed her. Aunt Victoria was sorry and scared, when Security came and probably told her to stop crying or asked her to leave; then aunt Victoria had been really, really mad: so aunt Victoria had left the garden right after that, on her own, while Dr. Ivanov was telling how maman had run Wing One.

There were a lot of things she wished she could talk about out loud with Florian and Catlin. But she *was* going to tell them, that was no problem. It just took longer.

There had been a lot of upset people there, at the services, and it was strange how they Felt different than the reporters.

The reporters had been sorry. Reseune was sorry too; but a lot of them Felt mad like her mad, which was maybe because it wasn't fair people had to die at all; but there had been so many different flavors of mad there, so many different flavors of being sorry, not at all like the reporters, but very strong, very complicated, all the way down past what she could pick up on their faces.

Justin and Grant had been there. Grant was one of the only azi.

A lot of grown people had said how maman had been their teacher, and they really loved her.

Dr. Schwartz had said maman and he used to fight a lot so loud that everybody in the halls could hear it, but that was because she never would take second best about anything; and he said whatever she set up at RESEUNESPACE was going to be all right, because that was the way maman always did things.

That made her remember her maman's voice echoing out of the bedroom, right through the walls: *Dammit, Ollie—* And made her feel warm all over, like maman was yelling at her: *Dammit, straighten up, Ari, don't give me any of that nonsense. That doesn't get anywhere with me.*

Like maman was back for a second. Like she was *there*, inside, just then. Or anytime she wanted to think about her. She wasn't at Fargone anymore.

Ollie was. And a lot of the Disappeareds might be.

She had thought on the plane coming home—who in the House just might know a lot of things.

And who she could scare into telling her.

ix

"You're a damn fool," Yanni said, and Justin looked him in the eye and said:

"That's no news. It's all there in the memo. Probably you think I have ulterior motives—which isn't the case. Nothing against John Edwards. Nothing against anyone. I don't even know I'm right. Just—" He shrugged. It was easy to go too far with Yanni, and he had probably gone there, high and wide. Time to stage a retreat, he reckoned. Fast. "I'll go get back to *my* business," he said. "I'll have the GY project in tomorrow morning."

"Stay put."

He sank back into the chair, under Yanni's scowl.

"You think the kid doesn't have enough stress," Yanni said.

"I don't mean that. You know I don't mean that."

"Son, Administration is just a little wrought up just now. So am I. I appreciate the fact you don't hate the kid, you really think you see something—but you know, we're all tired, we're all frayed around the edges, and I really hope you haven't gone anywhere else with this."

"No. I haven't."

"You know what I think you're doing?"

Not a rhetorical question. Yanni left a long, deathly silence for his answer.

"What, ser?"

"Sounds like your own damn craziness, to me, the same damn sink you come back to like a stone falls *down*, that's what it sounds like to me. Motivations and reward structures."

"I think I have a point."

"And you put it in writing." Yanni picked up the three-page memo and slid it into a slot at the edge of his desk. A red telltale flashed, and a soft hum meant even the ash had been scrambled. "That's a favor, son. I'm not supposed to wipe documents that bear on the Project. I just broke a regulation. As it happens—there are those of us who think you're right on the mark with this. And I like one of your arguments . . . if you don't mind my borrowing it for the upcoming staff meeting."

"Whatever you like. I'd just as soon you didn't mention the source."

Yanni gave him a long slow look. "Sometimes you worry me."

"I haven't got any ulterior motives. I don't *want* my name on it."

Another long look. "Motivational psych. —You haven't *had* the Rubin data. Just the structures. I told you I'd keep you off real-time. But I'd like you to do something for me, son. A favor. A real favor. I'm going to dump all Rubin's data on you. The whole pile.''

"He's, what, two?"

"Not the replicate. The original."

"Why?"

"I'm not going to tell you that."

"What do you want out of it?"

"I'm not going to tell you that either."

"I get the idea."

"All right." Yanni leaned on his elbows, hands locked in front of him. "You run the problem. I'll tell you what I think about it.''

"Is this an exercise?"

"I'm not going to tell you that."

"Dammit, Yanni—"

"You're right about the kid. She's smarter than those scores. You leave that in my lap. You take care of your work. I'll take care of the Project. All right?"

<hr />

X

<hr />

Uncle Denys took another helping of eggs. Ari picked at hers, mostly just moved them around, because breakfast upset her stomach.

"We could go out to eat tonight," uncle Denys said. "Would you like that?"

"No," she said. "I'm not hungry."

It was her ninth birthday. She just wanted to forget it was her birthday at all. She didn't want to complain about her stomach, because then uncle Denys would call Dr. Ivanov, and that would mean another shot, and her head being all fuzzy.

"Is there anything you *do* want?" uncle Denys said.

I want maman, she thought, mad, mad until she felt like she could throw the dishes off the table and break everything.

But she didn't.

"Ari, I know it's a terrible time for you. There's nothing I can do. I wish there were. Is there anything you'd like to do? Is there anything you want that I can get you?"

She thought. There was no good throwing an offer like that

away. If you could get something, you got it, and you might
be glad later. She had figured that out a long time ago.

"There is something I want for my birthday."

"What's that, dear?"

She looked uncle Denys right in his eyes, her best wishing-
look. "Horse."

Uncle Denys took in his breath, real quick. "Ari,
sweet, —"

"You asked."

"I'd think a broken arm is enough. No. Absolutely not."

"I want Horse."

"Horse belongs to Reseune, Ari. You can't just *own*
him."

"That's what I want, anyway."

"No."

That hurt. She shoved her plate away, and got up from the
table.

"Ari, I think a broken arm ought to do, don't you?"

She felt like crying, and when she did that she went to her
room. So she went that way.

"Ari," uncle Denys said, "I want to talk with you."

She looked back at him. "I don't feel good. I'm going to
bed."

"Come here."

She didn't. She went to her hall and shut the door.

And went and cried like a baby, lying on her bed, till she
got mad and threw Poo-thing across the room.

Then she felt like something had broken, because Poo-
thing came from maman.

But he wasn't real, anyway.

She heard somebody open the hall door, and then they
opened hers. She figured it was uncle Denys, and she turned
over and scowled; but it was Catlin and Florian, come to see
what was the matter with her.

"Ser Denys wants you," Florian said in a hushed voice.

"Tell him go to hell."

Florian looked distressed. But he would go do that and he
would get in a lot of trouble for her, she knew he would.

"Yes, sera."

"No," she said, and wiped her eyes and got up. "I will."

She wiped her eyes again and walked past him and Catlin, and went out to the living room.

It was a mistake to walk out on uncle Denys. When she did that, she let him Work *her*, and now she was having to walk back into the living room he owned and be nice.

Stupid, stupid, she told herself, and unraveled her mad and got a nicer expression on her face when she went to uncle Denys. Denys was in the dining room having his coffee and he pretended not to notice her for a second.

That was Working, too.

"I'm sorry, uncle Denys."

He looked at her then, took a quick sip of coffee, and said: "I did have a surprise planned for you today," he said. "Do you want some more orange juice?"

She moped over to the chair and climbed into it, hugging her cast with her good hand. "Florian and Catlin too," she said.

"Seely," uncle Denys said. And Seely came and got two more glasses and poured orange juice as Florian and Catlin quietly settled down across the table.

"Nelly's in hospital again," uncle Denys said. "Ari, you know it hurts her when you put her out and call somebody else."

"Well, I can't help it. Nelly fusses."

"Nelly doesn't know what to do with you anymore. I think it might be a good idea to let Nelly go work down in the Town, in the nursery. You think about that. But that's for you to decide."

She could not lose maman and Nelly in one week. Even if Nelly drove her crazy. She looked at the table and tried not to think about that.

"You think about it," uncle Denys said. "Nelly's the happiest when she has a baby to take care of. And you're not a baby. So you're making her unhappy—especially when you give her orders. But you just think about it. It's not like you couldn't see Nelly again. Otherwise she's going to have to take tape to re-train her and she'll have to do house management or something."

"What does Nelly want?"

"She wants you to be three years old. But that won't work. So Nelly's got to move or Nelly's got to change."

"Can Nelly have a job down in the baby lab? And live here?"

"Yes, she could do that. It's not really a bad idea." Uncle Denys set his cup down for Seely to pour more coffee, then stirred it. "If that's what you want."

"I *want* Horse."

Uncle Denys' brows came together. "Ari, you can't have what'll hurt you."

"Florian says there's a baby."

"Ari, horses are big animals. Nobody knows anything about riding them, not on Cyteen. We have them for research, not to play with."

"You could give me the baby one."

"God," uncle Denys said.

"Florian knows all about horses."

Uncle Denys looked at Florian and Florian went azi, all blank.

"No," uncle Denys said flatly. Then: "Let me talk to AG about it, Ari, all right? I don't know about horses. When you grow a bit, maybe. When you show me you're grown up enough not to *sneak* down there and break your neck."

"That's nasty."

"It's true, isn't it? You could have broken your neck. Or your back. Or your head. I don't mind if you do things: you'll fly a plane someday. You'll do a lot of things. But for God's *sake*, Ari, you don't sneak off and try to fly one of the jets, do you? You have to study. There's no second chance when the ground's coming at you. You have to know what can go wrong and how to deal with it, and you have to be big enough; and if you want to deal with a horse, you'd better be big enough to hold on to it, and you'd better show me you're grown up enough to be smarter than the horse is."

That was nasty too. But it was probably true.

"He surprised you," uncle Denys said, "because you didn't know what you were doing. So I suggest you study about animals. They're not machines. They think. And he thought: there's some fool on my back. And he was bigger and he got rid of her. Figure that one out."

She frowned harder. It sounded too much like what had happened. Only uncle Denys had gotten down to a Maybe about giving her Horse. That was something.

"I needed a saddle and a bridle."

"All right. So how do you make the horse wear it, hmmn? Maybe you'd better do some advance study. Maybe you'd better look some things up in library. Maybe you'd better talk to some people who might know. Anyway, you prove to me you know what you're doing and you prove to me you're responsible. Then we'll see about seeing about it."

That was halfway, anyway. For about two seconds she had forgotten how much she hurt, which threw her off for a moment when it all came back again, and she thought how she had been when maman went away to Fargone, and how she got over that.

It was awful to get over maman dying. But that was starting to happen. She felt it start. Like things were trying to go back the way they were, and uncle Denys was getting short with her and she was going to have to go back to classes and everything was going to be the way it was again.

She felt sad about feeling better, which was stupid.

She wished she could have told maman about Horse.

And then she still wasn't sure if maman had ever gotten her letters at all, no matter what they said, or if Ollie had. Thinking that made her throat swell up and the tears start, and she scrambled down from the table, ran for her hall and shut the door.

Then she stood there by Florian and Catlin's room and cried and pounded her fist on the wall and kicked it, and went in their room and got some tissue to wipe her eyes and blow her nose.

They came in. And just stood there.

"I'm all right," she said. Which probably confused hell out of them, maman would say.

"Ari," she heard uncle Denys calling her from the other room. The door was open. "Ari?"

She had given uncle Denys a hard morning. But that was all right, uncle Denys said; it was like getting well from something, sometimes you had aches and pains, and they got better, eventually. He wasn't mad at her.

"I've talked to AG," uncle Denys said at lunch. "As soon as they can schedule a tank, they're going to do a run for you."

"You mean a horse?"

"Don't talk with your mouth full. Manners."

She swallowed. Fast.

"Here's the work part. You have to go over all the data and write up a report just the way the techs do. You have to do it on comp, and the computer will compare your work against the real techs' input. And where you're wrong you have to find out why and write up a report on it. You have to do that from start to birth and then keep up with all the other stuff and all your other studies. If you want something born, you have to work for it."

That *was* a lot of work. "Do I get him, then?"

"Her, actually. We need another female anyway. Two males tend to fight. Some animals are like that. We're going to do another just like the one we have, instead of a new type, so we won't risk losing her. But if you don't keep up the work, you don't get the horse at all, because you won't have earned her. Understood?"

"Yes, ser," she said. Not with her mouth full. Horses grew up fast. She remembered that. Real fast. Like all herd animals. A year, maybe?

"They're real delicate," uncle Denys said. "They're a bitch to manage, frankly, but your predecessor had this notion that it was important for people to have them. Human beings grew up with other lifeforms on the motherworld, she used to say, and those other lifeforms were part of humans learning about non-humans, and learning patience and the value of life. She didn't want people on Cyteen to grow up without that. Her maman Olga was interested in pigs and goats because they were useful and they were tough and adaptable for a new planet. Ari wanted horses because they're a high-strung herd ungulate with a lot of accessible data on their handling: we can learn something from them for some of the other, more exotic preservation projects. But the other important reason, the reason of all reasons for having horses, she said, is that working with them does something to people. 'They're exciting to something in our own psychsets,' those are her exact words: 'I don't want humans in the Beyond to grow up without them. Our ancient partners are a part of what's human: horses, cattle, oxen, buffalo, dolphins, whatever. Dogs and cats, except we can't support carnivores yet, or tolerate a predator on Cyteen—yet. Earth's ecology is an interlocking system,' she used to say, 'and maybe humans aren't human without input from their old partners.' She wasn't sure about that. But she tried a lot of things. So it's not surprising you want a horse. *She* certainly did, although she was too old to try riding it—thank God. —Does it bother you for me to talk about her?''

"No." She gave a twitch of her shoulders. "It's just— funny. That's all."

"I imagine it is. But she was a remarkable woman. Are you through? We can walk back now."

_____ **xi** _____

Florian did the best he could. He and Catlin both.

He had even asked ser Denys if they were letting sera down somehow, or if there was something they ought to be doing to help her get well, and ser Denys had patted him on the shoulder and said no, they were doing very well, that when a CIT had trouble there were no tapes to help, just people. That if they were strong enough to take the stress of sera's upset without needing sera's help that was the best thing, because that was what CITs would do for her. "But don't let yourselves take damage," ser Denys had said. "That's even worse for sera, if something bad happened to you, too. You protect yourselves as well as her. Understand?"

Florian understood. He told Catlin, because they had agreed he would ask, she just wasn't good with CIT questions.

"We're doing right," he had said to her. "Sera's doing all right. We're doing what we're supposed to be doing. Ser Denys is happy with us."

"I'm not," Catlin said, which summed it up. Catlin was hurting worse than he was, he thought, because Catlin was mad about sera being hurt, and Catlin couldn't figure out who was responsible, or whether people were doing enough to help sera.

They were both relieved when sera had said she had an idea and a job for them to do. And when sera started back to classes and things started getting back to normal, they had classes then, down in the Town, ser Denys said they should and sera agreed. "Meet me after class," she said.

So they did.

And sera walked with them out to the fishpond and fed the fish and said: "We have to wait until a rainy day. That's next Thursday. I looked."

On the charts that showed when the weathermakers were going to try to make it rain, that meant. Usually the charts were good, when they were down to a few days. And sera told them what they had to do.

Catlin was happy then. It was an Operation and it was a real one.

Florian just hoped sera was not going to get herself into trouble.

Skipping study was easy: sera just sent a request down to Green Barracks and said they couldn't come.

Then they worked out a way to get to C-tunnel without going through the Main Residency Hall, which meant going down the maintenance corridors. That was easy, too.

So sera told them what she wanted, and they all set up the Operation, with a lot of variations; but the one that they were going to use, sera thought of herself, because she said it would work and it was simplest and she could handle the trouble if it went bad.

So Catlin got to be the rear guard and he got to be the point man because sera said nobody suspected an azi and Catlin said he was better at talking.

The storm happened, the students kept the schedule sera had gotten from Dr. Edwards' classbook, and sera whispered: "Last two, on the left," as the Regular Students came back from their classes over in the Ed Wing, right down the tunnel, right past them where they were waiting in the side tunnel that led to air systems maintenance. It was a good place for them: dark in the access, and noisy with the fans.

Florian let them get past just the way sera had said. They had talked about how to Work it. He let them string way out.

Then sera patted him on the back just as he was moving on his own: he went out in the middle of the hall just before the last few students could disappear around the corner.

"Sera Carnath!" he called out, and the last students all

stopped. He held up his fist. "You dropped something." And just the way sera had said, several of the students walked on, disappearing at the turn. Then more did, and finally Amy Carnath walked back a little, looking through the things she had in her arms.

He jogged up to her. Just one girl was waiting with Amy Carnath. He did a fast check behind to make sure no one was coming.

No one was. Catlin was supposed to see to that, back at the other turn, having a cut hand and an emergency if she had to, if it was some Older coming and not a kid.

So he gave Amy Carnath the note sera had written.

Dear Amy, it said. That was how you wrote, sera said. *Don't say a thing about this and don't tell anybody where you're going. Say you forgot something and have to go back, and don't let anybody go with you. I want to talk with you a minute. Florian will bring you. If you don't come, I'll see something terrible happens to you. Sincerely, Ari.*

Amy Carnath's face went very frightened. She looked at Florian and looked back at her friend.

Florian waited. Sera had instructed him not to speak at all in front of any of the rest of them.

"I forgot something," Amy Carnath said in a faint voice, looking at her friend. "Go on, Maddy. I'll catch up."

The girl called Maddy wrinkled her nose, then walked on after the rest of them.

"Sera, please," Florian said, and indicated the way she should go.

"What does she want?" sera Carnath asked, angry.

"I'm sure I don't know, sera. Please?"

Amy Carnath walked with him. She had her library bag. She could swing that, he reckoned, but sera said sera Carnath didn't know how to fight.

"This way," he said, when they got to the service corridor, and sera Carnath balked when she looked the way he pointed, into the dark.

And when sera stepped out from behind the doorway.

"Hello, Amy," sera said; and grabbed Amy herself, by the front of the blouse, one-handed, and pulled her, so Florian opened the door to the service corridor.

As Catlin came jogging up and into their little dark space.

Amy Carnath looked at her. Terrified.

"Inside," sera said. And pushed sera Carnath, not letting her go. Sera Carnath tried to protect her blouse from being torn, but that was all.

"Let me go," sera Carnath said, upset. "Let go of me!"

Florian pulled the penlight from his pocket and turned it on; Catlin shut the door; sera pushed Amy Carnath against the wall.

"Let me go!" sera Carnath screamed. But the door was shut and the fans were noisy.

"I'm not going to hurt you," sera said very calmly. "But Catlin will break your arm if you don't stand still and talk to me."

There were tears on sera Carnath's face. Florian felt a little sick, she was so scared. Even if she was the Target.

"I want to know," sera said, "where Valery Schwartz is."

"I don't know where he is," sera Carnath cried, biting her lip and trying to calm down. "He's at Fargone, that's all I know."

"I want to know where Sam Whitely is."

"He's down at the mechanics school! Let me go, let me go—"

"Florian has a knife," sera said. "Do you want to see it? Shut up and answer me. What do you know about my maman?"

"I don't know anything about your maman! I swear I don't!"

"Stop sniveling. You tell me what I ask or I'll have Florian cut you up. Hear me?"

"I don't know anything, I don't know."

"Why am I poison?"

"I don't know!"

"You know, Amy Carnath, you know, and if you don't start talking we're going to go down deep in the tunnels and Catlin and Florian are going to ask you, you hear me? And you can scream and nobody's going to hear you."

"I don't know. Ari, I don't know, I swear I don't."

Sera Carnath was crying and hiccuping, and Ari said: "Florian, —"

"I can't tell you!" sera Carnath screamed. "I can't, I can't, I can't!"

"Can't tell me what?"

Sera Carnath gulped for air, and sera pulled sera Carnath's blouse loose and started unbuttoning it, one-handed.

"They'll send us away!" sera Carnath cried, flinching away; but Catlin grabbed her from behind. "They'll send us away!"

Sera stopped and said: "Are you going to tell me everything?"

Sera Carnath nodded and gulped and hiccuped.

"All right. Let her go, Catlin. Amy's going to tell us."

Catlin let sera Carnath go, and sera Carnath backed up to a bundle of pipes and stood with her back against that. Florian kept the light on her.

"Well?" sera asked.

"They send you away," sera Carnath said. Her teeth were chattering. "If anybody gets in trouble with you, they can send them to Fargone."

"*Who* does?"

"Your uncles."

"Giraud," sera said.

Sera Carnath nodded. There was sweat on her face, even if it was cold in the tunnels. She was crying, tears pouring down her cheeks, and her nose was running.

"All the kids?" sera asked.

Sera Carnath nodded again.

Sera came closer and took sera Carnath by the shoulder, not rough. Sera Carnath thought sera was going to hit her, but sera patted her shoulder then and had her sit down on the steps. Sera got down on one knee and put her hand on sera Carnath's knee.

"Amy, I'm not going to hit you now. I'm not going to tell you told. I want to know if you know anything about why my maman got sent away."

Sera Carnath shook her head.

"*Who* sent her?"

"Ser Nye. I guess it was ser Nye."

"Giraud?"

Sera Carnath nodded, and bit her lips.

"Amy, I'm not mad at you. I'm not going to be mad. Tell me what the other kids say about me."

"They just say—" Sera Carnath gulped. "—They just say let you have your way, because everybody knows what happens if you fight back and we don't want to get sent to Fargone and never come back—"

Sera just sat there a moment. Then: "Like Valery Schwartz?"

"Sometimes you just get moved to another wing. Sometimes they take you and put you on a plane and you just have to go, that's all, like Valery and his mama." Sera Carnath's teeth started chattering again, and she hugged her arms around her. "I don't want to get sent away. Don't tell I told."

"I won't. Dammit, Amy! Who said that?"

"My mama said. My mama said—no matter what, don't hit you, don't talk back to you." Sera Carnath started sobbing again, and covered her face with her hand. "I don't want to get my mama shipped to Fargone—"

Sera stood up, out of the light. *Maman* and *Fargone* were touchy words with her. Florian felt them too, but he kept the light steady.

"Amy," sera said after a little while, "I won't tell on you. I'll keep it secret if you will. I'll be your friend."

Sera Carnath wiped her face and looked up at her.

"I will," sera said. "So will Florian and Catlin. And they're good friends to have. All you have to do is be friends with us."

Sera Carnath wiped her nose and buttoned her blouse.

"It's the truth, isn't it, Catlin?"

"Whatever sera says," Catlin said, "that's the Rule."

Sera got down beside sera Carnath on the steps, her casted arm in her lap. "If I was your friend," sera said, "I'd stand up for you. We'd be real smart and not *tell* people we were friends. We'd just be zero. Not good, not bad. So you'd be safe. Same with the other kids. I didn't know what they were doing. I don't *want* them to do that. I can get a lot out of my uncle Denys, and Denys can get things out of uncle Giraud. So I'm a pretty good friend to have."

"I don't want to be enemies," sera Carnath said.

"Can you be my friend?"

Sera Carnath bit her lip and nodded, and took sera's left hand when sera reached it over.

They shook, like CITs when they agreed.

Florian stood easier then, and was terribly glad they didn't have to hurt sera Carnath. She didn't seem like an Enemy.

When sera Carnath got herself back together and stopped hiccuping, she talked to sera very calm, very quiet, and didn't sound at all stupid. Catlin stopped being disgusted with her and hunkered down when sera said, and rested her arms on her knees. So did Florian.

"We shouldn't be friends right off," sera Carnath said. "The other kids wouldn't trust me. They're scared."

As if sera Carnath hadn't been.

"We get them one at a time," sera said.

xii

"Shut the door," Yanni said; Justin shut it, and came and took the chair in front of Yanni's desk.

Not *his* problem this time. Yanni's. The Project's. It was in those papers on Yanni's desk, the reports and tests that he had *not* scanned and run on the office computer, but on a portable with retent-storage.

He had not signed his write-up. Yanni knew whose it was. That was enough.

"I've read it," Yanni said. "What does Grant say, by the by?"

Justin bit his lip and considered a shrug and no comment: Yanni still made his nerves twitch; but it was foolish, he told himself. Old business, raw nerves. "We talked about it. Grant protests it's a CIT question—but he says the man doesn't sound like he's handling it well at all."

"We're six months down on this data," Yanni said. "We don't have a ship-call from that direction for another month and a half, we don't have anything going out their way till the 29th. Jane was worried about Rubin. If our CIT staff kept off Ollie he'll have tried to work on it, I'm sure of that, but he's azi, and he's going through hell, *damn* my daughter's meddling—she's a damn expert, *she* has to know CIT psych better than Ollie does, right?"

"No comment."

"No comment. Dammit, I can *tell* you what they've been doing these last few months. My daughter and Julia Strassen. I *never* wanted those two on staff. So they get a harmless job . . . on the Residency side, of course. With Rubin. Jane gets out there and gets a look at the Residency data and Jane and my daughter go fusion in the first staff meeting. I think it contributed to Jane's heart attack, if you want my guess."

Justin felt his stomach unsettled—Yanni's pig-stubborn daughter, thrown out to Fargone on an appointment she never wanted . . . and probably thought she would get promotion from, setting up RESEUNESPACE labs and administration along with Johanna Morley; then Yanni's old adversary-sometime-lover Strassen the Immovable suddenly put in as Administrator over her head the same as over her father's; *his* stomach was upset, and he figured what was going on in Yanni.

Dammit, Administration is crazy.

Crazy.

"I'd trust Strassen," he said quietly, since Yanni left it for him to say something.

"Oh, yes, damn right I'd trust Strassen. Jenna might be a good Wing supervisor, but hell if she's got her own life sorted out, and she's Alpha-bitch when she's challenged. So Jane dies. That means someone has to run things. Jenna listens to her staff, all right. But Rubin's mother is a complicated problem. A real power-high when Rubin got his Special status, a real resentment when Rubin got the lab facilities and a little power of his own. Rubin's psychological problems—well, you've got the list: depressions over his health, his relationship with his mother—all of that. Rubin acts like he's doing fine. Happy as a fish in water. While his mother wants to give network interviews till Jenna hauls her in. Stella Rubin didn't like that. Not a bit. That woman and the Defense Bureau go fusion from the start . . . and Rubin's situation has been an ongoing case of *can't live with her or without her*. Rubin plays the psych tests we give him, Rubin's happy so he can keep peace, *that's* what Jane estimated—not an honest reaction out of him since the Defense Bureau put the lid on mama. Six months ago, spacetime.

That's why I wanted you to look at the series. And the bloodwork—''

"Considering what's going to arrive out there in another six months or so."

"Ari's interviews, you mean."

"He's a biochemist. He's aware they're running some genetic experiments on him. What if someone picks up on it?"

"Especially—" Yanni tapped the report on his desk. "This shows a man a hell of a lot more politically sophisticated than he started. Same with his mother."

"Reseune can do that, can't it?"

"Let me give you the profile I've got: Rubin isn't the young kid they made a Special out of. *Rubin's* grown up. Rubin's realized there's something going on outside the walls of his lab, Rubin's realized he's got a sexual dimension, he's frustrated as hell with his health problems, RESEUNESPACE goes into a power crisis at the top and Rubin's hitherto quiet, hypochondriac mother, who used to focus his health anxieties *and* his dependencies on herself, is carrying on a feud with Administration and the Defense Bureau *and* reaching for the old control mechanisms with her son, who's reacting to those button-pushes with lies on his psych tests and stress in the bloodwork, while *Jenna*, damn her, has torn up Jane's reassignments list and declared herself autonomous in that Wing on the grounds Ollie Strassen can't make CIT-psych judgments."

"Damn," Justin murmured, gut reaction, and wished he hadn't. But Yanni was being very quiet. Deadly quiet.

"I'm firing her, needless to say," Yanni said. "I'm firing her right out of Reseune projects and recalling her under Security Silence. Six months from now. When the order gets there. I'm telling you, son, so you'll understand I'm a little . . . personally bothered . . . about this."

What in hell am I in here for? He knew this. It didn't take me to see it. What's he doing?

"You have some insights," Yanni said, "that are a little different. That come out of your own peculiar slant on designs, crazed that it is. I talked your suggestions over with committee, and things being what they were—I *told* Denys what my source was."

"Dammit, Yanni, —"

"You happened to agree with *him*, son, and Denys has the say where it concerns Ari's programs. Giraud was his usual argumentative self, but I had a long quiet talk with Denys, about you, about your projects, about the whole ongoing situation. I'll tell you what you're seeing here at Reseune. You're seeing a system that's stressed to its limits and putting second-tier administrative personnel like my daughter in positions of considerable responsibility, because they don't have anyone more qualified, because, God help us, the next choice down is worse. Reseune is stretched too thin, and Defense has their project blowing up in their faces. If Jane had lived six months longer, even two *weeks* longer, if Ollie could have leaned on Jenna and told her go to hell—but he can't, because the damn regulations don't let him have unquestioned power over a CIT program and he can't fire Jenna. He's got a Final tape, he can get CIT status, but Jenna's reinstated herself over his head with the help of other staff, and Julia Strassen declaring she's Jane's executor—so Jenna and Julia are the ones who have to sign Ollie's CIT papers, isn't that brilliant on our part? Jenna's going to pay for it. Now Ollie's got his status, from *this* end. But *that* won't get there for some few months either, and *he* doesn't know it." Yanni waved his hand, shook his head. "Hell. It's a mess. It's a mess out there. And I'm going to ask you something, son."

"What?"

"I want you to keep running checks on the Rubin data as it comes in, in whatever timeframe. Our surrogate with the Rubin clone is Ally Morley. But I want you to work some of your reward loops into CIT psych."

"You mean you're thinking of intervention? On which one of them?"

"It's the structures we want to look at. It's the feedback between job and reward. Gustav Morley's working on the problem. You don't know CIT psych that well, that's always been one of your problems. No. If we have to make course changes, you won't design it. We just want to compare his notes against yours. And we want to compare the situation against Ari's, frankly."

He was very calm on the surface. "I really want to think you're telling the truth, Yanni. Is this a real-time problem?"

"It's no longer real-time. I'll tell you the truth, Justin. I'll tell you the absolute truth. A military courier came in hard after the freighter that got us this data, cutting—a classified amount of time—off the freighter run. Benjamin Rubin committed suicide."

"Oh, God."

Yanni just stared at him. A Yanni looking older, tired, emotionally wrung out. "If we didn't have the public success with Ari right now," Yanni said, "we'd lose Reseune. We'd *lose* it. We're income-negative right now. We're using Defense Bureau funds and we're understaffed as hell. You understand now, I think—we were getting those stress indicators on Rubin before the Discovery bill came up, before Ari's little prank in the Town. We knew then that there was trouble on the Project. We'd sent out instructions which turned out to be—too late. We had pressure on the Discovery bill; we knew that was coming before it was brought out in public. We knew Ari was going to have to go public—and we had all of that going on. You may not forgive Giraud's reaction, but you might find it useful to know what was happening off in the shadows. Right now, Administration is looking at you—in a whole new light."

"I haven't got any animosity toward a nine-year-old kid, for God's sake, I've proved that, I've answered it under probe—"

"Calm down. That's not what I'm saying. We've got a kid out at Fargone who's the psychological replicate of a suicide. We've got decisions to make—one possibility is handing him to Stella Rubin, in the theory she's the ultimate surrogate for the clone. But Stella Rubin has problems, problems of the first order. Leave him with Morley. But where's the glitch-up that led to this? With Jenna? Or earlier, with the basic mindset of a mother-smothered baby with a health problem? We need some answers. There's time. It's not even *your* problem. It's Gustav Morley's and Ally's. There's just—content—in your work that interests Denys, frankly, and interests me. I think you see how."

"Motivational psych."

"Relating to Emory's work. There's a reason she wanted you, I'm prepared to believe that. Jordan's being handed the

Rubin data too. When you say you've got some clear thought on it—I'm sending you out to Planys for a week or so."

"Grant—"

"You. Grant will be all right here, my word on it. Absolutely no one is going to lay a hand on him. We just don't need complications. Defense is going to be damned nervous about Reseune. We've got some careful navigation to do. I'm telling you, son, Administration is watching you very, very closely. You've been immaculate. If you—and Jordan—can get through the next few years—there's some chance of getting a much, much better situation. But if this situation blows up, if anything—if *anything* goes wrong with Ari—I don't make any bets. For any of us."

"Dammit, doesn't anybody care about the *kid*?"

"We care. You can answer this one for yourself. Right now, Reseune is in a major financial mess and Defense is keeping us alive. What happens to her—if Defense moves in on this, if this project ends up—under that Bureau instead of Science? What happens to any of us? What happens to the direction all of *Union* will take after that? Changes, that much is certain. Imbalance—in the whole system of priorities we've run on. I'm no politician. I hate politics. But, damn, son, I can see the pit ahead of us."

"I see it quite clearly. But it's not ahead of us, Yanni. I live in it. So does Jordan."

Yanni said nothing for a moment. Then: "Stay alive, son. You, and Grant, —be damn careful."

"Are you telling me something? Make it plain."

"I'm just saying we've lost something we couldn't afford to lose. We. Everybody, dammit. So much is so damn fragile. I feel like I've lost a kid."

Yanni's chin shook. For a moment everything was wide open and Justin felt it all the way to his gut. Then:

"Get," Yanni said, in his ordinary voice. "I've got work to do."

xiii

Ari walked with uncle Denys out of the lift in the big hall next to Wing One, upstairs, and it was not the kind of hall she had expected. It was polished floors, it was a Residency kind of door, halfway down, and no other doors at all, until a security door cut the hallway off.

"I want to show you something," uncle Denys had said.

"Is it a surprise?" she had asked, because uncle Denys had never shown her what he had said he would show her; and uncle Denys had been busy in his office with an emergency day till dark, till she was *glad* Nelly was still with them: Seely was gone too.

"Sort of a surprise," uncle Denys had said.

She had not known there *were* any apartments up here.

She walked to the door with uncle Denys and expected him to ring the Minder; but:

"Where's your keycard?" he said to her, the way the kids used to tease each other and make somebody look fast to see if it had come off somewhere. But he was not joking. He was asking her to take it and use it.

So she took it off and stuck it in the key-slot.

The door opened, the lights came on, and the Minder said: *"There have been twenty-seven entries since last use of this card. Shall I print?"*

"Tell it save," uncle Denys said.

She was looking into a beautiful apartment, with a pale stone floor, with big furniture and *room*, more room than maman's apartment, more room than uncle Denys', it was huge; and all of a sudden she put together *last use of this card* and *twenty-seven* and the fact it was *her* card.

Hers. Ari Emory's.

"This was your predecessor's apartment," uncle Denys said, and walked her inside as the Minder started to repeat. "Tell it save."

"Minder, save."

"Voice pattern out of parameters."

"Minder, save," uncle Denys said.

"Insert card at console."

He did, his card. And it saved. The red light went off. "You have to be very careful with some of the systems in here," uncle Denys said. "Ari took precautions against intruders. It took Security some doing to get the Minder reset." He walked farther in. "This is yours. This whole apartment. Everything in it. You won't live here on your own until you're grown. But we are going to get the Minder to recognize your voice." He walked on, down the steps, across the rug and up again, and Ari followed, skipping up the steps on the far side to keep close to him.

It was spooky. It was like a fairy-tale out of Grimm. A palace. She kept up with uncle Denys as he went down the hall and opened up another big room, with a sunken center, and a couch with brass trim, and woolwood walls—pretty and dangerous, except the woolwood was coated in thick clear plastic, like the specimens in class. There were paintings on the walls, along a walkway above the sunken center. Lots of paintings.

Up more steps then, past the bar, where there were still glasses on the shelves. And down a hall, to another hall, and into an office, a *big* office, with a huge black desk with built-ins like uncle Denys' desk.

"This was Ari's office." Uncle Denys pushed a button, and a terminal came up on the desk. "You always have a 'base' terminal. It's how the House computer system works. And this one is quite—protective. It isn't a particularly good idea to go changing these base accesses around, particularly on my base terminal . . . or yours. Sit down, Ari. Log on with your CIT-number."

She was nervous. The House Computer was a whole different system than her little machine in her room. You didn't log-on until you were grown, or you got in a lot of trouble with Security. Florian said some of the systems were dangerous.

She gave uncle Denys a second nervous look, then sat down and looked for the switch on the keyboard.

"Where's the *on*?"

"There's a keycard slot on the desk. At your right. It'll ask for a handprint."

She turned in the chair and gave him a third look. "Is it going to do something?"

"It's going to do a security routine. It won't gas the apartment or anything. Just do it."

She did. The handprint screen lit up. She put her hand on it.

"Name," the Minder said.

"Ariane Emory," she told it.

The red light on the terminal went on and stayed on.

The monitor didn't come up from the console.

"What's it doing?"

"Checking the date," he said. "Checking all the House records. It's finding out you've been born and how old you are, since it's found similarities in that handprint and probably in your voiceprint, but it knows it's not the original owner. It's checking Archives for all the Ari handprints and voiceprints it has. It's going to take a minute."

It *wasn't* like the ordinary turn-on. She had seen uncle Denys do that, just talking to his computer through the Minder. She looked at this one working, the red light still going, and looked at Denys again. "Who wrote this?"

"Good question. Ari would have asked that. The fact is, Ari did. She knew you'd exist someday. She keyed a lot of things to you, things that are very, very important. When the prompt comes up, Ari, I want you to do something for me."

"What?"

"Tell it COP D/TR comma B1 comma E/IN."

Take program: Default to write-files. "What's B1? What's IN?"

"Base One. This is Base One. Echo to Instore. That means screen and Minder output into the readable files. If I thought we could get away with it I'd ask it IN/P, and see if we could snag the program out, but you don't take chances with this Base. There!"

The screen unfolded from the desktop and lit up.

Hello, Ari.

Spooky again. She typed: *COP D/TR, B1, E/IN*

Confirmed. Hello, Ari.

"It wants *hello,*" uncle Denys said. "You can talk to it. It'll learn your voiceprint."

"Hello, Base One."

How old are you?

"I'm nine."

Hello, Denys.

She took in a breath and looked back at Denys.

"Hello, Ari," Denys said, and smiled in a strange way, looking nowhere at all, not talking to her, talking to *it*.

It typed out: *Don't panic, Ari. This is only a machine. I've been dead for 11.2 years now. The machine is assembling a program based on whose records are still active in the House computers, and it's filling in blanks from that information. Fortunately it can't be shocked and it's all out of my hands. You're living with Denys Nye. Do you have a House link there?*

"Yes," uncle Denys said, and when she turned around to object, laid a finger on his lips and nodded.

"Uncle Denys says yes."

The Minder could handle things like that. It just took it a little longer.

Name me the rivers and the continents and any other name you think of, Ari. I don't care what order. I want a voice-print. Go till I say stop.

"There's the Novaya Volga and the Amity Rivers, there's Novgorod and Reseune. Planys, the Antipodes, Swigert Bay, Gagaringrad and High Brasil, there's Castile and the Don and Svetlansk. . . ."

Stop. That's enough. After this, you can just use your keycard in the Minder slot anywhere you happen to be before you log-on next, and state your name for the Minder. This Base is activated. I'm creating transcript continually. You can access it by asking the Minder to print to screen or print to file. If Denys is doing his job you know what that means. Do you know without being told?

"Yes."

Good. Log-on anytime you like. If you want to exit the House system just say log-off. Storing and recall is automatic. It will always find your place but it won't activate until you say hello. Denys can explain the details. Goodbye. Don't forget to log-off.

She looked at uncle Denys. Whispered: "Do I?" He nodded and she said: "Log-off."

The screen went dark and folded down again.

2415: 1/24: 2332

B/1: Hello, Ari.
AE2: Hello.
B/1: Are you alone?
AE2: Florian and Catlin are with me.
B/1: Anyone else?
AE2: No.
B/1: You're using House input 311. What room are you in?
AE2: My bedroom. In uncle Denys' apartment.
B/1: This is how this program works, Ari, and excuse me if I use small words: I wrote this without knowing how old you'd be when you logged-on or what year it would be. It's 2415. The program just pulled that number out of the House computer clock. Your guardian is Denys Nye. The program just accessed your records in the House data bank and found that out, and it can tell you that Denys ordered pasta for lunch today, because it just accessed Denys' records and found out the answer to that specific question. It knows

you're 9 years old and therefore it's set a limit on your keycard accesses, so you can't order Security to arrest anybody or sell 9000 Alpha genesets to Cyteen Station. Remembering what I was like at 9, that seems like a reasonable precaution.

The program has Archived all the routines it had if you were younger or older than 9. It can get them back when your House records match those numbers, and it can continually update its Master according to the current date, by adding numbers. This goes on continually.

Every time you ask a question it gets into all the records your age and your current clearance make available to you, all over the House system, including the library. Those numbers will get larger. When you convince the program you have sufficient understanding, the accesses will get wider. When you convince the program you have reached certain levels of responsibility your access will also get into Security levels and issue orders to other people.

There's a tape to teach you all the accesses you need right now. Have you had it?

AE2: Yes. I had it today.

B/1: Good. If you'd answered no, it would have cut off and said: log-off and go take that tape before you log-on again. If you make a mistake with your codes, it'll do that too. A lot of things will work that way. You have to be right: the machine you're using is linked to the House system, and it will cut you off if you make mistakes. If you make certain mistakes it'll call Security and that's not a good thing.

Don't play jokes with this system, either. And don't ever lie to it or enter false information. It can get you in a lot of trouble.

Now I will tell you briefly there is a way to lie to the system without causing problems, but you have to put the real information in a file with a sufficiently high Security level. The machine will always read that file when it needs to, but it will also read your lie, and it will give the lie to anyone with a lower Security clearance than you have. That means only a few people, mostly Security and Administration, can find out what you hid. This is so you can have some things private or secret.

Eventually you can use this to cover your Inquiry activity.

Or your Finances. Or your whereabouts. That file can't be erased, but it can be added to or updated. When your access time in the House system increases and the number of mistakes you make per entry decreases to a figure this program wants, you'll get an instruction how to use the Private files. Until then, don't lie to the program, or you'll lose points and it'll take you a long time to get beyond this level.

You've probably figured out by now you can't question the program when it's in this mode. You can stop this tutorial at any point by saying: Ari, wait. You can go out of this mode and ask a question and come back by saying, Ari, go on.

Don't ever think that this program is alive. It's just lines of program like the programs you can write. But it can learn, and it changes itself as it learns. It has a base state, which is like a default, but that's only in the master copy in Archives.

Sometimes this program transcribes what I tell you for your guardian Denys. Sometimes not. It's not doing that now. I'm writing to files only you can access, by telling the Minder you want to hear the file from this session, by hour and date. This is an example of a Private file. Do you understand how to access it?

AE2: Yes.

B/1: If you make a mistake the program will repeat this information.

Never ask for a Private file in front of anyone but Florian and Catlin. Not even Denys Nye can see the things I tell you in Private files. If he tries to do this, this program will send an order to Security. This program has just sent a message to Denys' Base that says the same thing. Trust me that I have a reason for this.

Sometimes a file will be so Private I will tell you to be totally alone. This means not even Florian and Catlin. Never ask to review those files when anyone else is present. They won't print out either, because they involve things very personal to you only, that not even your friends should know about you.

Many of these things involve your studies and they will simply come out of my own notes.

A lot of times they will come simply because you've asked a question and the computer has found a keyword.

You carry my keycard, my number, and my name. My rec-

ords exist only in Archives and yours are the current files. Don't worry about my being dead. It doesn't bother me at all at this point. You can call me Ari senior. There isn't any word in the language that says what we are to each other. I'm not your mother and I'm not your sister. I'm just your Older. I assume that word is still current.

Understand, Ari, there is a difference between myself, who say these words into a Scriber, —and Base One. Base One can use a language logic function to talk with you much more like a living person than I can, because it's real-time and I'm not, and haven't been since 2404.

That's the computer accessing my records, understand, to find out that date.

Base One can answer questions on its own and bring up my answers to certain questions, and you can talk back and forth with it.

But never get confused about which one is able to talk back and forth with you directly.

Have you got a question now? Ask it the right way and Base One will start talking to you. If you make a mistake the program will revert to the instruction you missed. Or you can ask for repeat. Good night, Ari. Good night, Florian and Catlin.

AE2: **Ari, wait.**

B/1: *I'm listening, Ari.*

AE2: **Are you Base One now?**

B/1: *Yes.*

AE2: **Who sent my maman Jane Strassen to Fargone?**

B/1: *Access inadequate. There is a reference from Ari. Stand by.*

Ari, this is Ari senior.

This is the first time you've asked a question with a Security block on it. I don't know what the question is. It means something is preventing you from reaching that information in the House computers and your clearance isn't high enough. The most probable reason is: Minority status. End segment.

AE2: **Ari, wait.**

B/1: *I'm listening, Ari.*

AE2: **Where is Valery Schwartz?**

B/1: *Access inadequate.*

AE2: Where's Amy Carnath?

B/1: Amy Carnath checked into the Minder in U8899. U8899 is: apartment registered to Julia Carnath. There is no record of check-out in that Minder.

AE2: Then she's home.

B/1: Please be specific.

AE2: Then Amy Carnath is home, isn't she?

B/1: Amy Carnath is home, yes.

2315: 1/27: 2035

AE2: Base One: look up Ariane Emory in Library.

B/1: Access limited. Ari has a message. Stand by.

Ari, this is Ari senior.

So you've gotten curious about me. I don't blame you. I would be too. But you're 9 and the program will only let you access my records up to when I was 4. That gap will narrow as you grow older, until you're able to read into my records equal to and beyond your current age. There's a reason for this. You'll understand more of that reason as you grow. One reason you can understand now is that these records are very personal, and people older than 9 do things that would confuse hell out of you, sweet.

Also at 9 you're not old enough to understand the difference between my accomplishments and my mistakes, because the records don't explain anything. They're just things the House computer recorded at the time.

Now that you've asked, Base One will automatically upgrade the information once a week. I'd give it to you daily, because there's going to be a lot of it, but I don't want you to get so involved with what I did from day to day that you live too much with me and not enough in the real world.

You can access anything about anybody you want in Archives through 2287, when I was 4. If the person you want wasn't born by then, you won't get anything.

This gap will constantly narrow as you grow, and as your questions and your own records indicate to Base One that you have met certain criteria. So the harder you study in school and the more things you qualify in, the faster you get answers. That's the way life works.

Remember what you do is your own choice. What I did was mine.

Good luck, sweet.

Now Library will retrieve all my records up to the time I was 4 and store it for your access in a file named BIO.

2315: 4/14: 1547

B/1: Stand by for your Library request.

AE2: Capture.

B/1: Affirmative: document captured; copyrighted: I must dump all data in two days unless you authorize the 20-credit purchase price.

AE2: Scan for reference to horse or equine or equestrian.

B/1: Located.

AE2: How many references?

B/1: Eighty-two.

AE2: Compare data to data in study file: HORSE. Highlight and Tempstore additional information or contradictions in incoming data. Call me when you're done.

B/1: Estimated time of run: three hours.

AE2: Log-off.

2316: 1/12: 0600

B/1: Good morning, Ari. Happy birthday.

AE2: Is this Base One?

B/1: Ari, this is Ari senior. You're 10 now. That upgrades your accesses. If you'll check library function you can access a number of new tapes.

Your test scores are one point better than mine in geography, three points under mine in math, five points under mine in language. . . .

CHAPTER
3

_____ I _____

Uncle Giraud called it the highest priced shop in the known universe, let alone Novgorod, and Ari loved it. She tried on a blouse that would absolutely _kill_ Maddy Strassen: it was bronze and brown, it was satin, and it had a scarf around the throat with a topaz and gold pin—real, of course, at _this_ place.

And she looked back at uncle Giraud with a calculated smile. It was a very grown-up smile. She had practiced it in the mirror.

The blouse cost two hundred fifty credits. It went into a box, and uncle Giraud put it on his personal card without saying a word.

She signed a picture of herself for the shop, which had a lot of pictures of famous people who shopped there: it had its own garage and a security entrance, and it was an appointment-only place, near the spaceport, where you couldn't just walk in.

Which was why uncle Giraud said it was a place they could go, the only place they could go, because of Security.

There was a picture of the first Ari. It was spooky. But she had seen those before. The first Ari was pretty even when she was almost as old as maman, and she had been a hundred twenty when she died. She had pretty, pretty eyes, and her hair was long and black (but she would have been on rejuv then and she would have dyed it) and parted in the middle the way Ari wore hers. She wanted to wear makeup like Ari senior, but uncle Denys said no, she could have a little, but not that much, and besides, styles changed.

Uncle Denys had given her cologne for last New Year's, that he said had been made especially for Ari by a perfumery in Novgorod. It smelled wonderful, like the greenhouse gardens when the tulips were blooming.

She was growing up, he said, and she knew that. All of a sudden one day a long time back Nelly had said she was getting too old to run around without her blouse on, and she had looked down and realized it was not that she was getting a little fat, but that something was changing.

At the time she had thought it was a damn nuisance, because she *liked* not having to wear a shirt.

By now she *definitely* was getting a shape, and even Catlin was, sort of. Nothing, of course, to match her cousin Maddy Morley-Strassen, who was a year older, transferred in from Planys with her maman Eva, who was aunt Victoria Strassen's daughter, and maman's niece; and a cousin of Amy Carnath through *Amy's* father Vasily Morley-Peterson, who was at Planys.

Maddy was—

An early developer, uncle Denys called it.

Maddy was not anybody she would want to be, but she was certainly not the sort to let get too comfortable.

So she bought a scarf for Maddy and a real gold pin for Amy and a pullover for Sam and one for Tommy, and *insisted* to carry them on the plane, besides the other things she got for everybody. It didn't matter that you could order a lot of it, she told uncle Giraud, it mattered it came from *Novgorod*, where the other kids didn't get to go, and she was too going to take it on the plane. She got a blouse for Catlin, for parties: black, of course, but gauzy; Catlin looked surprised when she saw herself in the mirror. And a shirt for Florian over on the men's side: black and satiny and with a high collar that was sort of like his usual uniform sweaters, but very, very elegant. And then the woman who owned the shop thought of a pair of pants that would fit Catlin, very tight and satiny. So that meant it was only fair Florian should get new pants too. And while they were doing that, *she* found a gunmetal satin pair of pants that just fit her, and that meant the sweater that went with them, which was bronzed lavenders on the shoulders shading down to gunmetal-sheen lavender and then gunmetal-and-black at the bottom. It was elegant. Uncle Giraud said it was too old for her before she put it on. When he saw her in it he said well, she *was* getting older.

She thought she could sneak some lavender eyeshadow when she wore it at Maddy's next party.

So take that, Maddy Strassen.

They brought so many packages out of *La Lune* that uncle Giraud and Abban had to put a lot of them in the security escort car, and she and Florian and Catlin had to sit practically on top of each other in the back seat.

Uncle Giraud said they were going to be into the next century going through Decon at Reseune.

That was the wonderful thing about Novgorod: because they had the Amity escarpment on the east and the terraforming had piled up the rock and put up towers to make the Curtainwall on the west, and because they had all those people and all that sewage and all that algae and the greenbelt and algae starting out even in the marine shallows, it was one of the few places in the world besides Reseune that people went out without D-suits and the only other airport besides Reseune where you could take your baggage right through without anything but a hose-down and an inspection.

There was an interview to go through, in the lounge at the airport, while Abban was supervising the baggage being loaded. But she knew a lot of the reporters, especially one of the women and two of the oldest men and a young man who had a way of winking at her to get her to laugh; and she didn't mind taking the time.

Ransom, uncle Giraud called it, for being let alone while she got to see the botanical gardens, except for the photographers.

"What did you do today, Ari?" a woman asked.

"I went to the garden and I went shopping," she said, sitting in the middle of the cameras and in front of the pickup-bank. She had been tired until she got in front of the cameras. But she knew she was *on*, then, and *on* meant sparkle, which she knew how to do: it was easy, and it made the reporters happy and it made the people happy, and it made uncle Giraud happy—not that Giraud was her favorite person, but they got along all right: she had it figured uncle Giraud was real easy to Work in a lot of ways, and sometimes she thought he really had a soft place she got to. He would buy her things, lots of things. He had a special way of talking with her, being funny, which he wasn't, often, with other people.

And he was always so nasty every time they had a party or anything in the House.

About Giraud and maman—she *never* forgot that. Ever.

"What did you buy?"

She grinned. "Uncle Giraud says 'too much.' " And ducked her head and smiled up at the cameras with an expression she knew was cute. She had watched herself on vid and practiced in the mirror. "But I don't get to come to the city but once a year. And this is the first time I ever went shopping."

"Aren't there stores in Reseune?"

"Oh, yes, but they're small, and you always know what's there. You can always get what you need, but it's mostly the same things, you know, like you can get a shirt, but if you want one different from everybody's you have to order it, and then you know what you're going to get."

"How are the guppies?"

Another laugh. A twitch of her shoulders. "I've got some green long-tails."

Uncle Denys had given her a whole lab. And guppies and aquariums were a craze in Novgorod, the first time in the world, uncle Denys said, that anybody had had pets, which people used to, on Earth. Reseune had gotten a flood of requests for guppies, ever since she had said on vid that they were something anybody could do.

And she got a place to sell her culls: uncle Denys said she should keep all the records on it, she would learn something.

Which meant that most every flight RESEUNEAIR's freight division made out, had some of her guppies on it, sealed in plastic bags and Purity-stamped for customs, and now it was getting to be an operation larger than the lab she did the breeding in: uncle Denys said it was about time she franchised-out, because guppies bred fast, and bred down, and the profit was in doing the really nice ones, which meant you had to get genesets. It was really funny, in some ways it was a lot easier to clone people than guppies.

"We hear," someone else said, "you've taken up another project. Can you tell us about the horse?"

"It's a filly. That's what you call a female baby horse. But she's not born yet. I had to study about her and help the techs get the tank ready; and I have to do a lot of reports—it's a *lot* of work. But she's going to be pretty just like her genesister. *She's* pregnant. She's going to birth not too long after my filly comes out of the tank. So we'll have *two* babies."

"Haven't you had enough of horses?"

"Oh, no. You have to *see* them. I'm going to ride mine. You *can*, they do it on Earth, you just have to train them."

"You're not going to break another arm, are you?"

She grinned and shook her head. "No. I've studied how to do it."

"How do you do it?"

"First you get them used to a saddle and a bridle and then you get them used to a weight on their back and then they don't get so scared when you climb on. But they're smart, that's what's so different, they're not like platytheres or anything, they *think* what they're going to do. That's the most wonderful thing. They're not like a computer. They're like *us*. Even pigs and goats are. You watch them and they watch you and you know they're thinking things you don't know about. And they feel warm and they play games and they do things just like people, just because they think of it."

"Could we get a clip of that?"

"*Could* we, uncle Giraud?"

"I think we could," Giraud said.

---

ii

Uncle Giraud was very, very happy with the session in Novgorod, Ari decided that on the flight back. She and

Florian and Catlin sat up front in the usual spot and drank soft drinks and watched out the windows, while Giraud and the secretaries and the staffers sat at the back and did business, but there was a lot of laughing.

Which was why uncle Giraud bought her things, she thought. Which was all right. Sometimes she almost warmed up to Giraud. That was all right too. It kept Giraud at ease. And she learned to do that, be very nice to people she knew quite well were the Enemy, and even like them sometimes: it didn't mean you weren't going to Get them, because they were bound to do something that would remind you what they were sooner or later. When you were a kid you had to wait, that was all. She had told that to Catlin and Florian, and she got Catlin in front of a mirror and made Catlin practice smiling and laughing until she could do it without looking like she was faking it.

Catlin was ticklish right around her ribs. *That* was a discovery. Catlin was embarrassed about it and said nobody was supposed to get that close anyway. She didn't like her and Florian laughing at first. But then Catlin decided it was half-way funny, and laughed her real laugh, which was kind of a halfway grin, without a sound. The other was fake, because Catlin was good at isolating muscles and making them do whatever she wanted to.

Catlin had laughed her real laugh when she saw herself in the gauzy blouse, in the shop in Novgorod, and her eyes had lit up the way they would when Florian showed them something he had learned in electronics. *Catlin* had a new skill.

Then Catlin had turned around to the shop-keeper with her stage-manners on and acted just like Maddy Strassen, which was funny as hell, maman would say, right down to Maddy's slither when she turned around to look at the satin pants in the mirror. It was a Maddy-imitation. Ari had nearly gotten a stitch, inside, especially seeing Giraud's face. But Giraud was fast, especially when she winked at him and cued him in it was a prank.

Florian had stood over in the doorway to the men's side being just straight azi, which meant he was having a stitch too, because Florian never had to practice laughing. Florian just did; and stopping himself was the trick, before he gave Catlin away.

Things were a lot better in Novgorod, and there was a lot less pressure, Ari picked that up. Giraud said he thought there was a market for *tapes* about animals people couldn't own, that it was a real good idea, and that getting two hundred fifty credits for a fancy guppy meant there was a market for a lot of things, and hell if they were going to franchise it out: they could *hire* it done over in Moreyville, and maybe there was a market for koi, too, and the people who had been making aquariums and filter systems on special order for Reseune research labs might want to invest in a whole new division of manufacture.

"That's the way it works," he said. "Everything is connected to everything else."

There were miners clear out in brown little outback domes who were spending a fortune on guppy rigs, especially for the bright-colored ones, and for green *weed*, because they liked the colors and the water-sound, out where there was nothing but pale red and pale gray-blue. At Reseune people said it was the contact with a friendly ecosystem, and it was good for people: miners swore the air off the tanks made the environment healthier. Reseune said it just made people *feel* healthier and gave them a sense of connection to everything that was green and bright and Terran.

Giraud just said it made money and maybe they could look in the genebanks and the histories and see if there was something else they were missing.

Meanwhile it didn't hurt anything that people thought of her as the kid who made all that available to people. It made it hard for the people who had been the first Ari's enemies.

That was Giraud, all right. But she was doing the same thing when she practiced how to smile for the cameras. She had met the Councillor for Information, Catherine Lao, who wore a crown of braids just like Catlin, and was blonde like Catlin, but about a hundred years old: and Councillor Lao had been a friend of Ari senior's, and was so happy to see how she was growing up, the Councillor said, *so* pleased to see her doing so well.

Ari tried not to like people right off: that was dangerous, because you missed things that way that you ought to see— Ari senior had told her that, but it just clicked with something she already knew, down inside. All the same, she liked

Councillor Lao a lot; and Councillor Lao was friendlier with her than with Giraud, no matter how hard the Councillor tried to hide it: *that* gave Ari a contrast to work with, which made anybody easier to read, and it made her think Councillor Lao really was someone she might like.

It didn't hurt at all that Catherine Lao was Councillor of Information, which meant the whole news-net, among other things, and libraries and publishing and archives and public education.

There was Admiral Gorodin too, who was Defense, and Defense had protected her stuff from people going through it; he was a lot different than Lao, kind of this way and that about a lot of things, not friendly, not hostile, just real interested and kind of prickly with Giraud, but coming at her like he had known her a long time.

She had even met Mikhail Corain, who was the Enemy, and said hello to him, and he tried his best to be nice. They had been in the Hall of State, in front of all the cameras. Councillor Corain had looked like he had indigestion, but he said he had a daughter about her age, and he hoped she enjoyed her trip to Novgorod, did she want to run for Council someday?

That was too close to ideas she had that she wasn't about to tell even Giraud or Denys, so she said she didn't know, she was busy with her schoolwork, which gave the reporters a stitch and made Corain laugh, a laugh like Catlin being Maddy, and he backed up and said the world had better look out.

So would he, she thought, a little worried about that: that had been a little nasty at the last, and she wished she could have thought of something else real fast to Get him in front of the cameras. But she didn't know what was going on that he could have been talking about, and uncle Giraud had said she had done exactly right, so she supposed she must have.

So it was the plane flight and touchdown at Reseune; and the reporters waiting for her at landing—so Amy and Tommy got to be on vid. She smiled for the cameras—they didn't have to do an interview, just there were some shots the news wanted, so they got them, and then the camera people folded up to catch their RESEUNEAIR flight back on up to Svetlansk, where they were covering a big platythere that had broken right through an oil pipeline—she would like to have *seen* that, she wanted to go, but uncle Giraud said she had been away from classes long enough, and she had *better* go see about her filly.

"Is she all right?" she asked, scared by that.

"Well, who knows?" uncle Giraud said, Working her for sure, but it was a good one. "You haven't checked on her in a week."

She didn't wait for baggage. She took the bus with uncle Giraud and Florian and Catlin and Amy and Tommy went too; and she didn't even go home first, she went straight over to the lab.

The filly was doing fine, the lab said; but the Super there gave her a whole packet of fiches and said that was what she had to catch up on.

It was a trap. She got a look at the filly on the monitor: she was looking less and less like a person and more and more like a horse now. That was exciting.

It was exciting when she went over to Denys' office and got permission to bring Amy and Tommy home with her, because her baggage was going to be there by now and she wanted to give them their presents.

"Don't mess the place up," uncle Denys said, because Nelly was working babies during the day and just showing up at night; and that meant Seely and Florian and Catlin had to do a lot of the pick-up. She didn't care about Seely, but she did about Florian and Catlin; so she was careful. "Give me a hug," uncle Denys said, "and be good."

She had forgotten to get something for uncle Denys. She was embarrassed. And made a note to order something from the gourmet shop in North Wing and put it on her own card, because she had an allowance.

Something like a pound of coffee. He would like that and he wouldn't care it didn't come from Novgorod.

Besides, she got to have some of that too.

So she told Base One to buy it and send it to his office when she got in, easy as talking to the Minder.

Amy and Tommy were real impressed.

They were real happy with their presents. She brought them out of her room and didn't show off the other things—

it's not nice, uncle Denys would say, to advertise what you've got and others don't.

Uncle Denys was right. Also smart.

Tommy loved his sweater. He looked good in it.

Amy looked a little doubtful about the tiny box, like a little box like that wasn't going to be as nice a gift, until she opened it.

"It's real," she told Amy, about the pin. And Amy's face lit up. Amy was not a pretty girl. She was going to be tall and thin and long-faced, and she had to take tape to make her stop slouching, but for a moment Amy looked pretty. And felt pretty, she guessed, which made the difference.

She wished Amy had the allowance she did, to buy nice things.

Then she got an idea.

And made a note to ask uncle Denys if *Amy* could take over the guppy project, Amy knew all about it, and she was sharp about what to breed to what, and very good with numbers.

She had enough to do with the filly, and she wanted to go back to just having a few pretty fish in the aquarium in her bedroom, and not having to do in the ugly ones.

iii

Justin dumped his bags in the bedroom and went and threw himself facedown on the bed, aware of nothing until he realized he had a blanket over him and that he was being urged to tuck up onto the bed. "Come on," Grant's voice said to him. "You're going to chill. Move."

He halfway woke up then, and rolled over and found the pillow, pulling it up under his head.

"Rotten flight?" Grant asked, sitting on the edge of the bed.

"Damn little plane; they had a hell of a storm over the Tethys and we just dodged thunderheads and bounced."

"Hungry?"

"God, no. Just sleep."

Grant let him, just cut the lights, and let him lie.

Which he dimly remembered in the morning, hearing noise in the kitchen. He found himself in his clothes, unshaven.

And the clock saying 0820.

"God," he muttered, and threw the cover over and staggered for the bath and the kitchen, in that order.

Grant, in white shirt and plain beige pants, looked informally elegant, was having morning coffee at the kitchen table.

Justin raked a hand through his hair and fumbled a cup out of the cabinet without dropping it.

Grant poured him half his cup.

"I can make some," he protested.

"Of course you can," Grant said, humoring the incompetent, and pulled his chair back. "Sit down. I don't suppose you're going in today. —How's Jordan?"

"Fine," he mumbled, "fine. He really is." And sat down and leaned his elbows on the table to be sure where the cup was when he took a drink, because his eyes were refusing to work. "He's looking great. So is Paul. We had a great worksession—usual thing, too much talk, too little sleep. It was great."

He was not lying. Grant's eyes flickered and took on a moment's honest and earnest relief. Grant had already heard the word last night, at the airport, but he seemed to believe it finally, the way they always had to doubt each other, doubt every word, without the little signals that said things were what they seemed.

And then Grant looked at the time and winced. "Damn. One of us had better make it in. Yanni's hunting hides this week."

"I'll get there," Justin said.

"You're worthless. Stay here. Rest."

Justin shook his head. "I've got a report to turn in." He swallowed down the last of the coffee at a gulp. "God. You go on first. I'll get the papers hunted down. I'll get there. Message Yanni I'm coming, I just have to get the faxes together, they messed everything up in Decon."

"I'm going." Grant dumped the last of his coffee into Justin's cup. "You need it worse. It seems to be a vital nutrient for CITs."

Damn. He had crashed incommunicado last night when

Grant had been waiting days for news, and now he stole Grant's coffee at breakfast.

"I'll make it up to you," he called to Grant in the next room. "Get a rez at *Changes* for lunch."

Grant put his head back in. "Was it that good?"

"Sociology ran the TR design all the way past ten generations and it's still clean. Jordan called it clean as anything they're running."

Grant pounded the doorframe and grinned. "Bastard! You could have said!"

Justin raised an eyebrow. "I may be a son of a bitch, friend, but the very one thing I can't possibly be is a bastard. And now even Giraud will have to own up to it."

Grant hurled himself out into the living room again, crying: "Late, dammit! This isn't fair!"

In a moment the front door opened and shut.

There flatly was no time to go over things in the morning, even working back to back in the same office. Grant ticked away at the keyboard with occasional mutters to the Scriber-input, a constant background sound, while Justin ran the fax-scanner on his notes and Jordan's and the transcription of the whole week's sessions, punched keys where it was faster and sifted and edited and wrestled nearly fourteen hundred hours of constant transcription into five main topics with the computer's keyword scanning. Which still might miss or misfile things, so there was no question of dumping it: he created a sixth topic for Unassigned and kept the machine on autoTab, which meant it filed the original locations of the information.

He had four preliminary work-ups and one report nearing turn-in polish before Grant startled him out of a profound concentration and told him they had ten minutes to get to the restaurant.

He ground the heels of his hands into his eyes, saved down and stretched and flexed shoulders that had been rigid for longer than he had thought.

"Nearly done on the Rubin stuff," he said.

But that was not what he and Grant talked about all the way downstairs and across to North Wing, through the door at *Changes* and as far as their table—small respite for ordering drinks, more report, another break for ordering lunch, and into it again.

"The next thing," he said, "is getting Yanni to agree to test."

Grant said: "I'd take it."

"The hell you will."

Grant lifted a brow. "I wouldn't have any worry about it. I'd actually be a damned *good* subject, since it couldn't put anything over on me I couldn't identify—I understand the principles of it a hell of a lot better than the Test Division is going to—"

"And you're biased as hell."

Grant sighed. "I'm curious what it feels like. You don't understand, CIT. It's quite, quite attractive."

"Seductive is what I'm worried about. *You* don't need any motivation, friend, —a vacation, maybe."

"A tour of Novgorod," Grant sighed. "Of course. —I still want to *see* the thing when you get through with it."

Justin gave him a calculated, communicative frown. They *still* had to worry about bugs; and telling Security how skilled Grant was at reading-absorption of a program was something neither one of them wanted to do.

That look said: *Sure you would, and if you internalize it, partner, I'll break your fingers.*

Grant smiled at him, wide and lazy, which meant: *You smug CIT bastard, I can take care of myself.*

A tightening of his lips: *Dammit, Grant.*

A wider smile, a narrowing of the eyes: *Discuss it later.*

"Hello," a young voice said, and Justin's heart jumped.

He looked at the young girl who had stopped beside their table, at a young girl in expensive clothes, clothes that somehow, overnight, seemed to have developed a hint of a waist; caught a scent that set his heart pounding in remembered panic, looked up into a face that was the child gone grave, shy—that had gotten cheekbones; dark eyes gone somber and, God, touched with a little hint of violet eyeshadow.

"Hello," he said.

"I haven't seen you in a while."

"No. I guess I've been pretty busy."

"I was back there." She indicated the area of the restaurant past the archway. "I saw you come in, but I was already started on my sandwich. I thought I'd say hello, though."

"It's good to see you," he said, and controlled his voice with everything he had, managing a cheerful smile: the kid could read people faster than any of Security's computers. "How's your classwork?"

"Oh, too much of it." Her eyes lit, kid again, but not quite. "You know uncle Denys is going to let me have a horse—but I have to birth it; *and* do all the paperwork. Which is his way of getting me to study." She traced a design on the table edge with her finger. "I had the guppy business—" A little laugh. "But I turned that over to Amy Carnath. It was getting to be too much work, and now *she's* drafted her cousin in on it. Anyway— What are *you* doing?"

"A government study. And some stuff of my own. I've been working hard too."

"I remember when you came to my party."

"I remember that too."

"What Wing do you work in?"

"I'm in Design."

"Grant too?" With a flash of dark eyes Grant's direction.

"Yes," Grant said.

"I'm starting to study that," she said. The finger started doing designs again. The voice was lower, lacking the little-girl pitch. It was a different, more serious expression, a different tone of voice than she gave the cameras. "You know I'm a PR, don't you?"

"Yes," he said calmly, oh, very calmly. "I knew that."

"My predecessor was pretty good at Design. Did you know her?"

God, what do I say? "I knew her, yes. Not very well. She was a lot older." *Best to create no mysteries.* "She was my teacher for a little while."

The eyes flashed up from their demure down-focus, mild surprise, an evident flicker of thought. "That's funny, isn't it? Now you know a lot more than I do. I wish I could just take a tape and know everything."

"It's too much to learn from one tape."

"I know." Another soft laugh. "I know where I can go if I get a question, don't I?"

"Hey, I can't help you dodge your homework, your uncle would have my skin."

She laughed, tapped the table edge with her finger. "Your lunch is getting cold. I'd better get back to the lab. Nice to see you. You too, Grant."

"Nice to see you," Justin murmured; and: "Sera," Grant murmured in courtesy, as Ari went her way.

Justin tracked her till he was sure she was out the door, then let out his breath and dropped his forehead against his hands. "God." And looked up at Grant. "She's growing up, isn't she?"

"It was a courtesy," Grant said. "I don't think it was more than that."

"No," he agreed, and got himself together, picked up his fork and prodded tentatively at a piece of ham, determined not to pay attention to the unease in his stomach. "Not a bit of malice. She's a nice kid, a damn nice kid." He took the bite. "Jordan and I talked about that, too. Damn, I'd like to see her test records."

Grant made a frightened move of his eyes toward the wall. *Remember the eavesdroppers.*

"They're using the other—" Justin went on doggedly: Rubin was not a word they could toss around in the restaurant. "—the other subject—to see what they *can* get away with. And we can't get the results, dammit, for fifteen years."

"A little late," Grant murmured.

A little late to do anything for Ari's situation, Grant meant; and gave him a brows-knit look that said: *For God's sake, let's not talk about this, here, now.*

It was only good sense. "Yes," Justin said, as if he were answering the former, and took another bite and a drink to wash it down. He was starved after the battering on the flight: food service had been limited. And sweating over the terminal had worked up an appetite nothing could kill.

"Talk to Yanni," Grant said when they were walking across the open quadrangle, on their way back to the office, "and call Denys, the way you're supposed to. For both our sakes."

"I have every intention to," Justin said.

Which was the truth. What else he meant to say, he hesitated to mention.

But it was in the transcripts from Planys.

His opinion, and Jordan's, both . . . for what little it was worth to an Administration worried about its own survival.

_____ iv _____

Down into the tunnels, and, with Florian's little manipulation of the lock, down into the ventilation service area, from a direction that did *not* have a keycard access involved: they always had to be first, because nobody else could get the door to their meeting-place open; and the last, because Florian and Catlin were the sharpest when it came to cleaning up and making sure they left no trace at all for the workmen to find.

They used several of these little nooks. They had them coded, so Ari had only to say: number 3, and Amy passed the word to Tommy and Maddy, and Tommy got Sam up from the port school.

So they waited for the knock, and all of them came together: Amy and Tommy and Sam. Maddy was with them. And a girl named 'Stasi Morley-Ramirez, who was the reason they were meeting in a place they didn't use very often.

'Stasi was a friend of Amy's and Maddy's, but Maddy had opened her mouth, that was what had happened.

'Stasi was scared, coming in here, she was real scared, and Ari stood there with her hands on her hips, glaring at her with Catlin on her left and the flashlight on the shipping can in front of them, which made their shadows huge and their faces scary—she knew that. She had practiced that with the mirror, too, and she knew what she looked like.

"Sit down," she told 'Stasi, and Amy and Tommy sat her straight down on a big waterpipe they used to sit on here, while Florian came up and stood behind her. So 'Stasi was the only one sitting. That was a psych.

"When you come down here," Ari said, "that's it. We either vote you in or you're in a lot of trouble, 'Stasi Ramirez. You're in a whole lot of trouble, because we don't like to lose a meeting-place. And if you tell Security, *I'll* fix you good, I'll see you and your maman get shipped out of here and you won't ever come back. Say you understand."

'Stasi nodded. Emphatically.

"So you tell us why you want in."

"I know all of them," 'Stasi said desperately, twisting around where she sat to look at Amy and Maddy and the rest.

"You don't know Sam."

"I know him," 'Stasi said. "I know him from the House."

"But you don't know him like friends. And Maddy can't vote, she's the one bringing you. And Amy and Tommy can't, they're friends of yours. So it's me and Sam and Florian and Catlin who get to say. —What do you think, Catlin?"

"What can she do?" Catlin asked in her flat way.

"What *can* you do?" Ari asked.

"Like what?" 'Stasi asked anxiously. "What do you mean?"

"Like can you wire locks or memorize messages or get past a Minder or get stuff out of the lab?"

'Stasi's eyes got wider and wider.

"Catlin and Florian can do all that. They can kill people, for real. Take your head off with a wire. Pop. Just like that. Sam can get tools and wire and stuff. Maddy can get office stuff." And eyeshadow. "Tommy can get all kinds of stuff and what Amy and I do, you don't need to know about. What can you get?"

'Stasi got a more and more desperate look. "My mama and my dad manage *Ramirez's*. A lot of stuff, I guess. What do you need?"

She knew that already. *Ramirez's* was a North Hall restaurant.

"Mmmmn," she said. "Knives and stuff."

"I could," 'Stasi said earnestly. "Or food. Or most anything like that. And my uncle's a flight controller. All sorts of airline stuff—"

"All right. That part's good enough. Here's the rest. If you get in and you do anything stupid and get caught, you don't talk about us. You say it was just you. But you don't *get* caught. And you don't bring anybody here without asking. And you don't tell anybody about us. Hear?"

'Stasi nodded soberly.

"Swear?"

'Stasi nodded.

'Stasi didn't talk much. Like Sam. That was a good sign. "I vote yes," Ari said. And Sam nodded, then. She looked at Florian and Catlin.

They didn't look like it was a bad idea. Catlin always frowned when she was considering somebody.

"They say all right," Ari said.

So everybody climbed over the pipe and sat down: it was clean. Florian and Catlin always made sure the sitting place was, because otherwise people could tell they were running around in dusty places.

And Florian and Catlin just squatted down when they were relaxing.

So they got down to business, which was her telling a lot about the trip to Novgorod—Sam had his new sweater on and so did Tommy, and Maddy wore her scarf, but Amy's pin was too good to wear to classes. Then they talked about the party Maddy was going to have, which *they* were all going to be invited to, and Maddy was happy, about 'Stasi getting in, and about being important for a while.

It was true Maddy was an early developer. The way Maddy sat and the way the light came up from their makeshift table showed that, real plain; and she was always slinking around and fluttering at the boys.

Tommy took it all right. It really bothered Sam: poor Sam had grown up big and he was in kind of a clumsy stage, because he grew so fast, Tommy said, but Sam was mostly always banging his head on things—like he was always misjudging how tall he was. He was quick as Florian when it came to fixing something, his fingers were so fast it was amazing to watch him, and he could figure out mechanical things very fast.

Sam also was in love with her, sort of, Sam always had been, like he wanted really truly to be a special friend, but she never let him, because she just didn't feel that close to Sam from her side; and it made her mad when she saw how he took Maddy seriously and worried about it, like he knew he wasn't really part of the House, and he lived down next to the Town. Maddy was rich and that wasn't ever going to come to anything, no more than Sam with her.

She had all this figured out, in a years-away mode, that none of them were really serious yet, but Sam was born serious, and Maddy was *on* ever since she learned there was a difference in boys and girls.

She knew. You didn't breed guppies and study horses without figuring out how *that* worked, and why all of a sudden boys and girls were getting around to teasing each other.

She wasn't terribly interested. She resented the whole process. It made everybody act stupid, and it was a complication when you were trying to set things up with people.

Then she saw Maddy fake a trip when they were going out and nudge Florian with her hip.

You didn't push Florian: people bumping him scared him. But he recovered fast and put his arm out and she grabbed it, lucky she hadn't landed against the wall, because Florian had learned in Novgorod not to react too suddenly when they were in crowds.

Maddy managed to put her hands on his shoulders and laugh and pretend to catch her balance before she got out the door.

What Maddy didn't see was the funny look Florian gave her retreating back.

But Ari did. He was still wearing it when he looked back at her, like he thought he had just been Got in some vague way and wasn't sure whether he had reacted right or not.

She didn't help him out either. And she doubted Catlin understood.

V

It was a long time since Justin had come into Denys Nye's office. The last visit came back all too strongly: the heavy-set man at the desk, every detail of the room.

Giraud Nye's brother. One never forgot that either.

"Yanni said," Justin began, at the door, "you were willing to talk with me."

"Certainly. Sit down."

He came and sat down, and Denys leaned forward, hands

on the desk. There was a dish of pastilles. Denys took one, offered the dish across the desk.

"No, ser, thank you."

Denys popped one in his mouth, leaned back with a creak of the chair, and folded his hands on his stomach. "Yanni sent me your work. He says you want to go Test. You're pretty confident about this one, are you?"

"Yes, ser. I am. It's a simple program. Nothing at all fancy. I don't think it'll have to run long."

"I don't think it's a problem that the Test Division can show us much about. Jordan says it'll run, it'll run without a glitch. The trouble with your work, after all, *isn't* what it does in generation one or even two. If it were, we—wouldn't have a problem with it, would we? We could just install and go."

Grant had arguments for the run too, azi-view. *Grant* understood how the Testers worked: Grant could do what the Testers did. But it was the last place he was going to say anything on that score, not if it cost him his chance, not if it was the one and only chance he would ever have.

Nothing—was worth Grant's safety.

"I value the Testers' opinion," he said quietly. "And their experience. They have a viewpoint the computers can't give me; that's why we go to them last, isn't it?"

"That's why their time is more valuable. But they still can't answer the multi-generational problem."

"I don't know, ser, I have a great deal of confidence in their emotional judgment. And the run would give me a lot if it could turn up anything, *any* sort of input. Jordan is saying it should run. He isn't saying that just because he's my father, ser. Not to me. Not on something that important."

Denys gave a slight, sad smile, and sighed. The chair creaked as he leaned forward and leaned his elbows on the table. And pushed a button. The bone-deep hum of the Silencer enveloped them, afflicting the nerves and unsettling the stomach. "But the problem is beyond a twenty-year study even if we gave you a full run with a geneset. That's the crux of it. Ultimately, proving whether you're right or wrong would take a Gehenna-style run. Twenty *generations*, not twenty years. We're just damn shy of planets to hand you.

And what do we do with the culture that turns out if you're wrong? Nuke it? That's the scale you work on, son.''

He heard *no* coming, in a slow, sarcastic way, and bit his lip and controlled his temper. "Kind of like Emory," he said, bitterly. Ultimate hubris, in Reseune. And almost said: *if your committee had had to vet her projects we'd still be a damn production farm.*

But then he was in no wise sure what Emory had done twenty or thirty generations down, or how far, or whether Union itself worked. Denys' Gehenna-reference chilled him.

"Kind of like Emory," Denys said slowly, without inflection. "I'll tell you, Sociology has been mightily upset with your designs—the suggestion that they might have turned up a flaw in the projection programs, you know. You've given the programmers over there some sleepless nights. And quite honestly, we haven't spilled the fact to Defense. You know how excited they get."

"I've never thought of going to them."

"Never?"

"No, ser. I don't see any percentage in doing it. Reseune—has its advantages. More than Planys does."

"Even if Defense might promise you residency with Jordan."

He took a breath and felt the unease of the Silencer to the roots of his teeth. It was hard to ignore. "I *have* thought of that. I hope to get him back here, ser, not—not put both of us there. He understands. He hopes for the same thing. Someday. Or we could have leaked this to Defense. Neither of us has."

"Jordan never has *liked* Defense," Denys said. "They certainly didn't help him at his hearing."

"You've counted on that," Justin said quietly. "He could have talked to them. He didn't. Not that I ever know of."

"No, you're quite right. He doesn't trust them. But mostly the consideration of your career. And Grant's. Let's be frank. We know—how far he could push us . . . and why he won't. Let me go on being honest with you. He has every motive to lie to us and to you: to convince us you're valuable in your own right, to make sure you're protected—if he gets careless. You're very naive if you think he wouldn't do that."

He ignored the body blows and kept his face unmoved. "He values Grant too," he said. "And I do. You always have a hostage. All you have to do is keep him untouched."

"Of course. That's why Grant doesn't travel."

"But once—alone—even for a few hours——that trip would be worth it to Grant. And to my father. What's a hostage worth, if the one you're holding him against—forgets his value?"

Denys gave a heavy sigh. "Son, I don't enjoy this situation; and I had far rather have peace with the Warrick clan, God knows how, without making a slip that gets someone hurt. I'm being utterly honest with you, I'm telling you my worries in the matter. I still believe in you enough to have you in on the Project on Yanni's say-so. We're solvent again, but we're sure as hell not taking chances or spending wildly, and you're asking for a major amount of effort here, on something that's already been a headache to Sociology——"

"You say yourself, if those projections are wrong, if Sociology is working on flaws, then Defense ought to be interested. I'd call that a major matter, ser, I don't know what more it takes to qualify."

Denys frowned. "I was about to say, young friend, —'but, over all, a benefit.' All right, you get your test subject. Six-month run."

"Thank you, ser." Justin drew a whole breath. "I appreciate your honesty." *Like hell.* "And I hope—from my side— you understand the meeting yesterday—"

"Absolutely," Denys said. "I do. I appreciate the call. Ari has lunch in there now and again. You can't stay in hiding. You handled it exactly right."

"I told her Ari was my instructor. Since she asked about my knowing her. I figured—I'd better say how I knew her— early."

"That falls in an area she can't research. But yes, I see your reasoning. I have no objection to it. Sometimes you have to make fast assessments with her—God knows. You should *live* with her." Denys chuckled, and leaned back again. "She's a challenge. I know that, believe me."

"I—" God, it was an opening. It was lying in front of him. "The other thing I wanted to talk with you about: the

Rubin sets, ser, I wish—wish you'd take a look at that, your-self; and my arguments. Working with Ari, the way you do, —I thought you—could give me a viewpoint—I don't have."

"On the Rubin case? Or regarding Ari?"

"I—see one bearing on the other. Somewhat. Ser."

Denys rocked his chair back and forth and lifted his brows. "Yanni told me."

"I just wonder if you'd take a look at the latest paper."

"I *have* looked at it. Yanni sent it over. I'll tell you, a lot you're doing is quite, quite good. I'm aware of your personal profile. I know what a strain it is for you to work real-time, or anything close to it, and I appreciate the stress you've undertaken—for that boy on Fargone. I know it's hard for Morley to appreciate how much pressure you're under . . . your tendency to internalize these cases. Damn bad thing for a clinical psychologist. About Ari, let me tell you, of *course* the cases are linked and of *course* your worry for the Rubin boy is going to spill over in worry about Ari, your personal mindset guarantees it. —But we *can't* hand you the whole of both projects, you do understand that, Justin, no more than we can find you a planet to test with."

"I just—" He had had enough people calling him a fool in his life he should be less sensitive; but Denys didn't bludg-eon, Denys was stinging and unexpected as a paper-cut. "—just hoped—if you had time, ser, you might want to con-sider contingencies."

Riposte to Denys.

Denys rocked forward again, leaned on the desk. "We're working an emergency course change with the Rubin baby. You're giving us a useful perspective on the Rubin case, be-cause we *have* a problem, but we sure as hell aren't in that situation with Ari—"

"*Rubin* worked till the thing blew up, forgive me if I mis-understand, but the matter went deeper than Jenna Schwartz and Stella Rubin—"

"Let me tell you, Justin, I *do* worry about someone who's so sure he's right he can't conceive of being wrong. I know Yanni's talked to you about that problem."

"*I'll send you my project papers. I'll pay for them.*

Enough for your damn committee. Point of information—is that interference?'' He drew a breath. "I happen to think it's *sane* to consider related data in a case where a committee is running an untested program. I'm not asking you for data; I'm not asking you even for data on the Rubin case that I damn well need to work with, because I know I haven't got a chance in hell of getting it. But I can hand it to you, at my own expense, since Reseune can't afford the faxes, in the theory you ought to have it available. I don't call that interference. Shred it if you like. But at least I'll have tried!''

Denys rubbed his lip, and picked up another pastille. Popped it into his mouth. "Damn, you're persistent.''

"Yes, ser.''

Denys looked at him a very long time. "Tell me. Does your own experience—as Jordan's replicate—bear on your confidence that you understand the Project?''

The question he had not wanted asked. Ever. His heart hit bottom. "I don't know. Everything bears on my ideas. How can I sort it out?''

"It's interesting to me. You were never aware of yourself as a replicate—until you were—how old?''

"Six. Seven. Something like. I don't remember.''

"Always in Jordan's shadow. Always willing to take Jordan's opinion over your own. I think there *is* something in you . . . possibly a very important something. But sometimes I see other things: Jordan's stubbornness; his tendency to be *right* beyond all reason.'' Denys shook his head and sighed. "You have a hell of a way of applying for finance. Attack the people who can give it to you. Just exactly like Jordan.''

"If politics matters more than what *is*, —''

"Damn, more and more like your father.''

Justin shoved the chair back and got up to leave. Fast. Before he lost his temper altogether. "Excuse me, then.''

"Justin, Justin, —remember? Remember who *funded* your research time? That was out of *my* budget, at a time we could hardly afford it. I take everything you've said as an honest intent to help. I assure you. I have your report; I'll have my secretary fax it for the committee. And any other material you want to send.''

He was left, on his feet, with the anger still running through him. It made a tremor in his muscles. He jammed his hands in his pockets to hide their shaking. "Then thank you, ser. What about my Test request?"

"God," Denys sighed. "Yes, son. You have it. No change in that. Just—do us all a favor. *Don't* intrude any further into the Project. Keep on being prudent as you have been. Ari's handling everything very well. She's accepted being Ari's replicate, taken everything in stride. But she likes you. And she doesn't know how her predecessor died. Her time-frame on Ari is constantly lagged. The Ari she knows is five going on six, and beyond that, she's seen only a few pictures. Remember that."

"When *will* she know?"

"I'm not sure," Denys said. "I tell you that honestly. We make decisions real-time on this side of the Project; there's no way for me to answer that question. But believe me—I will warn you, when it becomes—immediate. That's one of the things we worry about as much as you do."

vi

It was *shots* again. Ari winced as the hypo popped against her arm, not one hypo, but three, besides the blood tests she had had every few days of her life.

Nothing wrong with you, Dr. Ivanov had told her repeatedly. *We just do this.*

Which was a lie. Dr. Ivanov had finally said so, when she found out she was a replicate and asked whether the first Ari had had something wrong with her: *No, but the first Ari had tests just like yours, because her maman knew she was going to be somebody special, and because tests like these are valuable information. You're a very bright little girl. We'd like to know if something special goes on in your bloodstream.*

But the shots made her dizzy and sick at her stomach and she was tired of getting shots and having needles in her arm.

She frowned at the nurse and thought where she would like to give the nurse a hypo, right when her back was turned. But she took the thermometer under her tongue a second till it registered, then took it out and looked at it.

"A point under," she told the nurse. Who insisted to look at it. "I always am. Do I get to go now?"

"Wait here," the nurse said, and went out, leaving her sitting in the damn robe and a little cold, the way the hospital always was, people could *freeze* to death in this place.

In a moment Dr. Ivanov came in. "Hello, Ari. Feeling fine?"

"The shot made me sick. I want to go get an orange or something."

"That's fine. That's a good idea." He came and took her pulse again. And smiled at her. "A little mad?"

"I'm tired of this. I've been in here twice this week. I'm not going to have any blood left."

"Well, your body is going through some changes. You're just growing up, sweet, that's all. Perfectly normal. You know a lot of it. But you're going to take a tape this afternoon. If you have any questions you can call me or Dr. Wojkowski, whichever you'd rather—she might be a little better at this."

She wrinkled her nose, not with any clear idea, really, what he was talking about, except she was embarrassed sitting there in the robe, which was more than she used to sit there in, and suspecting that it had to do with sex and boys and that she was going to be embarrassed as hell if she had to listen to Dr. Ivanov explain to her what she had already figured out.

Do you understand? he would ask her every three lines, and: *Yes*, she would say, because he would not get through it without that.

But he didn't mention it. He just told her go on to library, she had the tape to do.

They gave it to her to take home to use, on the house machine, so it wasn't one of the skill ones, that she had to take with a tech.

It certainly wasn't, she decided, when she saw the title. It said *Human Sexuality*. She was embarrassed in front of the librarian, who was a man, and tucked it into her bag and took it fairly straight home, very glad that Seely was out and Nelly was at her day job and there wasn't anyone around.

She applied the patch over her heart and lay down on the couch in the tape lounge and took the pill. When the pill began to work she pushed the button.

And was awfully glad, in a vague, tape-dazed way, that she hadn't had to take this one with any tech sitting by her.

There *were* things she hadn't known, things a lot different than horses, and things the same, and things Dr. Edwards had sort of hit on in biology, but not really explained with pictures and in the detail the tape had.

When it was over she lay there recovering from the pill and feeling really funny—not bad. Not bad at all. But like something was going on with her she could not control, that she sure as hell didn't want uncle Denys or Seely to know about.

It certainly had to do with sex. And it was hard to get up finally and get her mind off it. She thought about doing the tape again, not that she was not going to remember, but because she wanted to try out the feeling again, to see if it was the way she remembered it.

Then she thought it might not feel the same, and she didn't want it not to. So she put the tape back in her bag and because she didn't want the thing lying around her room where Nelly would find it and look at her funny, she had a glass of orange juice to get her blood moving again and walked all the way back to the library to drop it in the turn-in slot.

Then she went to lunch and went to class, but her concentration was shot to hell. Even Dr. Edwards frowned at her when he caught her woolgathering.

She did her write-up on the filly. It was a long day, because people were mostly busy, uncle Denys and Seely and Nelly and everybody, because Florian and Catlin were off since three days ago on a training exercise that was not going to finish till the end of the week.

She went over to the guppy lab to see if Amy was there. Tommy was. Tommy was not who she wanted to see, but she sat and talked with him a little while. Tommy was doing some stuff with the reds that she could give him some information on.

She went home to do more homework. Alone.

"Ari," uncle Denys said, on the Minder, when she had had dinner and she was still doing homework in her room. "Ari, I want to talk with you in my study."

Oh, God, she thought. Uncle *Denys* was going to ask her about the tape. She had rather die.

But it was even more embarrassing to make a fuss about it. So she got up and slunk in and stood in uncle Denys' doorway.

"Oh. Ari. There you are."

I'm going to die. *Right here. On the spot.*

"I want to talk with you. Sit down."

God. I have to look at him.

She sat, and held on to the arms of the chair.

"Ari, you're getting older. Nelly's really fond of you—but she's really not doing much but housework anymore. She really lives with the lab babies. And she's awfully good at that. I wonder if you've thought any more whether you'd like—well, to see Nelly go over to lab full-time. It's the nature of nurses, you know, the babies grow up."

That was all it was. She drew a long breath, and thought about her room, and how she *liked* Nelly, but she liked Nelly better when she wasn't *with* Nelly, because Nelly always had her feelings hurt and was always upset when she wanted to spend more time with Florian and Catlin, and was constantly tweaking at her hair, her clothes, straightening her collar—sometimes Nelly made her want to scream.

"Sure," she said. "Sure, if *she's* all right. I don't think she's very happy."

She felt guilty about that, sort of, because Nelly had been maman's, because Nelly had been hers—because Nelly was—Nelly—and never would understand the way she was now.

And because she was so glad it was about that and not about the other thing she just wanted to agree and get out of there.

She was guilty the next morning when Nelly went to hospital not knowing what they were going to do with her tape this time.

"I'm really not upset," Nelly protested to uncle Denys at

the door, with her overnight kit in her hand. "I don't think I need to."

"That's fine," uncle Denys said. "I'm glad. But I think you're due for a check."

A Super said anything that he had to say, to keep an azi from being stressed.

So Nelly came and kissed her goodbye. " 'Bye, Nelly," Ari said, and hugged her around the neck, and let her go.

She was able to do that, because letting Nelly know would scare Nelly to death. Only when the door shut she bit her lip hard enough to bleed and said to uncle Denys:

"I'm going on to class."

"Are you all right, Ari?"

"I'm fine."

But she cried when she got out in the hall, and straightened her face up and wiped her eyes and held it in, because she was not a baby anymore.

Nelly was not going to get hurt; Nelly was going to hospital where they would slide her right over to a job she was happy at, and tell her she had done a wonderful job, her first baby was grown, and she had a whole lot of others that needed her.

It was foolish to cry. It was foolish to cry when it was just part of growing up.

The apartment was going to be lonely until suppertime. She went over to Amy's to do her homework, and told Amy about Nelly leaving, because she was finally able to talk about it.

"She was in the way anyway," she said. "She was always sniping at Florian and Catlin."

Then she felt mean for saying that.

"How are you feeling?" uncle Denys asked her again at dinner. "Are you all right with Nelly?"

"I'm fine," she said. "I just wish Florian and Catlin would get back."

"Do you want to call them home?"

Right at the end of one of their Exercises. It was very serious to them. So was she, but it was like taking something away from them. "No," she said. "They really like the overnights. Not—*like*, because they come back all scraped up; but, *like*, you know—they enjoy telling me about it. I don't need them that bad."

"I'm proud of you," uncle Denys said. "A good Super has to think that way."

She felt a little better then. And went to do her homework ahead, because she could, and she had rather do it and have something to fill her time and have it over with when Florian and Catlin got home.

Except she had a message from the computer when she went in her room.

"Ari," the Minder said. "Check Base One."

"Go ahead," she said, and looked at the screen.

Ari, this is Ari senior.

Sex is part of life, sweet. Not the most important part, but this is your coming-of-age lecture. I don't know how old you are, remember, so I have to keep it simple. Library says you've checked out Human Sexuality. *Have you had it?*

"Yes. Yesterday."

Good. You're 10 years old. This program is triggered by your medical records.

You're about to start your monthly cycles, sweet. Welcome to a damn unfunny fact of life. Housekeeping has been notified. You're going to have the appropriate stuff in your cabinet. Hell of a thing to get caught without. You've also had a shot that means you'll reject any pregnancy. So you don't have to worry about that, at least . . . because without that, your body's perfectly capable of it now.

I'm going to leave the what-to and what-with to the tape program, sweet. I figure you know. Probably it's given you some ideas. I know. I had it too. They're not bad ideas. I want you to listen to what I'm going to say next with everything you've got, like it was tape. This is private, it's about sex, and it's one of the most important things I'll ever have to tell you. Are you alone?

"Yes."

All right.

The ideas you have, sweet, are perfectly natural. Is your pulse a little elevated?

"Yes."

You feel a little flushed?

"Yes."

That's because you're thinking about sex. If I asked you to do complicated math you'd probably make a mistake right now. That's the important lesson, sweet. Biology interferes with logic. There's two ways to deal with it—do it and get it out of your head, because that feeling explodes like a soap bubble once you've done sex—or if it's somebody you really like, or somebody you don't like, who upsets you and makes you feel very, very strong reactions, you'd better think a whole lot about doing it, because that kind explodes all right, but it keeps coming back and bothering you. When you get into bed with somebody, you're not going to be thinking with your brain, sweet, you'll be thinking with the part of you that doesn't have anything but feeling, and that's damned dangerous.

When adults meet, sweet, and start getting to know each other, this is one of the main things that's different than kids. Kids are quite logical in some ways adults aren't. That's why they seem to see character so clearly. But when adults deal with each other, this feeling you've begun to get, gets right in the middle of their judgment.

Now there are some people who just let it take over. And the thing about this feeling is that it's playing totally off the emotional level, out of memories, out of what we're set up to believe is handsome or sexy, a whole lot of things that haven't got a damn thing to do with truth.

There are some people who learn early that they're very good-looking and that they can make anybody have this feeling about them—and they use it to get what they want. This doesn't mean they have any feeling inside at all. That's one reason to watch out who you go to bed with and who you let affect you that way.

There are other times when you get that feeling about somebody who doesn't have it for you, and that's one of the hardest things in the world to deal with. But you have to stop it then and let your brain take over, because you don't get everything you want in this world, and it's not fair to the other person at all. If you think about it you'll know how they'd feel, first if they didn't care for you as a friend and then if they did, and you kept insisting on having your way.

You can see how messy that gets.

Sometimes it happens the other way around. And if you don't see it happening or if you're too soft-hearted to say no, you can hurt somebody worse than if you say: I'm sorry, this won't work, *right off.*

Sometimes it works right on both sides, and watch out then too, sweet, because sex isn't the only thing in life, and if you let it be, that's all you'll ever have.

I'll tell you what the most important thing is, in case you haven't figured it out: It's being able to do what makes you the happiest the longest, and I don't mean sex and I don't mean chocolates, sweet, I mean being able. *Able means just exactly having the time, the money, the ability, and a thing to do that makes your life worth living long enough to get it done.*

You aren't going to have a clear sight of that thing until you've had a look at the world as it is, and had a chance to figure out what the world could be if you worked at it.

So when you get that feeling, *you think real clearly whether you can afford to give in to it and whether you're* able *to handle it without getting your whole life slanted in some direction that isn't smart. The time to give in to that feeling is when you can* afford *to, just the same as you don't spend money you haven't got, promise things you don't have time to do, or get involved in projects you can't finish. If it's a minor thing and nobody can get hurt, fine, do it. If it's got complications,* don't *do it until you know damn well you can handle it, and know how far the complications can possibly extend. At 10, you can't see everything. I was there. Believe me, I know. I got involved with somebody once, and I really liked him; unfortunately, he wasn't as smart as I am, and he wanted to tell me what to do and how to run my life, because he sensed I really was hooked on him, and he really liked ordering people around. So do I, of course. So when I got that figured out, which took longer than usual, because neurons work logic problems a hell of a lot faster than glands—I'm being facetious—anyway, I told him off, I reversed what was going on, and he hated it like hell. Hated me after that, too. So not only did the feeling go away, I lost a friend who would have stayed a friend if I hadn't let him do a power-move on me. I'm telling you about it now because you can learn about fire two ways: put your hand in it and understand it with the neurons below your neck or listen to me tell you about it and understand it with the ones up in your head. Your brain is the operations center that has to keep your hand out of the fire in the first place, so if you can believe me, and use the sense you were born with, you can save yourself all the pain and embarrassment of a real lesson.*

Brains and sex fight each other to control your life, and thank God brains get a head start before sex comes along. Sex is when you're the most vulnerable you'll ever be. Brains is when you're least. Brains have to win out, that's all, so they can make a safe time for sex to happen. Remember that.

Now, don't mistake: it's not bad to be vulnerable sometimes, but it's stupid to walk around that way: there are too many people just waiting for that chance. It's stupid to miss sex altogether for fear someone will take advantage of you— use the brain, sweet, and find somebody and some place and some time safe. Brains are nature's way of making sure you live long enough to spawn—if you were a frog. But you're better than a frog. So plan to live longer.

And for God's sake, don't ever use sex to get your own way where brains won't work. That's the dumbest thing in the world to do, because then you're operating without brains at all, aren't you? That's as plain as I can make it.

I want you to come back to this more than once, till you've understood what I'm saying.

If I could have learned this one thing early enough, I'd have been happier.

Good luck, Ari. I hope to hell you learn this part.

She thought about that a long time into the night, into a very lonely night, because Nelly was gone and Florian and Catlin were away; and she felt awful the next morning.

Then she found out why she felt awful and why her gut hurt, and mostly she just wanted to kill something. But she found the stuff in the bathroom, all right, read the instructions and got it all figured out: Dr. Wojkowski had given her a booklet with the package, which was very plain and echoed a lot of things the tape had said.

It was more biology than she wanted in one week, dammit. And she was embarrassed and mad when the Minder said uncle Denys was waiting breakfast.

"I'll get there when I can," she yelled at it.

And took her pill and got herself in order and went out to breakfast.

"Are you all right?" Denys asked.

She glared at him, figuring he damn well knew, everybody else did. "I'm just fine," she said, and ate without another word while he read his morning reports.

Florian and Catlin came home late, sore and tired and with bandages on Catlin's hand; and full of stories, what the Exercise had been, how Catlin had gotten her hand cut getting a piece of metal fixed for a trap, but it had worked, and they had survived all the way through the course. Which youngers didn't do.

She wished she had something better than losing Nelly to tell them. And she wasn't about to tell them why she was sulking in her bedroom and feeling rotten.

Certainly not Florian, anyhow. But she got Catlin apart from Florian and told Catlin what the trouble was. Catlin listened and made a face and said well, it happened: if you were on an Operation you could take stuff so it came early or later.

Never take azi-pills, maman had said, but it sure sounded attractive.

It was worth asking Dr. Wojkowski about. Damned if she was going to ask Dr. Ivanov.

It was also a damned nasty come-down from all the *interesting* stuff about sex. Not fair, she thought. Not fair.

Just when her friends were getting home.

And one of them was a boy, and azi, and she was his Super, which meant she had to be responsible.

Dammit.

Maman had had Ollie. She thought about Ollie a lot, when she thought about boys. Ollie was administrator of RESEUNESPACE, doing maman's job. But Ollie never wrote. And she figured he would if he wanted to. Or maman had never gotten the letters. Or never wanted them.

That hurt too much to think about. She knew what she thought: maman had never gotten them. Giraud had stopped them. And Giraud would stop any letters from getting to Ollie.

So she tried not to think about that part. Just Ollie, how nice he had been, how he had always been so patient and understood maman; and how maman could be down, and Ollie would come up and put his hand on her shoulder, and maman felt better, that was all.

There was Sam. Sam was going to be big and strong as Ollie. But Sam was one of those people Ari senior was talking about that liked you without you liking them that way.

She felt good about having figured that out before she ever heard it from Ari senior, like it proved her predecessor was giving her good advice.

She felt about the same about Tommy: Tommy was all right to work with, but he was stubborn, he was all right being Amy's cousin, and number two behind Amy; and that meant doing anything with Tommy was going to mess up things with Amy. That part of the first Ari's advice made that make sense, too: complications.

There were older boys—Mika Carnath-Edwards, Will Morley, Stef Dietrich, who were worth thinking about. But Mika was a lot older, that was no good; Will was just dull; and Stef was Yvgenia Wojkowski's, who was his age.

She sighed, and kept circling back to the same thought, and watching Florian when Florian wasn't watching her.

Florian was smarter and more fun than any of them. Even Sam.

Florian was so damned nice-looking, not baby-faced like Tommy: not clumsy like Sam. She found herself just watching him move, just staring at the way his jaw was, or his arms or—

Whatever.

He had a figure the others didn't, that was what, because he worked so hard. He could move the way they couldn't, because he had muscle Tommy didn't and he was limber like

Sam wasn't. And he had long lashes and dark eyes and a nice mouth and a jawline with nothing of baby about it.

He was also Catlin's partner. He was part of two, and they had been together forever, and they depended on each other in ways that had to do with things that could get you killed, if that partnership got messed up.

That was more serious than any hurt feelings. And they trusted her and depended on her in ways nobody else ever would, as long as she lived.

So she played Ari senior's advice over and over when she was alone in her room, silent, because of the Security monitoring, and told herself there had to be somebody safe, somewhere, somebody she couldn't hurt or who wouldn't mess things up.

Sex wasn't fun, she decided, it was a damned complicated mess, it gave you cramps and it tangled things up and made grown-ups not trust each other. And if you really fouled up you got pregnant or you got your best friends mad at each other.

No fair at all.

-------------------- vii --------------------

Spring happened. The eleventh. And the filly was getting restless in her tank, a knot of legs and body, for a long time now too big for the lens to see all of.

Florian loved her, loved her the moment she began to look like a horse and sera had brought him to the lab and let him look into the tank. And when it came to birthing her, which sera said felt like *she* had been pregnant all these months, she had to work so hard for her, and do all that paperwork—Florian knew who was the best person down in AG to help out with that, and who was strong enough to handle the filly and keep her from hurting herself, and who knew what to do.

He told sera, and sera told the staff in the AG lab, taking his advice right off. So up came Andy, a very pleased Andy, who shyly shook sera's hand and said in his quiet way, thank you, sera; because Andy loved Horse and all Horse's kind, and sera loved them in spite of the fact Horse had broken sera's arm . . . which was probably the worst moment of Andy's whole life.

So it was a very, very happy Andy who came up to the AG lab, and knew it was true what Florian had come down to the barns to tell him, that sera wasn't put out with Horse, sera loved him too, and sera wanted more of his kind, sera was working to birth another female, and was going to ride her, and show everybody what Horse and his kind could do.

"Sera," Andy said, bowing low.

"Florian says you're the best there is," sera said, and Andy knew then, Florian was sure, that his m'sera was the finest, the best, the wisest m'sera in all Reseune. And maybe farther.

"I don't know," Andy said, "sera. But I'll sure take care of her the best I can."

So the labor started in the evening, and they just watched, watched while the foal slid down the chute into the bed of fiber; and watched while the AG techs got the cord; and Andy took sponges and towels and dried the filly all over and got her up on her wobbly legs.

Sera got to touch her then, for the first time. Sera patted her and helped dry her, and Florian helped, until Andy said that was enough and picked the filly up—Andy was very strong, and he said there was no way any truck was going to take the filly down to the barn, he could carry her.

"I want to see her," sera said.

"We can walk down," Florian said, and looked at Catlin, who stood by all this, taking it in—he knew how Catlin thought—but a great deal bewildered by all the fuss, by babies, and by sera's worry over the filly—

It was healthy, it was all right: he could read Catlin's mind that well; so why was sera worried? Babies happened. They were supposed to be studying. They had an Exercise coming up.

"I'll go," he said to Catlin. "Sera and I will be back in about an hour."

"All right," Catlin said. Because Catlin had a lot of study to do. Because if he did that, Catlin was the one who was going to save them, he knew he was going to foul up, unless Catlin could brief him fast and accurately.

But for sera, for the filly, too, who was not at fault—no animal could choose its time to be born—he had not the least hesitation: training was training, and sera was—everything.

So Andy carried the filly down the hill to the horse barn, and Florian walked with sera, happy the way she was, *because* she was, and because now there were three horses in the world, instead of two.

Andy set the little filly down in a warm stall, and got the formula they had ready and warm, and let sera give it to the baby, which stood on shaky legs and butted with her nose as if that could get more milk faster. Sera laughed and backed up, and the filly wobbled after. "Stand still, sera," Andy called out. "Just hold it."

Sera laughed, and held on.

Down the way, in her stall, the Mare called out, leaning over the rail.

"I think she smells the baby," sera said. "That could be trouble. Or she might take up with her. I don't know."

"I don't either," Andy said.

"There being just three," sera said, "everything's like that, isn't it? The books don't say about a horse who never saw but one other horse in the world."

"And she's pregnant," Andy said in his quiet way, shy around a CIT, "and she's got milk already. And animals are like CITs, sera, they have their own ways, it's not all one psychset, and there isn't any tape for *them*."

Sera looked at him, not mad, just like she was a little surprised at all that out of Andy. But it was true, Florian knew it. One pig was trouble and its birthsisters weren't. It just depended on a lot of things, and when babies happened the way they did with pigs, with a boar and a sow, you were dealing with scrambled genesets and didn't know what you had—like CITs, too.

At least, with the filly, it was likely to be a lot like its genesister the Mare, which meant she was going to be easy to handle.

Bang! on the rails from down the row. The Mare called out, loud. And the azi who were standing in the barn to watch the new baby went running to get the Mare.

"This is all complicated," sera said, worried.

"Animals are like that," Andy said. "She's all right. It would be good if she would accept the baby. Animals know a lot. Some things they seem to be born knowing."

"Instinct," sera said. "*You* should cut a tape. I bet you know more than some of the damn books."

Andy grinned and laughed, embarrassed. "I'm a Gamma, sera, not like Florian. I'm just a Gamma." As one of the other AG-techs came running down to say the Mare was fine, they were going to move her to the little barn and get her out of here.

"No, do that, but pass her by here," Andy said. "But hold on to her. Let's see what she does. Sera, if she makes trouble, you better be ready to climb up over those rails to the side there and get into the other stall. Florian and I can hold the baby, and the boys can hold the Mare, but we sure don't want you to break another arm."

"I can help hold her."

"Please, sera. We don't know what will happen. Just be ready to move."

"He's the best," Florian said. "Andy's always out here; the Supers are always in the offices. Andy's birthed most everything there is. You should do what he says, sera."

"I'll move," sera said, which was something, from sera. But she *liked* Andy, and she realized right off that Andy had good sense, that was the way sera was. So she stood there watching anxiously as the techs led the Mare past, two of them, each with a lead on her.

The Mare pulled and they let her stop and put her head over the stall door. She snuffed the air and made a strange, interested sound.

The baby pricked up her ears, and stood there with her nose working hard too.

"Put the Mare in the next stall," Andy told the techs holding the Mare. "Let's just watch this awhile."

That was the way Andy worked. Sometimes he didn't know. Sometimes no one knew because no one in the world had ever tried it. But Andy didn't let his animals get hurt and he had a way of figuring what they were going to do even if Andy had never read a book in his life.

"She's *talking* to her," sera said, "that's what she's doing."

"They sure teach something," Andy said. "Animals sort of do tape on each other."

"They're a herd animal," sera said. "It's got to be *everything* to do with how they act. They want to be together, I think."

"Well, the little girl will fix on people," Andy said. "They're that way, when they're born from the tank. But the Mare could help this little horse. She's getting milk, already. And milk from a healthy animal is a lot healthier than formula. I'm just worried about how she'll act when hers comes."

"Politics," sera said. "It's always politics, isn't it?" Sera was amused, and watched as the Mare put her head over the rail of the next stall. "Look at her. Oh, she wants over here."

"Somebody's going to sit all night with the Mare, too," Andy said. "When we've got something we don't know about, we just hold on to the ropes and stay ready. But there's a chance the Mare will want this baby. And if she does, she's the best help we could get."

They were *very* late getting back up the hill. Florian wouldn't trade the time with sera and the filly for his own sake, but he was terribly sorry when he got back to the room, in a dark and quiet apartment, and said to Catlin: "It's me," when he opened the door.

"Um," Catlin said, from her bunk, and started dragging herself up on an arm. "Trouble?"

"Everything's fine. The baby's doing real well. Sera's happier than I've ever seen."

"Good," Catlin said, relieved. So he knew Catlin had been worrying all this time.

"I'm *sorry*, Catlin."

" 'S all right. Shower. I'll tell you the stuff."

He shut the door, asked the Minder for the bathroom light and started stripping on his way to the bath while Catlin got herself focused. He hardly ran water over himself and pulled on clean underwear and came out again, cut the light and sat there on his bed while Catlin, from hers, a calm, coherent voice out of the dark, told him how they were going to have one bitch of a problem tomorrow, they had to break past a Minder and get a Hostage out alive.

They said there were going to be three Enemies, but you never knew.

You never knew what the Minder controlled, or if there wasn't some real simple, basic wire-job on the door, which was the kind of trap you could fall into if you got to concentrating too much on the tech stuff.

They had to head down the hill at 0400. It was drink the briefing down, fix what could happen, and sleep for whatever time they could without getting there out of breath, because you never knew, sometimes they threw you something they hadn't told you about at all, and you had to cope with an Enemy attack before you even got to the Exercise.

Catlin never wasted time with what and where. She had showed him a lot in the years they had worked together, about how to focus down and think narrow and fast, and he did it now with everything he had, learning the lay of the place from maps he scanned by penlight, not wanting to shine light in Catlin's eyes, learning exactly how many steps down what hall, what the distance was and what the angles and line of sight were at any given point.

You hoped Intelligence was right, that was all.

It was eighty points on the Hostage, that was all they were saying. That meant in a hundred-point scale at least one of them was expendable. They could do it that way if they had to, which meant him, if it had to be: Catlin was the one who had the set-up best in her head and she was the one who would most likely be able to get through the final door, if he could get it open. But you didn't go into anything planning what you could give away. You meant to make the Enemy do the giving.

He did the best he could, that was all.

viii

It was Catlin on the phone. *Catlin* made a phone call; and Ari flew out of Dr. Edwards' classroom and down the hall to the office as fast as she could run.

"Sera," Catlin said, "we're going to be late. Florian's in hospital."

"What happened?" Ari cried.

"The wall sort of fell," she said. "The hospital said I should call, sera, he's real upset."

"Oh, God," she cried. "Catlin, dammit, how bad?"

"Not too. Don't be mad, sera."

"Catlin, dammit, report! What happened?"

"The Enemy was holding a Hostage, we had to get in past a Minder, and we did that; we got all the way in, but the Hostage started a diversion while they were trying to Trap the door. The Instructor is still trying to find out what happened, but their charge went off. The whole wall went down. It wouldn't really do that, it would blow out, but this was a set-up, not a real building, and it must have touched off more than one charge."

"Don't they *know*?"

"Well, they're dead. Really."

"I'm coming. I'm coming to the hospital right now. Meet me at the front door." She turned around and Dr. Edwards was there. So she told him. Fast. And told him call uncle Denys.

And ran.

"He thinks it's his fault," Catlin said, when she got there, at the front door, panting and sick at her stomach.

"He didn't tell me you had an Exercise today," Ari said. That was what she had thought all the terrible way down the hill. "He didn't tell me!"

"He was fine," Catlin said. "He didn't make a mistake. They shouldn't have been where they were, that's first." She pointed down the hall, where a man in black was talking to the doctors. "That's the Instructor. He's been asking questions. The Hostage—he's a Thirteen, he's the only one alive. It's a mess. It's a real mess. They're asking whether somebody got their charges mixed up, where the explosives kit was sitting, they think it was up against the wall right where they were working, and they hadn't Trapped everything they could have, so that was two charges more than they were using on the door. The whole set-up came down. Florian kind of threw himself backward and covered up, or he could have been killed too. Lucky the whole door just came down on him before the blocks did.''

Ari walked on past the desk with Catlin, down where the doctors were talking with the Instructor, and past, where Florian was, in the hall, on one of the gurneys. He looked awful, white and bruised and bleeding on his shoulder and on his arms and hands, but they had cleaned those up and sprayed them with gel.

''Why is he out here?'' Ari snapped at the med who was standing there.

''Waiting on X-ray, sera. There's a critical inside.''

''I'm all right,'' Florian muttered, eyes half-opening. ''I'm all right, sera.''

''You—'' *Stupid*, she almost said. But a Super couldn't say that to an azi who was tranked. She bit her lip till it hurt. She touched his hand. ''Florian, it's not your fault.''

''Not yours, sera. I wanted to go. With the filly. I could have said.''

''I mean it's *not your fault*, hear me? They say something blew up.'' She went over where the doctors and the Instructor were, right up to them. ''It wasn't Florian's fault, was it?'' Her voice shook. ''Because if it was, it was mine, first.''

''This is sera Emory,'' Dr. Wojkowski said to the frowning Security Instructor who looked at her like she was an upstart CIT brat. ''Florian and Catlin's Supervisor.''

The man changed in a hurry. ''Sera,'' he said, Catlin-like, stiff. ''We're still investigating. We'll need to debrief both of them under trank.''

''No,'' she said.

''Young sera, —''

''I said no. Let them alone.''

''Sera is correct,'' a hard voice said, from a man in ordinary clothes, who had come up on the other side of the group, a man a little out of breath.

It was Seely. She never thought she would be that glad to see Seely in her whole life.

Uncle Denys couldn't run. But Seely had, clear from Administration. And Florian and Catlin were right: Seely was Security, she knew it the minute he launched into the Instructor.

It was a *lot* better. Florian had had a piece of metal driven into his leg, that was the worst, but they had gotten that out, and he had sprains and bruises, and he was going to be sore, because they had pulled a lot of building blocks off the door that had fallen on him.

"Fools," was what Seely said when Ari asked him what he had found out, talking to Catlin and talking to the Instructor and the Hostage, when he came around, what little he could. When she heard it she drafted Seely into the room where Florian was starting to come around. "Tell *him*," she said, while Catlin came into the room behind Seely and stood there with her arms folded.

So Seely did. "Are you hearing me?" Seely asked Florian.

"Yes," Florian said.

"The Instructor is under reprimand. The amount of explosives allotted exceeded the strength of the set-up. The Hostage attempted a distraction according to his orders, while the team inside was Trapping the door. The Hostage doesn't know what happened at that point. He took out one team member. Apparently the two working with the door had set their kit close to them, probably right between them, and possibly the distraction, or the third boy falling against them— dropped the charge they were working with into two others they had in the kit."

"They didn't start Trapping the door they were behind until we got in past the Minder," Catlin said, walking close to the bed. "They thought they could get out and score points, because there was a third team coming in at our backs. They didn't tell us that. They were working with the Enemy and they were supposed to hit us from behind. But they were sticking to the Instructor's timetable and we got past the Minder too fast. . . ."

"Too *fast*?" Florian murmured, with a flutter of his eyes. "That's crazy. What was I supposed to do?"

". . . so the other team tried to improvise and tried to Trap the door when they knew we were ahead of what they expected. And the Hostage followed his orders, kicked the guard, but the guard fell into the two at the door and they dropped the charge right into their kit. Wasn't your fault. We couldn't fire into the room because of the Hostage. He was supposed to be on our side and cause *them* trouble. It was a double-team exercise. So it was the set-up that went wrong.''

"You didn't Trap the door," Seely asked Florian.

"I can't remember," Florian said. Then, blearily: "No. I wouldn't. No reason. Not in the plan."

"You didn't," Catlin said. "I was covering your back, in case the third Enemy was behind. You were going to blow the door and gas the room, remember?"

Florian grimaced as if it hurt. "I can't—remember. It's just gone. I don't even remember it blowing."

"Happens," Seely said, arms folded, just like Catlin. Ari sat there in a straight chair and listened. And wondered at Seely. "You may never get those seconds back. The shock jolted you. But you're all right. It wasn't your fault."

"You don't put your charges—" Florian said thickly, "under where you're working."

"You don't exceed your building limits with the charges in a training exercise, either, or set up a double-team course with a Murphy-factor in it like that in a dead-end room. You exceeded expectations. The other team fell below. End report. You'll be back in training next week. They won't."

"Yes, ser," Florian said quietly. "I'm sorry about them, though."

"He needs tape," Seely said, looking at Ari. "He shouldn't feel that way. That'll give him trouble in future."

That made her mad; and shouldn't. Seely was trying to help. "I'll decide," she said, afraid he was going to say that to uncle Denys too.

Seely nodded, very short, very correct. "I have business," he said, "if that's all, sera. You're doing everything right here."

"Thank you, Seely. Very much. Tell uncle Denys I might be over here for supper."

"Yes, sera."

Seely left.

Catlin walked over to the chair, arms still folded, and sat down.

"Catlin," Ari said. "Did *you* get hit?"

"Not much," Catlin said. "Most of my end of the hall was still standing." She flexed her left arm and wrist. "Sprain from moving the blocks. That's all."

"I went too *fast*," Florian said, like he was still a little tranked. "That's crazy. It was an old-model Minder."

"They made the mistake," Catlin said firmly, definite as the sun in the sky. "We didn't."

Ari bit her lip. *Florian* got to use the House library. Florian got into the manuals for the House systems. Florian knew a lot of things they didn't, down in the Town, because Florian and Catlin never stopped learning.

She went out in the hall, got permission for the phone, and called uncle Denys herself.

"Uncle Denys," she said, "Florian worked the course too fast. That's what they're saying. He got hurt for being better. That's lousy, uncle Denys. He could have gotten killed. Three people *did*. Aren't there any better Instructors down there?"

Uncle Denys didn't answer right off. Then he said: "I've got Seely's report up now. Give me a while. How is he?"

"He's damn sore," she said, forgetting not to say *damn* to uncle Denys. And told him what Dr. Wojkowski had said and what Seely and Catlin had said.

"I agree with you. If that's borne out in the report, we're going to have to do something. Do you want to spend the night down there, or is he going to need that?"

"I want to do it. With Catlin."

"All right," uncle Denys said, without arguing at all. "Make sure you get something to eat. Hear?"

Uncle Denys surprised her sometimes. She went back to the room, feeling a little like she had been hit with something too. Everything had been so good, and then everything went so bad. And then Seely and Denys both got reasonable, when she least expected it.

"They're going to fix things," she said to Catlin, because Florian's eyes were shut. "I just called uncle Denys. I think there's a foul-up somewhere higher up than the Instructor. I think you know too much for down there."

"Sounds right," Catlin said. "But it makes me mad, sera. They keep saying we're a little better than they expect. They wasted those azi. They were all right. They weren't the best in Green, but they didn't need to get killed. They lived right across the hall from us."

"Dammit," she said, and sat down with her hands between her knees. Cold all over and sick at her stomach, because it was not a game, what they did was never a game, Catlin was right from the start.

──────────────── ix ────────────────

Florian was still limping a little, but he was doing all right when he came into the barn with Catlin and Amy and the other kids. Ari watched him, watched a smile light his face when he saw the Mare and the filly—two fillies. One with a light mane and tail, that was Ari's; and one with black—that was Horse's daughter.

"Look at her!" Florian exclaimed. And forgot all about his limp; and came and patted the Mare on the shoulder, and hugged her around the neck. Which impressed hell out of the kids. Except Catlin, of course, who knew Florian wasn't scared of horses.

The Mare deserved it in Ari's estimation. The Mare mothered both babies, the one she had birthed and the one who was her genesister, which of course the Mare could not understand, except the Mare was just generous and took care of both of them.

"She's so big," Amy said.

They were a little scared of the fillies too. It was the first time they had ever been close to animals, and they were still afraid they were going to get knocked down—good guess, because they tended to spread out and get too close and dodge into each other's and the horses' way when the horses shied. Even Catlin, who backed up and tucked her hands behind her, stiff and azi, when 'Stasi nearly bumped into her. Maddy yelped and nearly got it from the Mare's backside, and Ari just dropped her face into her hands and looked up again, with the horses all off across the big barn arena and the kids looking a little foolish.

"You have to go a little slower," Andy said from behind them. "They don't want to step on you. But you smell funny to them."

The kids looked at Andy as if they thought he was joking or they had just been insulted.

"Come on," Ari said to Florian. "Let's see if we can get her."

"Wait, sera, I can," Florian said, and walked after her.

It was strange finally to come out in the open, and pretend they were mostly friends of Amy's, that everyone knew was her friend, and who, she figured, was safer from Disappearing than anybody else because her mama was a friend of uncle Denys and uncle Giraud. She didn't think it would happen anymore, but the kids worried; and that was the set-up she had worked out with Amy—because the kids were still worried.

But, she told them, they could go to places like seeing the new babies together and not have anybody get onto the fact she had friends, the same way she could buy things for people and not have uncle Giraud know they saw each other more than at parties. Andy wasn't in the House circuit, so Andy wouldn't tell everything he saw and neither would the azi in the barn. So they felt safer.

Florian caught the Mare with no trouble. He brought her back and the fillies came right along. That impressed the kids too.

It was strange how the kids looked at Florian and Catlin now, too, since Florian had come back still a little stiff and sore, and she had had Florian and Catlin tell what had happened down there in the Exercise—it was all right to tell them, she had explained to Florian and Catlin, because they were CITs and they were in the House, except Sam, and Sam was all right. So Florian had started telling it, but when he got to the part where he went down the hall, he couldn't remember past that point, and Catlin had to tell it, and about the hospital and everything.

It was the first time either one of them had said more than a sentence or two at a time to the kids, and it was something to get Catlin to tell a story; but once Catlin got warmed up, Catlin knew enough gory stories to get them all going, and all of a sudden the kids seemed to figure out that Florian and Catlin were real. That a whole lot of things were. That they had seen dead people. That they really could do what she said.

—Not, really, she thought, that they had ever doubted her, but that they had had no way to understand what it was like to walk down a hall toward an Enemy, carrying explosives which, thank God, had not gone off . . . or even that there were Enemies who could come right up on Reseune's grounds and try to blow things up or shoot people.

They started wondering why, that was one thing that was different. They wanted to know what went *on* in the Council and why people had wanted to take things from her in Court—and they got to questions where she couldn't give them all the answers.

"That's something I'm still trying to figure out," she had told them. "Except there are people who don't want azi to be born and they'd like to shut Reseune down."

"We do more than azi," Sam had said.

"Florian and Catlin wouldn't like not to be born," Amy had said.

"They might be born," Ari said, "but they'd bring them up like CITs and teach them like CITs. They wouldn't like it."

"Would you?" Amy had asked them, because they had started asking Florian and Catlin questions that didn't go through her.

"No," Florian had said, very quiet, while Catlin shook her head. Ari knew. Florian was too polite to say what he had said to her when she had talked with them about it before: that he didn't like most CITs, because they were kind of slow about things; a lot of CITs, he had said, worked harder trying to make up their minds *what* to do than they did doing what they'd decided, and he hated to be around people like that. And Catlin had said, a depth of thought which had surprised her, that she figured CITs had made azi to run things like Security because they knew they couldn't trust each other with guns.

"Do you *like* being azi?" 'Stasi had gotten far enough to ask, that time down in the tunnels.

Florian had gotten a little embarrassed, and nodded without saying a thing.

"I think he's sexy," Maddy had said outright, in school, not in Florian or Catlin's hearing. "I wish *I* had him." And giggled.

I'm glad you don't, had been Ari's thought.

That popped into her head again while Florian was leading

the horses back: he was so neat and trim in his black uniform, you couldn't see he was a kid if you didn't know the Mare's height. Florian and Catlin—were enough to make you jealous you couldn't walk like that and look like that and be like that.

Because CITs didn't take care of themselves like that, she thought, they ate too much and they spent too much of their time sitting down and, face it, she told herself, nature dealt Amy eyes that had to be corrected and made Tommy just average-looking, and didn't give Maddy any sense.

While Florian and Catlin looked like that and were so good at what they did that they were out of Green and into House Security, because they were just better than their predecessors—because they were taught *after* the War, Denys had said, using modern-day stuff that made them work harder and use what they had, and because she was right, they had learned a lot of classified stuff up in the House that the Instructors down in Green didn't even know about, that was different since sometime in the War, too. All of which came down to the fact that they started doing their tape in House Security, and that after this no Exercise with them involved could use a double-blind situation.

Like adult Security. Because their reactions had gotten so fast and so dangerous there was no way to make it safe if they got surprised, and they could push other teams past all their training.

She was damned glad Maddy *didn't* have their Contracts. Damned glad Maddy didn't have her hands on Florian and didn't have any chance to mess with that partnership, because she understood now beyond any doubt that it was life-and-death business with them. She had made Florian late for one study-session, Florian and Catlin had thrown everything they had into their Exercise, afraid they were going to fail it; and that had made them overrun the course and push another team to the point it got rattled and made a mistake, that was what had happened, so that three azi had gotten killed was, at least remotely, her fault. Not blamable fault, but it was part of the chain of what had happened, and she had to live with that.

She was terribly glad she hadn't done anything with Florian that would have put any more strain on him. Because he could just as well have been dead, and it would have been her fault, really, truly her fault.

Maddy was right. He was so damned pretty. She wanted so much to do with him exactly what Maddy wanted to do.

And Maddy would have no idea in her head why she couldn't.

She wished to hell Ari senior *could* talk back and forth, because she had tried to ask Base One if Ari had anything to say about Florian being in hospital or about whether it was safe to do sex with her azi, if they were Security. But Base One had said there was no such information.

She was so desperate she even thought about getting Seely off in a corner somewhere and asking *him* that question. But Seely was as much Seely as he had ever been—and not even sex could make her *that* desperate.

Yet.

_____ X _____

Her twelfth birthday, she had a big party—a dance in the Rec hall, with every kid in Reseune who was above nine and under twenty—uncle Denys begged off and said he had work, but that was because he hated the music.

He missed something, because Catlin learned to dance. Catlin got the idea of music—it's a mnemonic, Ari said, when Catlin looked puzzled at the dancing: the variations on the pattern are the part that makes it work.

Florian had no trouble at all picking it up—but he was too self-conscious to clown with it in public: that was the funny thing; and it was *Catlin* who shocked everybody, by trying to teach Sam a step he couldn't get—an azi out on the floor with a CIT. Everybody got to watching, not mad, just amazed, and Catlin, in a gauzy black blouse that covered just about what it had to with opaque places, and black satin pants that showed off her slim hips like everything, —smiled, did three or four fast steps and showed what you could *do* if you could isolate muscle groups and keep time with the music.

After that every boy in the room wanted to have one dance with Catlin, and it was funny as hell, because all the girls in the room didn't know whether to be jealous of an azi or not.

So Maddy Strassen flounced over and asked Florian, and the other girls started asking him, and the few older CIT kids who had azi their own age began showing them the steps, until the thing got all over the House by the next morning.

"You know," uncle Denys said about it at breakfast, "there *are* azi that could bother. You really ought to be careful."

"Seely was there," she said, tweaking uncle Denys just a bit. "And a lot of Security. They could have stopped it, anytime."

"Probably the music paralyzed their judgment. They were there to stop Abolitionists with grenades. They needn't have worried. They couldn't get past the noise."

"Well, none of the azi got pushed. Some would dance, some wouldn't, nobody pushed anybody. Florian said Catlin thought it was interesting. She's supposed to protect me, right? And she's not as social as Florian. But she can imitate anything physical and she can *act* like anybody. So she was having a great time out there. She was psyching everybody and getting the feel of how they moved and they never knew what she was doing. Want to know what she said?"

"What?"

"She said they were all soft and they were generally real vulnerable in their balance. That she could take out any one of them with an elbow."

Uncle Denys sneezed into his orange juice.

xi

More shots. They brought her period on. She swore she was going to get Dr. Ivanov. A call at his door at night and blam! a gift from Florian.

He probably had enough of her blood to transfuse most of Novgorod.

"I think I want a different doctor," she said to uncle Denys.

"Why?" uncle Denys asked, over his reports, at the supper table, which was the only place she saw him—at breakfast and at supper.

"Because I'm tired of getting stuck with needles. I'm going to be anemic."

"Dear, it's a study. It got started when you were born and

it's a very valuable study. You just have to put up with it, I don't care what doctor you have; and you'd hurt Petros' feelings. You know he's very fond of you.''

"He smiles very nice, right before he gives me something that makes me want to throw up.''

"You know, you have to watch, dear, your voice does tell what's going on with your cycles. That's something you don't want to make that public, isn't it?''

"I don't know why not! I don't know why they don't put it on the news! Why don't you hand the news-services the tapes from my bedroom? I bet I can give them some real thrills if I work at it, I bet the Security techs just love it!''

"Who said we were taping? That's a Security system.''

"Florian and Catlin are House Security, remember?''

Uncle Denys put down his reports, suddenly very serious.

So was she, not having intended to bring it up. Yet. Till they found out some other things. But he was off his balance: she had her opening; she Got him with it.

Good.

"Dear, all right—yes. There are tapes. They go into Archive, no one accesses them. They're just a historical record.''

"Of me having my period.''

"Ari, dear, don't be coarse.''

"I think it's coarse! I think it's a damn coarse thing to do to me! I want that system shut *down*, uncle Denys! I want it off, I want those tapes destroyed, I want Florian and Catlin to rip out that entire unit, *at the control board*.''

"Dear me, they *are* observant, aren't they?''

"Damn right they are.''

"Ari, dear, *don't* swear. You're not old enough.''

"I want that unit *off*! I want it *out*! I want those tapes *burned*! I want to move up to *my* apartment and I want Florian and Catlin to go over *that* and have access to all the control boards in all the secret little rooms in Security!''

"Ari, dear, calm down. I'll have them turn it off.''

"The hell! You'll just relocate the board somewhere else you think Florian and Catlin can't find it.''

"Well, then, you'd have a problem, wouldn't you? You have to believe me.''

"No, I don't, because I'll know if that unit is running.''

"How?"

"I'm not going to tell you. Ask Seely. I'm sure he can explain it."

"Ari, dear, your temper is running a bit high today, I'm sure you've noticed. And I really, really don't want to discuss things with you when you're *on* like this. I'm very, very fond of you, but no one likes to listen to a cultured twelve-year-old swear like a line soldier, and no one likes to be called a liar—as you once said in a very public place. So do you think you could lower the volume a little and discuss this rationally, or shall we say I'm sure Seely is still a little ahead of Florian? —If I wanted to continue the surveillance against your wishes. I appreciate the fact you're not a little girl anymore. I know there are very good reasons why you don't want to be taped in your bedroom, and the fact that you've objected is enough. We can't get any value out of a study if the subject is acting for the cameras, now, can we? So the taping will stop, not because you have the power to take out the units, but because it loses its value."

"I want the tapes burned!"

"I'm sorry, not even we can get at them. They've gone into the Archive vault, under the mountain out there, and they're irretrievable as long as you're active in the House computer."

"You mean while I'm logged in?"

"No, as long as you're an active CIT-number in the files. As long as you live, dear. Which is going to be a long, long time, and then you won't care, will you, whether somebody has a tape of a twelve-year-old girl in her underwear?"

"You've seen those tapes!"

"No, I know the twelve-year-old, that's quite enough. The taping will shut down. Florian can verify it, if you like, and Florian can remove the unit himself, with, I trust, some reasonable care not to damage the rest of the system."

"Today."

"Today." Uncle Denys looked very worried. "Ari, I *am* sorry."

He was acting with her. Working her. The way he had been Working the whole situation and trying to get her to believe him. The way she Worked him.

He was probably good enough to spot that too. If Seely

was ahead of Florian, uncle Denys was still ahead of her, she thought. Maybe.

But she could Work him right back by using her upset and letting it go on long enough to let him do the Shift on her, and do it a couple of times so he thought he Had her.

Then she could do what he was trying to get her to do and see where it led, without *being* led.

"I'm sorry, Ari."

She glared at him.

"Ari, this is a very bad time for this. I wish you'd come to me earlier."

Dammit, he wanted her to ask. She wanted to Work him to have to tell her whatever he was up to, but that would give it away for sure that she was onto him Working her. Which he might know anyway: you never knew how many layers there were with uncle Denys.

"You know there's a bill up to extend you the first Ari's Special status."

"I know."

"You know it's going to pass. There's not going to be any problem with it. There's no way the Centrists can stop it."

"That's nice, isn't it?"

"It was the one thing the Court didn't hand you with Ari's rights. The one thing they held back. So you'll have that. You'll have everything. You know Reseune is so proud of you."

Flattery, flattery, uncle Denys.

"You *are* going to be on your own in a few years. You'll leave this apartment and move to yours, and I won't be with you: I'll go back to being a fat old bachelor and see you mostly in and out of the offices and at parties."

Saying bad things on himself; humor; trying to get her to think about missing him.

She would. So you didn't let people Hook you, not when they were uncle Denys.

She didn't say a thing. She just let him go on.

"I worry, Ari. I really hope I've done all right with you."

Trying to scare her. Trying to talk like something was going to change. Another maman-event. Damn him anyway.

I hope you do *Disappear, uncle Denys.*

That wasn't quite the truth, but it was a real low move uncle Denys was doing and she wasn't about to show how mad it made her.

"We get along all right," she said.

"I'm very fond of you."

God. He's really pushing it.

"Ari? Are you mad?"

"I sure am."

"I'm sorry, sweet. I really am. Someday I can tell you why we do these things. Not now."

Oh, that's a hook, isn't it?

"You know Amy's mother invited you and Florian and Catlin to come over this evening."

"I didn't know that. No."

"Well, she did. Why don't you?"

"Because I feel lousy. And Amy didn't say anything about it."

"It's a surprise."

The hell.

"I think you've been studying too hard. I think an evening out would do you a world of good."

"I don't want to go anywhere! I feel lousy! I want to go to bed!"

"I really think you should go to Amy's."

"I'm not going to Amy's!"

Uncle Denys didn't look happy at all, and began getting up. "I'll call Dr. Ivanov. I think maybe he *did* give you something that's bothering you. Maybe he can send you something."

"The hell he can! I don't want any more shots, I don't want any more blood tests, I don't want any more cameras in my bedroom, I don't want any more people messing with me!"

"All right, all right. No medicine. Nothing. I'll talk to Petros." He frowned. "I'm really upset about this, Ari."

"I don't care." She got up from the table. She was wobbly from anger. It was out of control. She was. She hated the feeling, *hated* whatever they did to her.

"I mean I'm worried," uncle Denys said. "Ari, —you're using the computer tonight, aren't you?"

"What has that got to do with anything?"

"Just—when you do—remember I love you."

That hit her. Uncle Denys saying *I love you*? It was a Trap, for sure.

It hurt, because it was about the lowest try yet.

"Sure," she said shortly. "I'm going to my room, uncle Denys."

"Hormones," he said, as shortly. "It's hormones. Adolescence is a bitch. I'll be glad when you're through this. I really will."

She walked out, and shut the door between her hallway and the living room.

Florian and Catlin stepped out their door the instant she did.

Saying *What's the matter?* with their faces.

"I'm fine," she said. "Uncle Denys and I had a discussion about the taping. You're going to take the unit out first thing tomorrow."

"Good," Florian said in a vague, stunned way.

"I'm going to my room," she said. "I'm all right. Don't worry about me. Everything's fine."

She walked past them.

She closed the door of her room.

She looked at the computer on the desk.

Exactly, she figured, what he wanted her to do. She should frustrate hell out of him. Make him worry. Not touch the thing for days.

Not smart. The best thing was find *out* what he was wanting. Then deal with it.

"Base One," she said. "Is there a message?"

"No message," Base One said through the Minder.

That was not what she expected.

"Base One, what *is* in the system?"

The screen lit. She went over to it. There was only one item waiting for her.

The regular weekly update. Second week of April, 2290.

She sat down in front of the screen. Her hands were shaking. She clenched them, terrified, not sure why. But something was in it. Something Denys wanted was in that week, that year.

Second week of April.

Second week of April. Five years ago.

She had been at school. In the sandbox. She had started home.

"Selection one."

It came up. It started scrolling at the usual pace.

Olga Emory.

Deceased, April 13, 2290.

Ari senior had been at school. When her uncle Gregory had come to get her and break the news.

"Dammit!" she screamed, and got up and grabbed the first thing she found and threw it. Pens scattered clear across the bed and the holder hit the wall. She grabbed a jar and threw it at the mirror, and both shattered and fell.

As Catlin and Florian came running in.

She sat down on her bed. And grabbed up Poo-thing and hugged him, stroked his shabby fur, and felt like she was going to throw up.

"Sera?" Florian said.

And he and Catlin came and knelt down by the side of the bed where she was sitting, both of them, even though she had been breaking things and they must think she was crazy. It was terribly scary for them; it was scary for her to have them come that close when she was already cornered. She knew how dangerous they were. And there was nothing she could trust.

"Sera?" Catlin said, and got up by her, just straightened up, solid muscle, and flowed onto the bed and touched her shoulder. "Sera, is there an Enemy?"

She could have taken Catlin with her elbow. She thought about it. She knew Catlin did. Florian put his hand on hers, on the edge of the bed. "Sera, are you hurt? Has something happened?"

She reached up with her other hand and touched Catlin's, on her shoulder. Florian edged up onto the bed on her other side, and she got her breath and got her arm behind Catlin and her hand locked onto Florian's and just sat there a moment. Poo-thing fell. She let him.

"They sent maman away," she said, "because Ari's mother died."

"What, sera?" Florian asked. "What do you mean? When did she die?"

"The same day. When Ari was the same age. Her uncle

came to get her. Just like uncle Denys came for me.'' Tears ran out of her eyes and splashed onto her lap, but she wasn't crying, not feeling it, anyway; the tears just fell. ''I'm a replicate. Not just genetic. I'm like you. I'm *exact.*''

''That's not so bad,'' Catlin said.

''They sent my maman away, they sent her on a long trip through jump, it made her sick and she *died*, Catlin, she *died*, because they wanted her to!''

Catlin tapped her shoulder, hard, leaned up to her ear and whispered: ''Monitors.''

She felt the shock of that reminder in her bones and caught her breath, trying to think.

The scrolling stopped on the screen in front of them.

''Ari, check Base One,'' the Minder said.

She made a second gasp after air. Like she was drowning. She held onto Florian and Catlin.

''Ari, check Base One.''

Uncle Denys had known what would come up.

Uncle Denys hadn't wanted her to go on-line tonight. Go to Amy's, he had said.

Then *told* her to check the computer.

''Ari, check Base One.''

''Base One, dammit!'' She disentangled herself from Florian and Catlin and thought it was Unusual that uncle Denys and Seely hadn't tried to get in to see about her when the mirror broke. And then she thought that it wasn't Unusual at all.

Not with the room monitored.

She sat down at the terminal, in front of the monitor.

Ari, it said. *This is Ari senior. By now you've gotten the update. By now you know some things you may not have figured out before. Are you upset?*

''Of course not.'' She felt Florian beside her. She grabbed his arm and held it, hard. ''Go on, Ari.''

Your access is upgraded. You are no longer on time-lag. Data is available through April 13, 2295.

She grabbed Catlin's shoulder, on the other side of her. ''Go on, Ari.''

That's when I was 12. Updates will still be weekly. Good night, Ari.

She clenched down until her fingers hurt; and then she realized what she was doing and let up. "Log-off," she said. And sat there shaking.

Catlin patted her shoulder and gave her the handsigns they had made up for Tomorrow, Outside.

Florian signed: Tonight. Take-out Monitor.

She shook her head, and signed: Stay.

And took them each by a hand.

Knowing that five more years of data were in the files. But she had an idea what was in it.

Exactly what was in it.

Dammit. Dammit. Dammit.

Security was still taping. "Florian," she said, "Catlin, we *are* going to Security. Right now."

Catlin made the sign for Seely.

"They won't stop us. Get your stuff. Come on. We're going to go kill that thing. *Hear that, uncle Denys?*"

He didn't answer. Of course not.

She went and washed her face while Florian was getting his small tool kit. While Catlin was getting whatever she thought she might need. Which probably included a length of fine wire.

They walked out into the living room. Uncle Denys was reading at the dining table beyond the arch. Like most evenings.

He looked at her.

She said: "We're going down to Security, in case you missed it."

"I'll advise them," uncle Denys said. *"Don't* break anything, Florian."

Seely was not in the room. Seely should have been. Maybe Seely was monitoring from the office.

She stood there and stared at uncle Denys a long, long while.

"Like your maman," uncle Denys said, "I've tried to help you."

"They could kill you."

"Yes. I know that. You know that. You could do that anytime, if you put your mind to it. We have to take chances like that. Because I'm your friend. Not your uncle. Not really. I've been your friend for as long as you've lived."

"Which how long?"

"As long as you've lived. You're Ari. One *is* the other. That's what this is about. Neither one of you betrayed the other one. You *are* the one who did all these things—in a very direct sense. Think about it."

"You're crazy! Everybody in this House is crazy!"

"No. Go see about Security. I'll tell them. Your accesses have upgraded considerably tonight. You *have* real authority in some things. You don't have to live here. You can take your apartment, if you want to. It'll be very large, for a young girl and two azi. But you have the key. If you want to go there, you can. Florian can access the Security system there, and vet it for you. Or you can come back here when you're through. Or you can go over to Amy's. Her mother won't ask any questions."

"Does everybody in Reseune know what I am?"

"Of course. Everybody knew the first Ari. And you began, at least on paper, the day after she died."

"Damn you."

"Same temper, too. But she learned to control it. Learned to *use* it, not let it use her. There's a lot of Cyteen history in those data files, too. A lot of Reseune history. A lot of things your education has just—avoided, until now. Once upon a time there was a man who could see the future. He began trying to change his life. But that *was* his future. Someday you'll access yours—as far as you want to. Think about it."

"I'm not doing anything you tell me from now on."

"Ask yourself why five years. Why not six? Why not four? Ask the computer what happened April 13, 2295."

"You tell me."

"You can look it up. You have the access."

"I want all my stuff up at my apartment."

"That's fine. Tell Housekeeping. They can do that first thing in the morning. You'd better pack at least the basics—for the apartment where you're going. Or buy it. *Necessaries* is open round the clock. If you need anything—like advice on how to fill out the paperwork, whatever, —call me. I certainly don't mind helping you."

Trust Denys to get to the mundane, the depressing workaday details of anything.

"I'll manage."

"I know you will, dear. I'm still here. If I can help you I

want to. Florian, Catlin, don't let her hurt herself. Please. And take some pajamas."

"Dammit, uncle Denys, —"

"Dear, *somebody* has to take care of things. It's usually me. Do you want to go to your apartment, —or do you want to come back and live here for a little while, till you've figured out what it takes to *run* an apartment on your own?"

"No. No, I don't. I'll manage."

"I'll send Housekeeping *for* you. They can't go in up there. But I'll have a package waiting at your door, and send your things on tomorrow. Practical things, Ari. I'll fill out your supply forms for you, and your budget report, you have to have that, or you foul up accounting. I'll give you copies so you know how to set it up in your Base."

"Thank you."

"Thank you, Ari. Thank you for being reasonable about this. This is different from Ari senior, understand. She was fourteen when she moved out of this apartment. But you're overrunning your course too, by a little. Please. Take care of yourself. Can you give me a kiss?"

She stood there, frozen. *Out of this apartment.* She swallowed a lump of nausea. And shook her head. "Not right now. Not right now, uncle Denys."

He nodded. "Sometime, then."

She clenched her jaw and motioned to Florian and Catlin that they were leaving.

2418: 4/14: 0048

AE2: Minder, this is Ari Emory. Florian and Catlin are with me. Print out all entries since I was here last.

B/1: There are two messages.

Welcome to your own home. If you get scared and you want to call me or Security, please don't hesitate. But you're as safe there as here. Trust Florian and Catlin. Take their advice when it comes to your safety.

Drop by the office tomorrow if you feel like it. There's so much you need to know. I let you go because you're not a child, and I wouldn't bring your Security and mine into conflict: my bet would still be on Seely, but I truly don't want to put that to the test.

Attached to your Housekeeping list will be Security's standard recommendations and Seely's for basic Security set-up. Give it to Catlin and Florian. They'll understand. They probably don't need it, but a checklist never hurts even with experienced personnel.

Don't let Housekeeping in unless Florian or Catlin is watching, Seely always did that for us, in case you never noticed.

Refrigerate the eggs and use the ham immediately: it'll have thawed. I wasn't going to send perishables, but you haven't got any breakfast otherwise. I put in a box of cocoa.

You're responsible for everything now. But if it gets too much for you, please, call or come by the office.

You'll have to have an office now, in Wing One. You won't need it, but now that this apartment is active, you'll use at least one secretary and one clerk, which you can request from the Wing One administrator, Yanni Schwartz. Do that, or you'll be diverting valuable time from your studies filling out silly forms, which, I'm sorry, are necessary. I've assigned you an office in I-244, and you'll need to set that up with Wing One Security. Again, let Florian read Security's recommendations on that.

I'm upping your personal allowance to 10,000 cr. per month. That may sound like a fortune, but you have to pay 1200 per month for the office and 5000 for the clerk and secretary. The rest will go fast, believe me, so you're going to have to keep track of that. Of course I'll help you if you need something special: but you should learn good habits.

Your secretary can manage the credit account, but should not have certain accesses. Again, let Florian and Catlin talk to Seely.

The first Ari's system of protections is still in Base One: for God's sake don't dismantle it until you've devised a better one. Florian will advise you there is a security problem with that: it's been in place when other people, mainly myself, could access some of the keyword functions from the top. But it's better than nothing at the bottom, where your secretaries will work.

Read the building safety recommendations relative to fire exits and storm drill. Your area has special protections, but there are special things to learn.

Never mind: just read everything I send you and pass it to Florian and Catlin if it involves security or safety of any kind.

I still love you. It's much more complicated than that, but I am glad you were here and would be more than glad to have you back. There were a lot of times I came to odds with Ari senior. But we were friends. As I am and will always be yours.

Everything in the apartment is exactly the way your predecessor left it the day she died. You will want to dispose of a great deal of the clothing. Styles change. Pack what you don't want and notify Housekeeping to remove it.

Your key will also work at my apartment until you're fourteen. That's only two more years. It seems impossible.

Meanwhile be good. Please keep your-doctor appointments: it is necessary for your health, and you'll recall your maman saw you kept them, so it's not just me. You still have obligations, as everyone does who lives in Reseune, and your independent status doesn't excuse you, it only adds more of them, including obeying adult rules; and if medical says a Supervisor comes in for a check, they come in or they can lose their license. I'll add the obligation to keep your school schedule. I've indicated to Base One that you are extremely mature and responsible. Please don't make me a liar.

So many people have loved you. Jane loved you most of all. She never wrote to you because she felt that was best for you—she knew there was a time she had to cut the cord and let you go, for your own sake. So do I know that. So I wish you well, but I will still, because you are only twelve and because that apartment is very large and Reseune is much larger, be extremely concerned that you are well and taking care of yourself adequately. I know that you are much older than your chronological age, and that you have Base One to draw on, which is no small thing; you have handled Housekeeping and lab requisitions and finance; you have dealt with reports and lab scheduling; you have lived with the security systems and the regulations of the House all your years; and you have two equally adept companions. I would trust the three of you to handle yourselves in a Security crisis; I am not, on the other hand, sure that you will not leave the oven on in the kitchen or have the watering system overflowing the garden. Ari, however much you disdain trivia and accuse me of obsession with it, I remind you again that clean laundry only happens when you remember to send it to Housekeeping.

If this were Novgorod I could never countenance this move; but Housekeeping, like Security, is capable of coping with crises: and I am sure your mistakes will reach my desk. Reseune itself is my House, and you have elected to move to another of its Rooms.

Let me explain something further to you. I have encouraged you to this departure: I did so when I brought you here and told you that this would be yours.

You and I know the limits of your frustration, but Florian and Catlin do not, and neither, for that matter, does Seely. I believe you are emotionally mature enough to understand that the threats to your safety are real, and that indeed you are capable of giving an order which your companions will obey, which they must, I stress, obey—and they will kill, at your order, whether or not that order comes from a mature judgment.

I showed you this apartment because I felt that one day you would need this place to go to, a safety valve in a situation increasingly volatile and unpredictable. You are operating with a world-knowledge and maturity greater than many functioning adults, within a system of surveillance, interventions and monitoring which would stress an azi, with the internal emotional experience and stability of a pubescent child. I feared the explosion that has happened. I was glad to see it turn the direction it did. It is not unprecedented. I set you up for it. As you will see.

In 2295, when the first Ari was your age, I wasn't born yet. Giraud was four. Neither of us remembers that year, but Giraud does recall, when he was five, that the first Ari and her guardian Geoffrey Carnath had a spectacularly public argument at a New Year's party. Giraud doesn't himself remember what was said; Jane Strassen said it regarded Ari's showing up in makeup, but that was hardly an excuse for a screaming argument. Archives does say that Security had to mediate a severe problem between Ari and Geoffrey New Year's Day, when he ordered Florian and Catlin into detention for three days and Ari required unexplained medical treatment that may have included sedation.

There was, you will find, no taping on Geoffrey or the first Ari. We don't precisely know what happened. The public record of the problem involved Ari's demand to have a key to her own room. Years later, to me, she said Geoffrey had taken indecent liberties with Florian. Look that up, if you don't un-

derstand what I mean. Certainly Ari made certain things up. But while her early relationship with Geoffrey was friendly, it came to increasing stress and repeated altercations that finally resulted in a family council and Ari's being granted her own residency, independent of her legal guardian.

It's come true, hasn't it? Certainly not because of any such thing between myself and your staff, but because you're growing and you need more room. Perhaps that's the way it ought to be. Like your maman, I've done what I knew to do, the best I knew. And that includes letting you go. We have offended against your dignity as far as you are justly willing to tolerate it; and hope that if Geoffrey could be forgiven, so can we, in time.

Ari, incidentally, moved to a much more modest apartment: the present splendor, like much of Reseune, was her own creation. But you don't inherit her beginnings. You inherit what she held at the height of her power and intellect. In all things. You will think about that statement later.

Be good. Be reasonable.

End message. Store to file or dump?

AE2: Store to file. Put that on the couch, Florian, is it clean?

Fl2: Yes, sera.

AE2: There's print coming you both need to read.

Fl2: Yes, sera. Are you upset, sera?

AE2: Nothing. Go on. Stop worrying about me. You've got work to do. Base One, continue.

B/1: Second message.

Ari, this is Ari senior.

Welcome.

You're 2 years early.

This program is adjusting itself.

There's a Householding tape in the cabinet in the den. You need that.

You are 12 years old. This program does not provide for that contingency. It will treat you as if you were 14.

A list of accesses and authorizations will print.

Recommended tapes will print.

Base One access has been removed from your guardian's apartment. Security monitoring has been redirected to Base One.

Lethal security measures have been disabled for your protection. When you are 16 you will have the option to reactivate them.

You may run a security check on any individual from Base One. Ask for Security 10. The activity will not leave a mark on any file of lower security clearance than your own.

I hope you are happy here. Your taste and mine may not coincide, but most everything in this apartment is both real and handmade, from the tables to the vases to the paintings on the walls. The paintings in particular are originals and they don't truly belong to me or to you. They belong to the people of Union, someday, when there are museums where they can be protected: they come from Earth, and from the first starships, and from the beginnings of Cyteen as a human world. Guard them in particular, whatever you feel or whatever you understand about me right now: if you would harm any of these things you are a barbarian, and my geneset has gone wrong in you; there are conditions of responsibility involved with your permissions and accesses, and they will either expand or terminate. This program can protect Reseune and itself against misuse.

You don't know me yet, as you don't know yet the good and the bad that you are capable of reaching.

I came to live on my own to escape an intolerable situation with my guardian, and because I was at that time a Special, I was given certain rights of majority. I maintained a speaking relationship with my guardian. We were never close, but once the situation was relieved, I saw that he was only a man, with human faults, some of which were considerable, and some virtues, once I was not living within his reach. The faults did not manifest until late. They were sexual in nature, and I need not go into them: your database now reaches to the year 2297. That will tell you as much as you need to know, perhaps more than you want to know, and I certainly hope your own experiences have been happier.

Whatever has happened, whether your parting from your guardian was amicable or otherwise, you are still a minor even at 14, and it would be foolish of you to do other than cooperate with Administration until you have the experience to outmaneuver it. I could not win against my situation except by protesting to Security and establishing an independent *residency. If House Security has become corrupt you have a serious problem. Do you feel this is the case?*

AE2: I don't know.

B/1: A list of precautions will print. This program will search all House activity and advise you of any actions which may involve yourself or your rights. The list will print. This option is also available under Security 10, which can read into House Security but which cannot be read by them.

Remember that a negative or a positive result in any single question itself means nothing. You have to interpret your own situation. Remember a person with a higher security clearance than yours can install false information in the House system.

Florian and Catlin have survived to be here with you. Good. Are they physically and mentally well?

AE2: Yes.

B/1: Do you believe their loyalty to you is absolute and without exception?

AE2: Yes.

B/1: Is there any condition under which they would disobey you?

AE2: No.

B/1: Beware of absolute answers. Would you like to reconsider?

AE2: No.

B/1: This program accepts them. Security 10 can revise any estimation. Do not permit Florian or Catlin to take tape outside your personal supervision, not for two seconds, outside your direct observation. You can obtain their drugs with your supervisor's clearance. Advise them of this. Under no circumstances must they take any drug you do not provide or permit any intervention without your presence. You must run an intervention to do this. You are not yet qualified in this procedure. A routine will print. Follow instructions meticulously. Read the cautions and observe them. So much as a chance sound could do them great harm.

Their instruction is the most necessary security measure you will take.

Now name the individuals at Reseune or elsewhere you would like investigated by the Security accesses of this program. I urge you begin with your closest friends and your known enemies, and add anyone else whose behavior is not ordinary. You may amend this list by Security 10. The program will provide you the security status of these individuals.

Name as many as you wish.

AE2: Florian and Catlin. Amy Carnath. Sam Whitely. Dr. John Edwards. Denys Nye. Giraud Nye. Madelaine Strassen. Tommy Carnath-Nye. Julia Strassen. Dr. Petros Ivanov. Dr. Irina Wojkowski. Instructor Kyle GK. AG tech Andy GA. Mikhail Corain.

Dr. Wendell Peterson. Victoria Strassen.

Justin Warrick. Grant, Justin Warrick's Companion. I don't know his prefix.

B/1: Immediate security flag on Justin Warrick, Grant ALX, Julia Strassen. Your clearance is not adequate to access those records.

AE2: Ari, wait. Define: security flag.

B/1: Security flag indicates person with limited accesses in area queried.

AE2: Ari, go on.

B/1: Persons with security clearance exceeding yours: Denys Nye; Giraud Nye; Dr. John Edwards; Dr. Petros Ivanov; Dr. Wendell Peterson; Dr. Irina Wojkowski; Mikhail Corain.

You will be messaged at any change in relative clearances.

Now before I finish I will tell you one other thing I did not then understand. My guardian Geoffrey Carnath behaved badly, but he did not intend me personal harm. He knew my value. Whoever has caused your birth surely must know yours. Geoffrey and I were cold but cordial and did not publicize our differences even within the House, certainly not outside, because it could harm Reseune.

Base One can now contact one point outside Reseune: are you now in any danger you yourself cannot handle?

AE2: No. I don't think so.

B/1: Base One can call House Security or the Science Bureau Enforcement Division through Security 10. It will call both if it detects your voice raised in alarm on the keyword Mayday. The consequences of a false alert could be considerable, including political ones endangering your life or status. Never pronounce that word unless you mean it. You may set various emergency responses through the Security 10 keyword function.

If absolutely no other means is available to you to reach the Science Bureau to apply for legal majority, use the Mayday function. Under ordinary circumstances a quiet note to Security or a phone call should be adequate and Reseune should assist you. I reached my legal majority at 16, by a tolerably routine application to the Science Bureau. You may apply at any time you think this has become advisable. I do not advise doing this before 16, except if your life or sanity is threatened. The ordinary age of majority is, as you should know by now, 18.

Cast off all emotional ties to Denys Nye.

Protect Reseune: someday it will be in your hands, and it will give you the power to protect everything else.

You are 14 years old. Time itself will bury any enemy you do not yourself make—as long as you don't make a mistake that lets them bury you.

I am your safest adviser. You are the successor I choose; I aim for your mental and physical safety from interests that may have gained power since my death, or who might want to profit from your abilities. You would not be wise to believe that of everyone in Reseune.

CHAPTER 4

---

i

Uncle Denys was right. It was a huge place. It was very quiet, and at the same time filled with strange noises—motors going on, expansion of metal in the ducts, or small sounds that might have been a step, or a breath, though the Minder would surely sound an alarm if there were a living presence.

If it had not been tampered with. If Base One itself was reliable.

Ari knew which bedroom had been the first Ari's. The closets were full of her clothes. The drawers had more clothes, sweaters, underwear, jewelry, real jewelry, she thought. And the smell of the drawers and the closet was the smell of home—the scent *she* wore. The same smell as permeated her closet at home—at uncle Denys' apartment.

There was a room which had belonged to the first Florian and another which had belonged to the first Catlin. There were uniforms in their closets which were a man's and a woman's. Which bore their numbers. And party clothes in satin and black gauze.

There were things in the bureau drawers—there were guns,

and odd bits of electronics, and wire—as well as personal things.

"They were Older," Catlin said.

"Yes," Ari said, feeling a chill in her bones, "they were."

There were, constantly, the sounds, the small whisperings that the rooms made.

"Come on," she said, and brought them out of the first Catlin's room.

She kept telling herself the Minder would react to an intruder.

But what if one had already been there?

What if the Minder were in someone's control?

She took them back to Ari's bedroom, back at the far end of the house. They brought the guns that they had found, even though Catlin said they ought not to rely on charges that old. They were better than nothing.

"Stay with me," Ari said to them, and sat down on the bed and patted the place beside her.

So they got beneath the covers in their clothes, because the night seemed cold, and she was in the middle of the huge bed, Ari's bed, and Florian and Catlin were on either side of her, tucked up against her for warmth, or to keep her warm.

She shivered, and Florian put his arm around her on the right side and Catlin edged closer on her left, until she was warm.

She could not tell them the things they needed to know, like who the Enemy was. She did not know any longer. It was ghosts she imagined. She had read the old books. She was afraid of things she reckoned Florian and Catlin did not even imagine, and they were foolish to name.

No one had slept in this bed, on these sheets, since the first Ari died. No one had used her things or turned back the covers.

The whole bedroom smelled of perfume and musty age.

She knew it was foolish to be afraid. She knew that the sounds probably had to do with heating and cooling of metal ducts and unfamiliar, wooden floors. And the countless systems this place had.

She had read Poe. And Jerome. And knew there was no ghost to haunt the place. Things like that belonged to old

Earth, which believed the nights were full of spirits with unfinished business, anxious to lay hands on the living.

They had no place in so modern a place, so far from old Earth, which had had so *many* dead: Cyteen was new, and they were only stories and silliness.

Except in the dark around their lighted rooms, in the unexplained noises and the start and stop of things that were surely the Minder doing its business.

She wanted to ask Florian and Catlin if they felt anything like that, in their azi way of looking at things: she wondered in one part of her, cold curiosity, if CITs could feel ghosts because of something in CIT mindsets—shades of value, her psych instructor said. Flux-thinking.

Which Florian and Catlin could do, but it was something they were just now learning to do.

Which meant if she told them about ghosts they could get very disturbed: Catlin was so literal, Catlin believed what she said, and if she started talking about Ari being dead and still *in* this place—

No. Not a good idea.

She tucked the sheets up around her chin and Florian and Catlin both tucked themselves up against her, warm and dependable and free of wild imagination, never mind the fact that Catlin also had a gun with her under the covers, which ought to make her more nervous than thumps in the night.

The whole thing was unreal. Uncle Denys had called her bluff, that was what he had done, and hoped she *would* foul up and come back.

No, Base One had altered itself. It kept saying she was fourteen. It complained she was low in her test scores. Dammit, she was twelve; twelve; twelve; she was not ready to grow up.

And here she was, in a mess because she did not know whether to believe Base One anymore; or where everybody was pushing her life.

By setting her free. It was crazy. They set her free; and she didn't have to listen to Base One, she could ignore it, she didn't have to read the data, she didn't have to know what happened to Ari senior between seven and fourteen, that was seven *years*, dammit, she was supposed to jump over.

She wanted to be a kid. She wanted to take care of the Filly and have her friends and have fun and be just Ari Emory, just nobody-Ari, not—somebody who was dead.

And they—the They who did things in Reseune, like uncle Denys and uncle Giraud and dead Ari—they shoved her into this huge, cold place and told her to live by herself with no maman and no uncle Denys and no Nelly or Seely, nobody to take care of anything if it went wrong.

It had started out feeling good, and then feeling like an adventure, and now, at 0300 and snuggled down in a strange, huge bed with two kid azi, it started feeling like a terrible mistake.

I wonder if I can get Base One to back up and say I'm twelve again.

Or have I gotten myself into a mess and I can't back up and I can't catch up with it, it's just going to keep going, faster and faster, until I can't handle it anymore.

If I say no, Base One will stop all my accesses and take my Super license, and if they take that, they'll take Florian and Catlin—

They can't do that. Everybody across Union knows me, knows Catlin and Florian, I could call Mayday—

Not if I lose those accesses. Base One has to do that.

I daren't lose them. If I lose that I lose everything. I stop being Ari. I stop being—

—Ari.

I've got to do good, I've got to hold on to this, I can't do those things uncle Denys said, I can't foul up. I'm going to look like a fool, I know I'm going to do something wrong the very first day out—

I wish—

I wish I knew whether I like Ari. I wonder what did *happen to her?*

Are they going to do it to me, the way they did everything else?

But in this place Base One is supposed to take care of me. If that's lying, then everything is lying and I'm in bad trouble.

I can't foul up tomorrow. I can't look like I've had no sleep. I've got to do better than I usually do, that'll Get uncle Denys, throw me out, dammit, bug my room, put tapes of me under the mountain. I bet he can get at them, I bet he can, I bet his Base can retrieve it.

That whole list of people with higher clearances than mine—can lie to the system and lie to me and I can't find it out.

Unless I get a higher clearance . . . and the way I get that is when I do something that gets Base One to do it.

Which means doing everything Ari wants.

Nothing Ari wants, me-Ari, myself, for me. If I'm not the same. If there is a me. If there ever was a me that isn't Ari. Or if she's not me.

If I was her, how old would I be? A hundred fifty and twelve, a hundred sixty-two. That's older than Jane, no, she was born—Jane was a teenager, Jane was a hundred forty-two when she died, and she held the first Ari when she was a baby, so if I'm twelve and Jane was my maman when she was a hundred thirty-four and I was born—and if uncle Denys is right and I was begun on paper the day after Ari died—

It could take more work than making the Filly. And that was tons of figuring. And I'm not an azi, I'm not a production geneset, so that's nothing fast. So say it was a year, and then nine, ten months, and everything works out that Ari was a hundred—twenty-something.

You can live longer than that. I wonder if that's when I'm going to die. I wonder what she died of.

Rejuv usually doesn't go till you're a hundred forty if you get it started early, and she was pretty, she was pretty when she was older, she was on it early, for sure—

That's depressing. Don't think of that. It's awful to know when you're going to die.

It's awful to read ahead what's going to happen to you. I don't want to read that stuff in the files. I don't want to know.

And it's real stupid not to.

There was a man who could see the future. He tried to change his. But that was his future.

That was his future.

Like changing it—can't work. Because then you go off what the Base wants and you're frozen, locked up, no accesses.

I have to do well. I have to do everything they want and then when I grow up I can Get them good.

Damn. That's exactly what Ari said I should do.
How do I get away from her?
Can I get away from her—and still be me?

—————————————— **ii** ——————————————

She was very careful to keep on time when the Minder woke
her, shower fast, grab breakfast—Florian and Catlin cooked
it: the eggs got too done, and the cocoa was lumpy, but it was
food, and she swallowed it down and headed out for class
. . . Florian and Catlin to clean up and then wait for the de-
liveries from Housekeeping and check them out and get their
stuff installed in their rooms; and stay put, and debug the
place, as soon as Housekeeping brought some batteries up for
some of the first Florian's stuff. *They* had an excuse to miss
classes today. She didn't, and there was no stopping by the
fishpond this morning: she had to stop by the pharmacy, and
she was going to walk through Dr. Edwards' door right on
the minute.

Dr. Edwards was very relieved to see her: he said that
without saying a word; and was uncommonly easy on her in
the work—she noticed that and looked up sideways and gave
him her wickedest grin. "I suppose uncle Denys told you
what happened last night."

Oh, he didn't want to talk about that. "In a general kind of
way. You know he'd be worried."

"You tell him I was on time and we didn't burn up anything in the kitchen."

"I'll tell him. Don't you want to tell him yourself?"

"No," she said cheerfully, and went back to her frog
eggs.

She really put her mind to it in Designs, worked with no
nonsense, blasted through two lessons and actually enjoyed
it: she got Dr. Dietrich to give her a complete manual on one
of the Deltas in Housekeeping management, so she could see
the whole picture of a Design, because that was the way she
liked to learn, get the idea what the whole thing looked like
so that the parts made sense.

She *wanted* an Alpha set, but Dr. Dietrich said it was better to learn a more typical kind and then work on the exotic cases. That made sense.

Dr. Dietrich said it shouldn't be anybody she knew. That she wasn't ready for that.

Nice that she wasn't ready for *something*. It made her feel like there was at least a floor to stand on. She had learned a very good word in Dr. Dietrich's class.

Flux. Which fairly well said what she was caught in.

She didn't have class with any other kids until just before noon, when she had Economics with Amy and Maddy.

Amy and Maddy *hadn't* known about her moving out. They thought she was putting one on them. So she put her card in the nearest House slot in One A, and it started spitting out all these messages she hadn't known she was going to get, like Housekeeping asking for a verification on an order for a special kind of battery—she knew who had asked that, and punched yes—and a note from Yanni Schwartz telling her that her office in 1-244 was keyed to her card, and he had a secretary and a clerk going to set up in there, whose names were Elly BE 979 and Winnie GW 88690, and their living allowances were now on her card, along with the equipment requisition for another couple of terminals and on-line time on the House system; and a message from Dr. Ivanov that her prescription was waiting at the pharmacy.

That impressed Amy and Maddy, all right.

They looked like they still weren't sure she hadn't set this up to Get them, but she told them that tomorrow they were going to get a chance to see, she would take them up where she lived now, all on her own.

And they went funny then, like something was going different.

That was something she hadn't thought about.

She was thinking about it all the way to the pharmacy, and then she had that package to worry about, up past the Security guards into the lonely terrazzo hallway that was all hers down to the barrier-wall. She used her keycard on the door, and let herself in. The Minder told her that Florian and Catlin were there, and quick as that they showed up from the hall to the kitchen.

"Did Housekeeping get here?" she asked.

"Yes, sera," Florian said. "We've got everything put away. We went all over the apartment."

That meant the batteries Florian had wanted had gotten there. "Housekeeping was in order," Catlin said. "We made them set the boxes in the kitchen, no matter what they were, and we went over everything piece by piece before we put it away. We're warming up lunch."

"Good," she said. "Class was fine. No problems." She walked all the way back through the halls to her office to put down the carry-bag.

Her office, when she had automatically started for her bedroom. But now there was a room for everything. She unloaded the manual there; and took the carry-bag back past Florian and Catlin's rooms to her own bedroom.

Poo-thing was there, right on her bed where he always was. She picked him up and thought it would be really rotten if uncle Denys had bugged him. She picked him up and set him down again against the pillows.

And sat down and kicked off her shoes, and took out the pills from her carry-bag, the prescription pharmacy had fussed about until they nearly made her late for school, no matter what her keycard said and no matter what the House system told them she was authorized to have.

"75's," Florian said, looking at the pill-bottle, after lunch. Ham-and-cheese sandwiches. With nothing burned. "That's all right. That's right for a deep dose."

"Do you want to see what I have to tell you?" She had run out the print, and she had the paper in her lap. "I've told the Minder, no calls, no noises. I've got everything on the list. But I'd feel better if you looked at it."

She passed the printout over; they read it, one after the other.

"Sounds reasonable," Catlin said. "I haven't any trouble about it."

"I don't see any problem," Florian said. "It won't take half a minute. If there's no tape to do."

It still scared her. It scared her more than anything else.

But she did what it said. They took their pills and she followed what the paper said; and left them to sleep, then.

And went into her office, shut the door, and used the keyboard with Base One, because she wanted no noise in the apartment at all while they were that far down.

She told Base One the routine was run.

And Base One said: *This Base now recognizes their cards.*

She read, mostly, late, because she wanted them to wake up before she could rest. She scanned Ari senior's data, on the words *Geoffrey Carnath.* And she *had* understood uncle Denys in what he had said happened. She scanned it all the way to the end, when Ari moved out. She read the worst things and sat there feeling strange, just strange, like it was bad, but nobody had died, that was the worst, if somebody had died.

Then they might Disappear someone else.

And she was mad. Mad about things another Ari's guardian had done a long, long time ago, which weren't there, but the Security reports were, right up to when Ari had turned herself and Florian and Catlin over to Security, saying her uncle was abusing Florian.

That was the way Security wrote it. But she knew what had happened. Sort of. She couldn't make a picture in her mind, but she knew, all the same.

And Ari talked about getting along with her guardian.

I'd have killed him. Like I'd have killed uncle Denys if he'd gone after me.

Because you don't play games with Security. Not with Seely, not with Denys.

But then where would I be? In a lot of trouble.

In a lot of trouble.

Her stomach went upset. She had known she was in a corner, deep down. Geoffrey Carnath's security had gotten the better of the first Ari's. They must have had a fight. Something must have happened.

Florian and Catlin had gone to detention. Ari had gone to hospital.

Ari, hospital, she typed, for that date.

Sedation, it said. Geoffrey Carnath's order.

Florian, security.

A medic had seen him. He was hurt. So was Catlin. And they had run tapes on him and Catlin. She got the number on them.

She chased the case through files for an hour and chased the move-in order, and the Family council meeting—where senior staff, knowing what had happened, had given Ari senior a place of her own, with her own key and no one to watch over her, because that was what she demanded to have, because she was threatening to go to the news-services and Geoffrey Carnath was too much trouble for even the whole Family to fight him over the guardianship.

True. Everything true, as far as Base One went. Things like that had happened to the first Ari.

They had taken maman. But uncle Denys and uncle Giraud had never done what Geoffrey Carnath had done to the first Ari.

She sat there a long time staring at the screen, and then started looking up some of the words the report had used.

And sat there a long time after, feeling her stomach upset.

She was terribly, terribly relieved when Florian called to her on the Minder and said that he was awake, and all right, just a little sleepy yet.

"I'm here," Catlin said then, a little vaguely; but Catlin made it into the hall before Ari did. Leaning on the wall. "Is there a problem?"

"Nothing," Ari said, "nothing right now. Go sleep, Catlin. Everything's fine. I'm going to fix dinner myself. I'll call you."

Catlin nodded and went back into her room.

There were a lot of things in the apartment, once they started going through it—a lot of Ari senior's clothes that were very nice but too large yet. Ari senior had been—a bit more on top. And taller. That was spooky too, figuring out in the mirror what size she was going to be. Someday.

There was jewelry. Terribly expensive things. Not near as much as maman's, mostly gold, a lot of what could be rubies, just lying in the chest on the bureau—all these years—but who in the House would steal?

There was a wine cabinet taller than she could reach, which wouldn't have spoiled, she knew that, it was probably real good by now; and there was whiskey and other things under the counter that wouldn't have been hurt by all these years of sitting there.

There was a big tape library. A lot were about Earth and about Pell. A lot were on technical things. A lot were Entertainment. And a *lot* of those . . . had a 20 Years and Over sticker. And titles that made her embarrassed, and uneasy.

Sex stuff. A lot of it.

It was like looking through Ari senior's drawers in her bedroom, like it was private, and she would hate if she were grown-up and dead, to have some twelve-year-old kid going through *her* drawers and finding out *she* had stuff like that in her library, but it was interesting too, and scary. The first Ari had said there was nothing wrong with the thoughts she had had, just that she was too young and shouldn't be stupid.

But it was all right when you were Older.

She remembered how the first tape felt. And she closed up the cabinet door and wondered what was in them, and whether they would be like the other one. They were just E-tapes. They weren't deep or anything like it. They couldn't hurt you.

If they were hers like everything else in the apartment, then she could do whatever she wanted with them—when she was settled in, when she was sure everything was safe.

It wasn't like being stupid with *people*, where sex could hurt you.

Kids were supposed to be curious. And there was no way anybody could find out she was using them. Just Catlin and Florian, and they wouldn't mess with her stuff. She could do private things now, real private, and uncle Denys couldn't know.

When she got settled in. You didn't do Entertainment tapes just anytime you wanted, no more than you had all the food you wanted. You got your regular work done.

Even if you thought about how interesting it would be, and what there was to find out, and how the teaching-tape had felt.

Meanwhile the cabinet stayed closed.

"It's all right, come on," she said, and brought Amy and Maddy past the Security guards and up the lift.

She used her keycard on the door and let them in. The Minder told her that Florian and Catlin were not there, they were off in classes doing make-up work, the way she had told them they should.

She saw Amy and Maddy look at each other and look around at the huge front room, real impressed.

Something said to her she ought not let anyone see *all* of where she lived, or know how things were laid out: she knew Catlin would worry about that. But she showed them the middle of it, which was the big room in front and the kitchen and the breakfast room with the glassed-in garden where nothing was growing yet—and back to the main front room and into the other wing, where there was the big sunken den and the bar and then her office, and her bedroom and the bedrooms that had been Florian's and Catlin's (and were again).

They had oh'ed over this and that at the start, when she said that there were rooms down past the kitchen, mostly offices and stuff. And over the garden. But when they got this far, into still another living room with more rooms yet to go, they just stared around them and looked strange.

That bothered her. She was used to figuring people out, and she couldn't quite figure what they were thinking, except maybe they were worried about there being something dangerous about this, or her, or uncle Denys.

"We don't have to meet down in the tunnels anymore," she said. "We can be up here and there's no way they can find out what we're doing, because Florian and Catlin have this place checked over so nobody can bug us. Not even uncle Denys."

"They can still find out who we are," Amy said. "I mean, they know me and Maddy, maybe Sam, but they don't know all of us."

That was it. She had wondered over and over how much to tell them—particularly Maddy. She worried about it. But there were things they had to know, before they got the wrong ideas. "It's all right," she said, then took a deep breath and made up her mind on a big secret. "Let me tell you: I've got it set up so if any of you or your families gets a Security action, I know it the second it goes in."

"How can you?" Maddy asked.

"My computer. The Base I've got. My clearance is higher than yours—maybe not higher than somebody who could put a flag on and keep me from finding out stuff, but I've got my

Base fixed so if there's information I'm not accessing it tells me it's going on.''

"How?" Maddy asked.

"Because I'm in the House system. Because I've got a real high Base and a lot of clearances a kid isn't supposed to have. They come with this place. Lots of things. You don't have to worry. I've got an eye on you. If anything goes into the system about you, it calls me right then.''

"Anything?"

"Not private stuff. Security stuff. And I'll tell you something else.'' Another deep breath. She shoved her hands into her belt and thought very carefully what she was saying and how much she was giving away; but Amy and Maddy were the highest-up in the gang. "You tell this and I'll skin you. But you two don't have to worry anymore. None of my friends do. I know why the Disappearances happened, and I don't think it's going to happen anymore. Except if I asked it to. If there was somebody I really, really wanted not to see again. Which isn't any of you, as long as you're my friends.''

"*Why* did they?" Amy asked.

"Because—'' *Because things had to happen to me. Like Ari senior. That's too much, a whole lot too much about my business.* She shrugged. "Because I wasn't supposed to know things, because my uncles figured they'd tell.''

They were quiet a long time. Then Amy said, very carefully: "Even your maman?"

A second shrug. "Maman. Valery. Julia Strassen.'' She wanted off the subject. "I know why they did it. That's all.'' *My maman agreed to go, but I'm not telling anybody that. They'd think she didn't like me. And that wouldn't be so.* "I know a lot of things. Now they have to watch out, because I know they can't do anything to me, because anything they do from now on, they know I'll hold a grudge. And I will, if they Get any of my friends . . . because I know who they are, and they know how far they can go with me.''

"Then who are they?" Amy asked.

"My uncles. Dr. Ivanov. Lots of people. Because of me being a PR of Ariane Emory. That's what. This was her place. Now it's mine, because I'm a PR. Everything she had is mine. The way there used to be a Florian and a Catlin, too, and they died; and they replicated them for me.''

That took some thinking on their part. They knew about the replicate bit. They knew about a lot of things—like Florian and Catlin. But they never knew how it fit.

''I'll tell you,'' she said while she Had them, ''why they won't do anything that makes me mad. Reseune needs me, because if I'm a PR I have title to a whole lot of things they want real bad; and because if I'm a minor it's going to be a while before the first Ari's enemies can do anything against me, because of the courts, because if my uncles do any more to me than they've already done they're in a lot of trouble, because they know I'm onto them. I don't forget about maman. I don't forget a lot of things. So they're not going to bother my friends. You can figure on that.''

They looked at her without saying anything. They were not stupid. Maddy might be silly and she had no sense, but she was not at all stupid when it came to putting things together, and Amy was the smartest of all her friends, no question about it. Amy always had been.

''You're serious,'' Amy said.

''Damn right I'm serious.''

Amy grunted and sat down on the big couch with her hands between her knees. And Maddy sat down. ''This isn't any game,'' Amy said, looking up at her. ''It's not pretend anymore, is it?''

''Nothing is pretend anymore.''

''I don't know,'' Amy said. ''I don't know. God, Ari, you could park trucks in this place. —Isn't there *any*body here at night, or anything? Aren't you scared?''

''Why? There's nothing I can't order from Housekeeping, same as being at uncle Denys's. There's Security watching us all the time. We cook our food, we clean up, we do all that stuff. We can take care of ourselves. The Minder would wake us up if there was any trouble.''

''I'll bet somebody comes in at night,'' Maddy said.

''Nobody. The Minder isn't easy to get by; not even Housekeeping gets in here without one of us watching them every minute. That's how the security is here. Because my Enemies are real too. It's not pretend. If somebody sneaks in here, they're dead, for-real dead.'' She sat down, at the other side of the corner. "So this is mine. All of it. And they can't bug it. Florian and Catlin have been over it from end to end. We can have our meetings up here often as we like and we don't have to worry about Security. We can do a lot of stuff up here, with no Olders to get onto us."

"Our mothers will know," Amy said. "Security's going to tell them."

"It's safe," Ari said.

"They still might not like it," Amy said.

"Well, they wouldn't like the tunnels either, would they? That didn't scare you any."

"This is different. They'll *know* we're here. They *know* people can get in trouble, Ari, my mama is worried about me getting in too much with you, she's real worried, and she didn't want me to take on the guppy business, remember?"

"She said it was all right, then."

"She still worries. I think somebody talked to her."

"So she'll let you. She won't mind."

"Ari, this is—real different. She's going to think you can get in trouble up here without any Olders. And then we could be. They could say it was us. And we'd all be at Fargone. Bang. That fast."

So she got an idea of the shape of what was wrong with Amy and Maddy, then, even if she couldn't see all of it.

"We're not going to get in any trouble," she said. "We'd get in a lot more if they caught us in the tunnels. I'm telling you I can *tell* if something's going on in Security. And Florian and Catlin *are* Security. They find out a lot of things, like stuff that doesn't go in the system."

"Not really Security," Maddy said. "They're kids."

"Ever since those kids got killed, they're Security, that's where they take their lessons. That's what their keycards say. And they work office operations a lot of the hours they're there. Real operations. They can come in and out of there and they find out a lot of things."

Like about taping in my apartment. But she wasn't about to tell them that either.

"Our mothers don't know about the tunnels," Amy said, "but they're going to know about us coming here."

"Not if you don't tell them right off. Security's not going to run to them the first day, are they? Then you can say you've *been* doing it, it's all right. How else do you get away with stuff? Don't be stupid, Amy."

They still looked worried.

"Are you my friends?" she asked them, face on. "Or aren't you?"

"We're your friends," Amy said. The room was quiet. Real quiet.

And she felt a little cold inside, like something *was* different, and she *was* older, somehow, and was getting more and more that way, faster than Amy, faster than anybody she knew. Overrunning the course, she thought, remembering Florian going down that hallway too soon, too fast for the other team.

Who had had about a quarter of a second, maybe, to realize it had stopped being an Exercise and they were about to die for real.

I've got to be nice, she thought. *I don't want anybody to panic. I don't want to scare them off.*

So she talked with them like always, she bounced up to get them all soft drinks and show them the bar and the icemaker.

And all the stuff in the cabinet that opened up. The wine and everything.

"God," Maddy said, "I bet we could have a party with this."

"I bet we can't," Ari said flatly. Because that cabinet of wine was expensive stuff, and Maddy wasn't going to pay for it out of *her* allowance, that was sure; besides, she thought, a drunk Maddy Strassen squealing and clowning around Base One was a real scary thing to think about. Not mentioning the other kids, like the boys Maddy hung around.

Maddy thought that was a shame.

Amy said their mamas would smell it on them and they'd be in real trouble and so might Ari, for giving it to them.

Which was the difference between Maddy and Amy.

That night there was a message from uncle Denys on Base One. It said: "Of course I was checking up on you, Ari. You've done very well. I hoped you would."

"Message to Denys Nye," she answered it. "Of course I knew you were watching. I'm no fool. Thanks for sending my stuff over. Thanks for helping out. I won't be mad, maybe by next week. Maybe two weeks. Recording me was a lousy trick.''

That would Work him fine. Let him worry.

---

iii

The Tester's name was Will, a Gamma type, a warehousing supervisor what time he was not involved in test-taking, plain as midday and matter-of-fact about internal processes Gamma azi were not usually aware of.

Phlegmatic of disposition, if he were a CIT: older, experienced. And stubborn.

"I want to see you in my office," the message from Yanni had said, and Justin had gathered his nerve and gone in with his notes and his Scriber to sit listening while Will GW 79 told him and Yanni what he had told the Testing Super.

It was good news. *Good* news, no matter how he turned it over and looked at all sides of it.

"He said," Justin reported to Grant when he got back to the office, Grant listening as anxiously as he had: "Will said he got along with it fine. Why Yanni called me in—it seems Will's told his super he wants to take it all the way. He *likes* it. His medical report is absolutely clean. No hyper reactions, no flutters. His blood pressure is still reading like he was on R&R. He wants to Carry the program. Committee's going to consider it."

Grant got up from where he was sitting and put his arms around him for a moment. Then, at arm's length: "Told you so."

"Not saying the Committee's going to approve." He tried desperately hard to keep his mental balance and not go too far in believing it was working. Discipline: equilibrium. Things didn't work so well when the ashes settled out. There were always disasters, things not planned for; and Administration's whims. He found the damnedest tendency in his hands to shake and his gut to go null-G, every time he thought about believing it was going to work. He wanted it too badly. And that was dangerous. "Damn, now *I'm* scared of it."

"I told you. I told you *I* wasn't scared of it. You ought to believe me, CIT. What did Yanni say?"

"He said he'd be happier if the Tester was a little less positive. He said addictions feel fine too . . . up to a point."

"Oh, *damn* him!" Grant threw up his hands and stalked the three clear paces across the cluttered office. "What's the matter with him?"

"Yanni's just being Yanni. And he's serious. It *is* a point he has to—"

Grant turned around and leaned on his chair back. "*I'm* serious. You know that frustrates hell out of me. They aren't going to know anything a Tester can't tell them; they've had their run in Sociology, let them believe what the man's saying."

"Well, it frustrates me, too. But it doesn't mean Yanni's going to go down against it. And it's had a clear run. It's had that."

Grant looked at him with agitation plain on his face. But Grant took a deep breath and swallowed it, and cleared the expression away in a transition of emotions possible only in an actor or an azi. "It's had that, yes. They'll clear it. They have to use sense sooner or later."

"They don't have to do anything," he admitted, feeling the pall of Grant's sudden communications shutdown. "They've proved that. I just have some hope—"

"Faith in my creators," Grant repeated quietly. "Damn, it deserves celebrating." The last with cheerfulness, a bright grin. "I can't say I'm surprised. I knew before you ran it. I told you. Didn't I?"

"You told me."

"So be happy. You've earned it."

One tried. There was a mountain of work to do and the office was not the place to discuss subtleties. But walking the quadrangle toward dark, an edge-of-safety shortcut with weather-warnings out and a cloud-bank beyond the cliffs and Wing Two: "You started to say something this afternoon," Justin said. He had picked the route. And the solitude. "About Yanni."

"Nothing about Yanni."

"Hell if there wasn't. Has he been onto you for something?"

"Yanni's conservatism. That's all. He knows better than

that. Dammit, he knows it's going through. He just has to find something negative.''

"Don't blank on me. You were going to say something. Secrets make me me nervous, Grant, you know that.''

"I don't know what about. There's no secret.''

"Come on. You went 180 on me. What didn't you say?''

A few paces in silence. Then: "I'm trying to remember. Honestly.''

Lie.

"You said you were frustrated about something.''

"That?'' A small, short laugh. "Frustrated they have to be so damn short-sighted.''

"You're doing it again,'' Justin said quietly. "All right. I'll worry in private. No matter. Don't mind. I don't pry.''

"The hell.''

"The hell. Yes. What's going on with you? You mind telling me?''

More paces in silence. "Is that an order?''

"What the hell is this 'order'? I asked you a question. Is there something the matter with a question?'' Justin stopped on the walk where it crossed the sidewalk from Wing Two, in the evening chill with the flash of lightning in the distance. "Something about Yanni? *Was* it Yanni? Or did *I* say something?''

"Hey, I'm glad it worked, I *am* glad. There's nothing at all wrong with me. Or you. Or Will.''

"Addictions. Was that the keyword?''

"Let's talk about it later.''

"Talk where, then? At home? Is it that safe?''

Grant gave a long sigh, and faced the muttering of thunder and the flickering of lightnings on Wing Two's horizon. It was a dangerous time. Fools lingered out of doors, in the path of the wind that would sweep down—very soon.

"It's frustration,'' he said. "That they won't take Will's word on it. That they know so damn much because they're CITs.''

"They have to be careful. For Will's sake, if nothing else. For the sake of the other programs he tests, —''

"CITs are a necessary evil,'' Grant said placidly, evenly, against the distant thunder. "What would we azi possibly do without them? Teach ourselves, of course.''

Grant made jokes. This was not one of them. Justin sensed that. "You think they're not going to listen to him."

"I don't know what they're going to do. You want to know what's the greatest irritation in being azi, Supervisor mine? Knowing what's right and sane and knowing they won't listen to you."

"That's not exactly an exclusive problem."

"Different." Grant tapped his chest with a finger. "There's listening and listening. They'll always *listen* to me, when they won't, you. But they won't *listen* to me the way they do you. No more than they do Will."

"They're interested in his safety. *Listening* has nothing to do with it."

"It has everything to do with it. They won't take his word—"

"—because he's in the middle of the problem."

"Because an azi is always in the middle of the problem, and damn well outside the decision loop. *Yanni's* in the middle of the problem, he's biased as hell with CIT opinions and CIT designs, does that disqualify him? No. It makes him an *expert*."

"I listen."

"Hell, you wouldn't let me touch that routine."

"For your own damn—good, —Grant." Somehow that came out badly, about halfway. "Well, sorry, but I care. That's not a CIT pulling rank. That's a friend who needs you stable. How's that?"

"Damn underhanded."

"Hey." He took Grant by the shoulder. "Hit me on something else, all right? Let's don't take the work I'd test my own sanity on and tell me you're put out because I won't trust my judgment on it either. I'd give you anything. I'd let you—"

"There's the trouble."

"What?"

"Let me."

"*Friend*, Grant. Damn, you're flux-thinking like hell, aren't you?"

"Ought to qualify me for a directorship, don't you think? Soon as we prove we're crazy as CITs we get our papers and then we're qualified not to listen to azi Testers either."

"What happened? What happened, Grant? You want to level with me?"

Grant looked off into the dark awhile. "Frustration, that's all. I—got turned down—for permission to go to Planys."

"Oh, damn."

"I'm not his son. Not—" Grant drew several slow breaths. "Not qualified in the same way. Damn, I wasn't going to drop this on you. Not tonight."

"God." Justin grabbed him and held on to him a moment. Felt him fighting for breath and control.

"I'm tempted to say I want tape," Grant said. "But damned if I will. *Damned* if I will. It's politics they're playing. It's—just what they can do, that's all. We just last it through, the way you did. Your project worked, dammit. Let's celebrate. Get me drunk, friend. Good and drunk. I'll be fine. That's the benefit of flux, isn't it? Everything's relative. You've worked so damn long for this, we've both worked for it. No surprise to me. I knew it would run. But I'm glad you proved it to them."

"I'll go to Denys again. He *said*—"

Grant shoved back from him, gently. "He said maybe. Eventually. When things died down. Eventually isn't *now*, evidently."

"*Damn* that kid."

Grant's hands bit into his arms. "Don't say that. Don't— even think it."

"She just has lousy timing. *Lousy* timing. *That's* why they're so damn nervous. . . ."

"Hey. Not her timing. None of it's—her timing. Is it?"

Thunder cracked. Flashes lit the west, above the cliffs. Of a sudden the perimeter alarm went, a wailing into the night. Wind was coming, enough to break the envelope.

They grabbed each other by the sleeve and the arm and ran for shelter and safety, where the yellow warning lights flashed a steady beacon above the entrance.

----

iv

"Dessert?" uncle Denys asked. At *Changes*, at lunch, which

was where she had agreed to meet him; and Ari shook her head.

"You can, though. I don't mind."

"I can skip it. Just the coffee." Denys coughed, and stirred a little sugar in. "I'm trying to cut down. I'm putting on weight. You used to set a good example."

Fifth and sixth try at sympathy. Ari stared at him quite steadily.

Denys took a paper from his pocket and laid it down on the table. "This is yours. It did pass. Probably better without you—this year."

"I'm a Special?"

"Of course. Did I say not? That's one reason I wanted to talk with you. This is just a fax. There was—a certain amount of debate on it. You should know about that. Catherine Lao may be your friend, but she can't stifle the press, not—on the creation of a Special. The ultimate argument was your potential. The chance that you might *need* the protection—before your majority. We used up a good many political favors getting this through. Not that we had any other choice—or wanted any."

Seventh.

She reached out and took the fax and unfolded it. Ariane Emory, it said, and a lot of fine and elaborate print with the whole Council's signatures.

"Thank you," she said. "Maybe I'd like to see it on the news."

"Not—possible."

"You were lying when you said you hated the vid. Weren't you? You just wanted to keep me away from the news-services. You still do."

"You've requested a link. I know. You *won't* get it. You know why you won't get it." Uncle Denys clasped his cup between two large hands. "For your own health. For your well-being. There are things you don't want to know yet. Be a child awhile. Even under the circumstances."

She took the paper and carefully, deliberately slowly, folded it and put it in her carry-bag, thinking, in maman's tones: *Like hell, uncle Denys.*

"I wanted to give you that," uncle Denys said. "I won't keep you. Thank you for having lunch with me."

"That's eight."

"Eight what?"

"Times you've tried to get me to feel sorry for you. I told you. It was a lousy thing to do, uncle Denys."

Shift and Shift again. Working only worked if you used it when it was time. No matter if you were ready.

"The taping. I know. I'm sorry. What can I say? That I wouldn't have done it? That would be a lie. I *am* glad you're doing all right. I'm terribly proud of you."

She gave him a nasty smile, fast and right into a sulk. "Sure."

" 'To thine own self be true'?" With a smile of his own. "You know who planned this."

She ran that through again. It was one of his better zaps, *right* out of the blind-side, and it knocked the thoughts right out of her.

Damn. There weren't very many people who could Get her like that.

"I wonder if you can imagine how it feels," uncle Denys said, "to have known your predecessor—my first memories of her are as a beautiful young woman, outstandingly beautiful; and having the same young woman arriving at the end of my life—while I'm old—is an incredible perspective."

Trying to Work her for sure. "I'm glad you like it."

"I'm glad you accepted my invitation." He sipped at his coffee.

"You want to do something to make me happy?"

"What?"

"Tell Ivanov I don't *need* any appointment."

"No. I won't say that. I can tell you where the answer is. It's in the fifteenth-year material."

"That's real funny, uncle Denys."

"I don't mean it to be. It's only the truth. Don't go too fast, Ari. But I am changing something. I'm terminating your classes."

"What do you mean, terminating my classes?"

"Hush, Ari. Voices. Voices. This is a public place. I mean it's a waste of your time. You'll still see Dr. Edwards—on a need-to basis. Dr. Dietrich. Any of them will give you special time. You have access to more tapes than you can possibly do. You'll have to select the best. The answer to what you are is in there—much more than in the biographical material. Choose for yourself. At this point—you're a Special. You have privileges. You have responsibilities. That's the way it always works." He drank two swallows of the coffee and set the cup down. "I'll put the library charges to my account. It's still larger. —You can see your school friends anytime you like. Just send to them through the system. They'll get the message."

He left the table. She sat there a moment, figuring, trying to catch her breath.

She *could* go to classes if she wanted to. She could request her instructors' time, that was all.

She could do anything she wanted to.

Shots again. She scowled at the tech who took her blood and gave them to her. She did not even *see* Dr. Ivanov.

"There'll be prescriptions at pharmacy," the tech said. "We understand you'll be using home teaching. Please be careful. Follow the instructions."

The tech was azi. It was no one she could yell at. So she got up, feeling flushed, and went out to the pharmacy in the hospital and got the damned prescriptions.

Kat. At least it was useful.

She got home early: no interview with Dr. Ivanov, no hanging around waiting. She put the sack in the plastics bin and read the ticket and discovered they had billed her account thirty cred for the pills and probably for Florian and Catlin's too.

"Dammit," she said out loud. "Minder, message to Denys Nye: Pharmacy is your bill. *You* pay it. I didn't order it."

It made her furious.

Which was the shot. It *did* that to her. She took half a dozen deep breaths and went to the library to put the prescription bottles in the cabinet under the machine.

Damn. It was nowhere near time for her cycle. And she felt like that. She felt—

On. Like she wished she had homework tonight, or something. Or she could go down and see the Filly, maybe. She had been working too hard and going down there too little, leaving too much of the Filly's upbringing to Florian, but she didn't feel like that, either. The shots bothered her and she hated to be out of control when she was around people. It was going to be bad enough just trying not to be irritable with Catlin and Florian when *they* got home, without going around Andy, who was too nice to have to put up with a CIT brat in a lousy, prickly mood.

She knew what was going on with her, it had to do with her cycles, damn Dr. Ivanov was messing with her again, and it was embarrassing. Going around other people, grown-ups, likely they could *tell* what was going on with her, and that made her embarrassed too.

The whole thing was probably on Denys' orders. She bet it was. And she tried to think of a way to get them to stop it, but as long as Ivanov had the right to suspend her Super's license if she dodged sessions—she was in for it.

Dammit, there wasn't anything in the world those shots and those check-ups had to do with her dealing with azi, not a thing—but she couldn't prove it, unless maybe she could do what the first Ari had done and call Security, and get them to arrange a House council meeting.

God, and sit there in front of every grown-up she knew in the whole House and explain about the shots and her cycles? She had rather die.

Don't go up against Administration, Ari senior had told her, out of the things she had learned.

Except it was Ari senior doing it to her as much as it was Denys.

Damn.

Dammit, dammit, dammit.

She opened the tape cabinet, looking for something to keep her mind busy and burn some of the mad off. One of the E-tapes. Dumas, maybe. She was willing to do that tape twice. She knew it was all right.

But it was the adult ones that she started thinking about, which made her think about the last sex tape she had had, which was a long time back. And it was just exactly what she was in the mood for.

So she pulled one out that didn't sound as embarrassing as the others, *Models*, it was called; and she took it to the library, told the Minder to tell Florian and Catlin when they came in that she was doing tape and might be fifteen more minutes—she checked the time—by the time they got the message.

And locked the tape-lab door, tranked down with the mild dose you did for entertainment, set up and let it run.

In a while more she thought she should cut it off. It was different than anything she had thought.

But the feelings she got were interesting.

Very.

Florian and Catlin were home by the time the tape ran out. She ought not, she thought, stir about yet; but it was only a tiny dose, it was not dangerous, it only made her feel a little tranked, in that strange, warm way. She asked the Minder was it only them—silly precaution—before she unlocked the door and came out.

She found them in the kitchen making supper. Warm-ups again. "Hello, sera," Florian said. "Did it go all right to-day?"

Lunch with Denys, she realized. And remembered she was still mad, if she were not so tranked down. It was strange—the way things went in and out of importance in the day. "He stopped my classes," she said. "Said I didn't have to go to class anymore except just for special help. Said I had too many tapes to do."

So what do I start with? That *stupid thing. Like I had all kinds of time.*

"Is it all right, sera?" Catlin was worried.

"It's all right." She shoved away from the doorframe and came to put napkins down. The oven timer was running down, a flicker of green readout. "I can handle it. I will handle it. Maybe he's even right: I've got a lot to go through. And it's not like I was losing the school." She leaned on a chair back. The timer went. "I'll miss the kids, though."

"Will we meet with them?" Florian asked.

"Oh, sure. Not that we won't." She grabbed her plate and held it out as Florian used the tongs to get the heated dinner from the oven. She took hers and sat down as Florian and Catlin served themselves and joined her.

Dinner. A little talk. Retreat to their rooms to study. It was the way it always had been—except she had her own office and they had their computer terminals and their House accesses through the Minder.

She went to her room to change. And sat down on the bed, wishing she had left the cabinet alone and knowing she was in trouble.

Bad trouble. Because she was good at saying no to herself when she saw a reason for it . . . but it got harder and harder to think of the reasons not to do what she wanted, because when she did refuse she got mad, and when she got mad that feeling was there.

She went and read Base One . . . long, long stretches of the trivial housekeeping records Ari senior had generated, just the way they themselves were doing, until she ran them past faster and faster. Who *cared* whether Ari senior had wanted an order of tomatoes on the 28th September?

She thought about the tape library, about pulling up one of the Recommendeds and getting started with it. And finally thought that was probably the thing to do.

"Sera." It was Florian's voice through the Minder. "Excuse me. I'm doing the list. Do you want anything from Housekeeping?"

Bother and damnation.

"Just send it." A thought came, warm and tingly, and very, very dangerous. Then she said, deliberately, knowing it was stupid: "And come here a minute. My office."

"Yes, sera."

Stupid, she said to herself. *And cruel. It's mean to do, dammit. Make up something else. Send him off on a job. God. . . .*

She thought about Ollie. The way she had thought about him all afternoon. Ollie with maman. Ollie when he had looked young and maman had. Maman had never had to be lonely . . . while Ollie was there. And Ollie never minded.

"Sera?" Florian said, a real voice, from the doorway.

"Log-off," she told Base One, and turned her chair around, and got up. "Come on in, Florian. —What's Catlin doing?"

"Studying. We have a manual to do. Just light tape. It—isn't something you need to Super, —is it? Should I stop her?"

"No. It's all right. Is it something really urgent?"

"No."

"Even if you were late? Even if you didn't get to it?"

"No, sera. They said—when we could. I think it would be all right. What do you want me to do?"

"I want you to come to my room a minute," she said, and took him by the hand and walked him down the hall to her bedroom.

And shut the door once they were inside and locked it.

He looked at that and at her, concerned. "Is there some trouble, sera?"

"I don't know." She put her hands on his shoulders. Carefully. He twitched, hands moved, just a little defensive reaction, even if he knew she was going to do it. Uneasiness at being touched, the way he had reacted with Maddy once. "Is that all right? Do you mind that?"

"No, sera. I don't mind." He was still disturbed. His breathing got faster and deeper as she ran her hands down to his sides, and walked around behind him, and around again. Maybe he thought it was some kind of test. Maybe he understood. Another twitch, when she touched his chest.

She knew better. That was the awful thing. She was ashamed of herself all the way. She was afraid for Catlin and for him and none of it mattered, not for a moment.

She took a hard grip on his shoulder, friend-like. "Florian. Do you know about sex?"

He nodded. Once and emphatically.

"If you did it with me, would Catlin be upset?"

A shake of his head. A deep breath. "Not if you said it was right."

"Would you be upset?"

Another shake of his head. "No, sera."

"Are you sure?"

A deep nod. Another breath. "Yes, sera." Another. "Can I go tell Catlin?"

"Now?"

"If it's going to be a while. She'll worry. I think I ought to tell her."

That was fair. There were complications in everything. "All right," she said. "Come right back."

―――――――――――――――― v ――――――――――――――――

He left sera to sleep, finally—he had slept a little while, but
sera was restless. Sera said she was a little uncomfortable,
and he could go back and sleep in his own bed, she was fine,
she just wanted to sleep now and she wasn't used to company.

So he put his pants on, but he was only going to bed, so he
carried the rest, and slipped out and shut the door.

But Catlin's room had the light on, and Catlin came out
into the hall.

He stopped dead still. He wished he had finished dressing.

She just stood there a moment. So he walked on down as
far as her room, past his own.

"All right?" she asked.

"I think so," he said. Sera was in a little discomfort, he
had hurt sera, necessarily, because sera was built that way:
sera said go on, and she had been happy with him, overall.
He hoped. He truly hoped. "Sera said she wanted to sleep, I
should go to bed. I'll do the manual tomorrow."

Catlin just looked at him, the way she did sometimes when
she was confused, gut-deep open. He did not know what to
say to her. He did not know what she wanted from him.

"How did it feel?"

"Good," he said on an irregular breath. Knowing then
what he was telling her and how her mind had been running
and was running then. Partners. For a lot of years. Catlin was
curious. Some things went past her and she paid no attention.
But if Catlin was interested this far, Catlin wanted to figure it
out, the same way she would take a thing apart to understand
it.

She said finally—he knew she was going to say—: "Can
you show me? You think sera would mind?"

It was not wrong. He would have felt a tape-jolt about it if
it were. He was tired. But if his partner wanted something,
his partner got it, always, forever.

"All right," he said, trying to wake himself up and find
the energy. And came into her room with her.

He undressed. So did she—which felt strange, because
they had always been so modest, as much as they could, even
in the field, and just not looked, if there was no cover.

But he was mostly the one who was embarrassed, because he had always had sex-feelings, he understood that now—while Catlin, who was so much more capable than he was in a lot of ways, missed so much that involved what sera called flux-values.

"Bed," he said, and turned back the covers and got under, because it was a little cold; and because bed was a comfortable, resting kind of place, and he knew Catlin would feel more comfortable about being up against him skin against skin in that context.

So she got in and lay on her side facing him, and got up against him when he told her she should, and relaxed when he told her to, even when he put his hand on her side and his knee between hers. "You let me do everything first," he said, and told her there was a little pain involved, but that was no more than a don't-react where Catlin was concerned. You didn't surprise her in things like that.

"All right," she said.

She *could* react, he found that out very fast, with his fingers.

He stopped. "It gets stronger. You want to keep going with this? Does that feel all right?"

She was thinking about it. Breathing hard. "Fine," she decided.

"You let that get started again," he said, "then you do the same with me. All right? Just like dancing. Variations. All right?"

She drew a deep, deep breath, and she took his advice, until he suddenly felt himself losing control. "Ease up," he said. "Stop."

She did. He managed all right then, finding it smoother with her than with sera—but of course it would be. Catlin would listen, even when it was hard to listen, and he had a far better idea this time what he was doing.

He warned her of things. She was as careful with him as he was with her, not to draw a surprise reaction: he had more confidence in her in that way too.

She did not put a mark on him. Sera had, a lot of them.

He finished; and said, out of breath: "Most I can do, Catlin. Sorry. Second round for me. I'm awfully tired."

She was quiet a minute, out of breath herself. "That was

all right.'' In the thoughtful way she had when she approved of something.

He hugged her, on that warm feeling. She didn't always understand why he did things like that. He didn't think she had understood this time, just that it was temporary reflex, a sex thing, but when he kissed her on the forehead and said he had better get back to his own bed:

"You can stay here," she said, and sort of fitted herself to him puzzle-fashion and gave him a comfortable spot it was just easier not to leave.

They had to get up before sera anyway.

_____ vi _____

Ari woke up at the Minder-call, remembered what she had done last night, and lay there for a minute remembering.

A little scared. A little sore. It had not been quite like the tapes—like real-life, a little awkward. But someone had said—the tape, she thought—that happens; even sex takes practice.

So they were twelve pushing thirteen real hard. Which was young. Her body wasn't through growing, Florian's wasn't. She knew that made a difference.

The tape had said so. "Does Ari have any reference on sex?" Ari asked Base One.

But Base One only gave her the same thing it had always given, and she had read that so often she had it memorized.

She had been irresponsible, completely, last night, that was what kept eating at her. She could have hurt them, and the worst thing was she still could: this morning she was still _on_, —a whole lot cooler and calmer, but sex was just like the tape, hard to remember what it felt like the minute it was over, a damn cheat, leaving just a curiosity, something you kept picking at like a fool picking at a scab to see if it hurt— again.

It was hard to remember a whole lot of things when _that_ got started.

Like responsibility. Like people you cared about.

Like who _you_ were.

Ari senior was right. It messed up your thinking. It *could* take over. Real easy.

Sex is when you're the most vulnerable you'll ever be. Brains is when you're least.

Damn those shots! They're Working me, that's what they're doing, they're Working me and I can't stop it, Dr. Ivanov can pull my license if I don't take them, and I know what they're doing, dammit!

That stuff is still in my bloodstream. I can still feel it. Hormones gone crazy.

And I still want to pull Florian in and try it again like a damn fool.

Fool, fool, fool, Ari Emory!

"Are you all right?" she cornered Florian to ask, before breakfast, in the hallway. Carefully. *Care* about things. It was the only antidote.

"Yes, sera," Florian said, looking anxious—perhaps for being pulled alone out of the kitchen and far down the hall and backed against the wall, perhaps thinking they were going to go through it again.

Calm down. Don't confuse him. You've done enough, fool. She could hear maman, could hear maman clear when she did something stupid—*Dammit, Ollie!* "You're sure. I want you not to try to make me feel good, Florian. If I did something wrong, tell me."

"I'm fine." He took a deep breath. "But, sera, —Catlin and I—she—I—Sera, I slept with her last night. We—did sex too. It felt all right—then. It *was* all right, —wasn't it?"

Surge of hormones. *Bad* temper. Panic. She found her breath coming hard and folded her arms and turned away, looking at the stonework floor a moment until she could jerk herself sideways and back to sense.

Stupid, Ari. Real stupid. Look what's happened.

She's his partner, not me, what in hell am I being jealous for? I did a nasty thing to him and he doesn't even know it's not right.

Oh, dammit, Ari. Dammit!

Flux. That's what sex sets loose. A hell of a flux-state. Hormones. That's what's going on with me.

I wonder if I could write this up for one of Dr. Dietrich's damn papers.

"But she's all right," she said, looking around at Florian—at a painfully worried Florian. "She *is* all right this morning, isn't she? I mean, you don't think it's messed anything up between you. *That's* what I'm worried about."

His face lightened, a cloud leaving. "Oh, no, sera. No. Just—we got to thinking about it— Sera, Catlin was just curious. You know how she is. If it was there she wants to know about it, and if it involved me—she—really needs to know, sera, she really needs to understand what's going on." The frown came back. "Anything I do—is her, too. It has to be."

She put her hand on his arm, took his hand and squeezed it hard. "Of course it does. It's all right. It's *all right*, Florian. I'm only upset if you two are. I don't blame you. I don't care what you did. I only worry I could have hurt you."

"No, sera." He believed everything. He would do anything. He looked terribly relieved. She took his arm through hers and held on to his hand, walking him back down the hall toward the kitchen where rattles and closings of doors said Catlin was busy.

"But Catlin's not as social as you. And sex is a hell of a jolt, Florian, an awful hormone load." *But it's the flux-values it goes crazy with. Flux and feedback loop, brain and hormones interacting. That's what's going on with me. CIT processing. The whole environment fluxing in values. Even Florian doesn't flux-think that heavy.* "It didn't bother her—really?"

"I really don't think so. She said it—was sort of like a good workout."

A little laugh got away from her, just surprise on top of the angst, that left her less worried and more so, in different directions. "Oh, damn. Florian. I don't know everything I ought to. I wish I was azi, sometimes. I do. *Keep* an eye on Catlin. If her reactions aren't up to par, or yours aren't, I want to know it, I want to know it right then—call me if you have to stop an Exercise to do it, hear?"

"Yes, sera."

"I just worry—just worry because I'm responsible, that's all. And experimenting around with us makes me nervous, because I can't go and ask, I just have to try things and I really need you to tell me if I do wrong with you. You object, hear me, you *object* if you think I'm doing something I shouldn't."

"Yes, sera." Automatic as breathing.

They reached the kitchen. Catlin was setting out plates. Catlin looked up at them, a little query in the tension between her brows.

"No troubles with me," Ari said. "Florian told me everything. It's all right."

The tension went away, and Catlin gave one of her real smiles.

"He was real happy," Catlin said, the way she could go straight to the middle of something.

Of course Florian had been happy. His Super took him to bed and told him he was fine; sent him away in a heavy flux-state to deal with a Catlin fluxed as Catlin could get—her Super locking her out of the room and doing something emotional and mysterious with her partner.

So they wake up with *that* load on them.

Fool, Ari. Upset them twice over, for all the wrong reasons. Can I do anything right?

They ate breakfast. Pass the salt. More coffee, sera?— While her stomach stayed upset and she tried to think and look cheerful at the same time.

Then: "Florian," she said, finally. "Catlin."

Two perfectly attentive faces turned to her, open as flowers to light.

"About last night—we're really pretty young yet. Maybe it's good to get experience with each other, so we don't get fluxed too badly if we do it with other people, because it's a way people can Work you. But the last thing we need to do is start Working each other, not meaning to, even if it is fun, because it sure gets through your guard. It got through mine."

It was Catlin she was talking to, most. And Catlin said: "It does that." With her odd laugh, difficult to catch as her true smile. "You could use that."

"You sure could," she said finally, steadier than she had been. The flux diminished, steadily, now that she knew her way. "But it's hard for CITs. *I'm* having flux problems . . . nothing I can't handle. You'll have to get used to me being just a little *on* now and again; it doesn't last, it doesn't hurt me, it's part of sex with CITs, and I know I'm not supposed to discuss my psych problems with you—but now I'm onto it, I've got my balance. Nothing at all unnatural for a CIT. You know a little about it. I can tell you a lot more. I think maybe I should—use *me* for an example, to start with. You aren't used to flux—" Looking straight at Catlin. "Not real strong, anyway. You did fine when Florian got hurt. But that's something you knew about. This is all new, it feels good, and it's an Older thing. Like wine. If you feel uneasy about it, you tell Florian or you tell me, all right?"

"All right," Catlin said, wide-open and very serious. "But Florian's had tape about it already, so he's all right. If he doesn't get a *no* with me it's just something he's the specialist at, that's all. But I can learn it all right."

Trust Catlin. Ari paid earnest attention to her eggs, because Catlin was real good at reading her face, and she came near laughing.

Hormones were still crazy. But the brain was starting to fight back.

The brain has to win out, Ari senior had said. But the little gland at the base of the brain is the seat of a lot of the trouble. It's no accident they're so close together: God has a sense of humor.

----

vii

"We're giving permission," Yanni said, "for Will to assimilate the routine. *I* think—and the board thought—he'd already done it to a certain extent, from the time it started working. With its touch with deep-set values, it's not at all surprising . . . and I agree with the board: it's cause for concern."

Justin looked at the edge of Yanni's desk. Unfocused. "I agree with that," he said finally.

"What do you think about it?"

He drew a breath, hauled himself back out of the mental shadows and looked at Yanni's face—not his eyes. "I think the board's right. I didn't see it in that perspective."

"I mean—what's your view of the problem?"

"I don't know."

"For God's sake, wake *up*, son. Didn't think, don't know, *what in hell's* the matter with you?"

He shook his head. "Tired, Yanni. Just tired."

He waited for the explosion. Yanni leaned forward on his arms and gave a heavy sigh.

"Grant?"

Justin looked at the wall.

"I'm damn sorry," Yanni said. "Son, it's temporary. Look, you want a schedule? He'll get his permit. It's coming."

"Of course it is," he said softly. "Of course it is. Everything's always coming. I know the damn game. I've had it, Yanni. I'm through. I'm tired, Grant's tired. I know Jordan's getting tired." He was close to tears. He stopped talking and just stared, blind, at the wall and the corner where the shelves started. A Downer spirit-stick, set in a case. Yanni had some artistic sense. Or it was a gift from someone. He had wondered that before. He envied Yanni that piece.

"Son."

"Don't call me that!" He wrenched his eyes back to Yanni, breath choking him. "Don't—call me that. I don't want to hear that word."

Yanni stared at him a long time. Yanni could rip him apart. Yanni knew him well enough. And he had given Yanni all the keys, over the years. Given him a major one now, with his reaction.

Even that didn't matter.

"Morley's sent a commendation on your work with young Benjamin," Yanni said. "He says—says your arguments are very convincing. He's going to committee with it."

The Rubin baby. Not a baby now. Aged six—a thin, large-eyed and gentle boy with a lot of health problems and a profound attachment to young Ally Morley. And in some measure—his patient.

So Yanni started hitting him in the soft spots. Predictably. He was not going to come out of this office whole. He had known that when Yanni hauled him in.

He stared at the artifact in the case.

Non-human. A gentle people humans had no right to call primitive. And of course did. And threw them into protectorate.

"Son—Justin. I'm telling you it's a temporary delay. I told Grant that. Maybe six months. No more than that."

"If I—" He was cold for a moment, cold enough at least to talk without breaking down. "If I agreed to go into detention—if I agreed to cooperate with a deep probe—about everything that's ever gone on between myself and Jordan— would that be enough to get Grant his permit?"

Long silence. "I'm not going to give them that offer," Yanni said finally. "Dammit, no."

He shifted his eyes Yanni's way. "I haven't got anything to hide. There's *nothing there*, Yanni, not even a sinful thought—unless you're surprised I'd like to see Reseune Administration in hell. But I wouldn't move to send them there. I've got everything to lose. Too many people do."

"I've got something to lose," Yanni said. "I've got a young man who's not a Special only because Reseune wouldn't dare bring the bill up—wouldn't dare give you that protection."

"That's a piece of garbage."

"I gave you a chance. I've taken risks with you. I didn't say I thought Will's got a problem. I'm saying that testing your routines—may have to absorb Test subjects. By their very nature. Once they've run, it takes mindwipe to remove them. That doesn't mean they're not useful."

Defense Bureau.

Test programs with mindwipe between runs—

"Justin?"

"God. God. I try to help the azi—and I've created a monstrosity for Defense. My God, Yanni—"

"Calm down. Calm down. We're not talking about the Defense Bureau."

"It *will* be. Let them get wind of it—"

"A long way from Applications. Calm down."

It's my work. Without me—they can't. If something happened to me—they can't—not for a long while.

Oh, damn, all the papers, all my notes—

Grant. . . .

"Reseune doesn't give away its processes," Yanni said reasonably, rationally. "It's not in question."

"Reseune's in *bed* with Defense. They have been, ever since Giraud got the Council seat."

Ever since Ari died. Ever since her successors sold out—sold out everything she stood for.

God, I wish—wish she was still alive.

The kid—doesn't have a chance.

"Son, —I'm sorry, Justin. Habit. —Listen to me. I see your point. I can see it very clearly. It worries me too."

"Are we being taped, Yanni?"

Yanni bit his lip, and touched a button on his desk. "Now we're not."

"Where's the tape?"

"I'll take care of it."

"Where's the damn tape, Yanni?"

"Calm down and listen to me. I'm willing to work with you. Blank credit slip. Let me ask you something. Your psych profile says suicide isn't likely. But answer me honestly: is it something you ever think about?"

"No." His heart jumped, painfully. It was a lie. And not. He thought about it then. And lacked whatever it took. Or had no reason sufficient, yet. *God, what does it take? Do I have to see the kids walking into the fire before I feel enough guilt? It's too late then. What kind of monster am I?*

"Let me remind you—you'd kill Grant. And your father. Or worse—they'd live with it."

"Go to hell, Yanni."

"You think other researchers didn't ask those questions?"

"Carnath and Emory built Reseune! You think ethics ever bothered that pair?"

"You think ethics didn't bother Ari?"

"Sure. Like Gehenna."

"The colony lived. Lived, when every single CIT died. Emory's work, damned right. The azi survived."

"In squalor. In abominable conditions—like damned *primitives*—"

"*Through* squalor. Through catastrophes that peeled away every advantage they came with. The culture on that planet is an azi culture. And they're unique. You forget the human brain, Justin. Human ingenuity. The will to live. You can send an azi soldier into fire—but he's more apt than his CIT counterpart to turn to his sergeant and ask what the gain is. And the sergeant had better have an answer that makes sense to him. You should take a look at the military, Justin. You have a real phobia about that, pardon the eetee psych. They do deal with extreme stress situations. The military sets will walk into fire. But an azi who's too willing to do that is a liability and an azi who likes killing is worse. You take a look at reality before you panic. Look at our military workers down there. They're damned good. Damned polite, damned competent, damned impatient with foul-ups, damned easy to Super as long as they think you're qualified, and capable of relaxing when they're off, unlike some of our assembly-line over-achievers. Look at the reality before you start worrying. Look at the specific types."

"These are survivors too," Justin said. "The ones who outlived the War."

"Survival rate among azi is higher than CITs, fifteen something percent. I have no personal compunction about the azi. They're fine. They like themselves fine. Your work may have real bearing on CIT psych, in behavioral disorders. A lot of applications, if it bears out. We deal with humanity. And tools. You can kill a man with a laser. You can save a life with it. It doesn't mean we shouldn't have lasers. Or edged blades. Or hammers. Or whatever. But I'm damned glad we have lasers, or I'd be blind in my right eye. You understand what I'm saying?"

"Old stuff, Yanni."

"I mean, do you *understand* what I'm saying? Inside?"

"Yes." True. His instincts grabbed after all the old arguments like he was a baby going for a blanket. About as mature. About as capable of sorting out the truth. Damn. Hand a man a timeworn excuse and he went after it to get the pain to stop. Even knowing the one who handed it to him was a psych operator.

"Besides," Yanni said, "you're a man of principle. And humans don't stop learning things, just because they might be risky: if this insight of yours is correct you're only a few decades ahead of someone else finding it on his own. And who knows, that researcher might not have your principles—or your leverage."

"Leverage! I can't get my brother a visit with his father!"

"You can get a hell of a lot if you work it right."

"Oh, *dammit*! Are we down to sell-outs, now? Are we through doing morality today?"

"Your brother. Grant's a whole lot of things with you. Isn't he?"

"Go to hell!"

"Not related to you. I merely point out you do an interesting double value set there. You're muddy in a lot of sensitive areas—including a little tendency to suspect every success you have, a tendency to see yourself perpetually as a nexus defined by other people—Jordan's son, Grant's—brother, Administration's hostage. Less as a human being than as a focus of all these demands. *You* have importance, Justin, unto yourself. You're a man thirty—thirty-one years old. Time you asked yourself what Justin is."

"We *are* into eetee psych, aren't we?"

"I'm handing it out free today. You're not responsible for the universe. You're not responsible for a damn thing that flows from things you didn't have the capacity to control. Maybe you *are* responsible for finding out what you *could* control, if you wanted to, if you'd stop looking at other people's problems and start taking a look at your own capabilities—which, as I say, probably qualify you as a Special. Which also answers a lot of questions about why you *have* problems: lack of adequate boundaries. *Lack* of them, son. All the Specials have the problem. It's real hard to understand humanity when you keep attributing to everyone around you the complexity of your own thinking. You have quite a few very bright minds around you—enough to keep you convinced that's ordinary. Jordan's, particularly: he's got the age advantage, doesn't he, and you've always confused him with God. You think about it. You know all this with the Rubin kid. Apply it closer to home. Do us all a favor."

"Why don't you just explain what you want me to do? I'm real tired, Yanni. I give. You name it, I'll do it."

"Survive."

He blinked. Bit his lip.

"Going to break down on me?" Yanni asked.

The haze was gone. The tears were gone. He was only embarrassed, and mad enough to break Yanni's neck.

Yanni smiled at him. Smug as hell.

"I could kill you," Justin said.

"No, you couldn't," Yanni said. "It's not in your profile.

You divert everything inward. You'll never quite cure that tendency. It's what makes you a lousy clinician and a damned good designer. *Grant* can survive the stress—if you don't put it on him. Hear me?''

"Yes."

"Thought so. So don't do it. Go back to your office and tell him I'm putting his application through again."

"I'm not going to. It's getting too sensitive. *He's* hurting, Yanni. I can't take that."

Yanni bit his lip. "All right. Don't tell him. Do you understand *why* it's a problem, Justin? They're afraid of the military grabbing him."

"God. *Why?*"

"Power move. You can tell him that. I'm not supposed to tell you. I'm breaking security. There's a rift in Defense. There's a certain faction that's proposing the nationalization of Reseune. That's the new move. Lu's health is going. Rejuv failure. He's got at most a couple more years. Gorodin is becoming increasingly isolated from the Secretariat in Defense. He may get a challenge to his seat. That hasn't happened since the war. An election in the military. There's the head of Military Research, throwing more and more weight behind the head of Intelligence. Khalid. Vladislaw Khalid. If you're afraid of something, Justin, —be afraid of that name. That faction could *use* an incident. So could Gorodin's. Fabricated, would serve just as well. You're in danger. Grant— more so. All they have to do is arrest him at the airport, claim he was carrying documents—God knows what. Denys will have my head for telling you this. *I* wanted to keep you out of it, not disrupt your work with it—Grant's not getting a travel pass right now. *You* couldn't get one. That's the truth. Tell Grant—if it helps. For God's sake—tell him somewhere private."

"You mean they *are* bugging us."

"I don't know. I can answer for in here. We're off the record right now."

"You *say* we are—"

"I *say* we are. If Gorodin survives the election we're sure is going to be called—you'll be safer. If not—nothing is safe. We'll lose our majority in Council. After that I don't lay bets *what* will stay safe. If we lose our A.T. status, so will Planys. You understand me?"

"I understand you." The old feeling settled back again. Game resumed. He felt sick at his stomach. And a hell of a lot steadier with things as-they-were. "If you're telling me the truth—"

"If I'm telling you the truth you'd better wake up and take care of yourself. Next few years are going to be hell, son. Real hell. Lu's going to die. It's an appointive post. Lu could resign, but that's no good. Whoever gets in can appoint a new Secretary. Lu's wrecking his health, holding on, trying to handle the kind of infighting he's so damn good at. Gorodin's in space too much. Too isolate from his command structure. Lu's trying to help Gorodin ride out the storm—but Lu's ability to pay off political debtors is diminishing rapidly, the closer he comes to the wall. He's balancing factions within his own faction. Question is—how long can he stay alive—in either sense?"

viii

The Filly made the circuit of the barn arena again, flaring her nostrils and blowing, and Ari watched her, watched Florian, so sure and so graceful on the Filly's back.

Beside her, arms folded, Catlin watched—so did Andy, and a lot of the AG staff. Not the first time any of them had seen Florian and the Filly at work, but it was the first time the AG staff and Administration was going to let *her* try it. Uncle Denys was there—uncle Giraud was in Novgorod, where he spent most of his time nowadays: they were having an election—a man named Khalid was running against Gorodin, of Defense, and everybody in Reseune was upset about it. *She* was, since what she heard about Khalid meant another court fight if he did what he was threatening to do. But an election took months and months for all the results to get in from the ends of everywhere in space, and uncle Denys took time out of his schedule to come down to the barn: he had insisted if she was going to break anything he wanted to be there to call the ambulance this time. Amy Carnath was there; and so was Sam; and 'Stasi and Maddy and Tommy. It made

Ari a little nervous. She had never meant her first try with the Filly to turn into an Occasion, with so much audience.

Florian had been working the Filly and teaching her for months—had even gone so far as to make a skill tape, patched himself up with sensors from head to foot while he put the Filly through every move she could make, and kept a pocket-cam focused right past her ears—all to teach *her* how to keep her balance and how to react to the Filly's moves. It was as close to riding as she had come until today. It felt wonderful.

Uncle Giraud said, being uncle Giraud, that tape had real commercial possibilities.

Florian brought the Filly back quite nicely, to a little oh and a little applause from the kids—which upset the Filly and made her throw her head. But she calmed down, and Florian climbed down very sedately and held the reins out to her.

"Sera?" he said. Ari took a breath and walked up to him and the Filly.

She had *warned* everybody to be quiet. It was a deathly hush now. Everyone was watching; and she so wanted to do things right and not embarrass herself or scare anyone.

"Left foot," Florian whispered, in case she forgot. "I'll lead her just a little till you get the feel of it, sera."

She had to stretch to reach the stirrup. She got it and got the saddle and got on without disgracing herself. The Filly moved then with Florian leading, and all of a sudden she felt the tape, felt the motion settle right where muscle and bone knew it should, just an easy give.

She felt like crying, and clamped her jaw tight, because she was not going to do that. Or look like a fool, with Florian leading her around. "I've got it," she said. "Give me the reins, Florian."

He stopped the Filly and passed them over the Filly's head for her. He looked terribly anxious.

"*Please*, sera, don't let her get away from you. She's nervous with all these people."

"I've got her," she said. "It's all right."

And she was very prudent, starting the Filly off at a sedate walk, letting the Filly get used to her being up instead of Florian, when for months and months she had had to stand at the rail and watch Florian get to ride—and watch Florian take a few falls too, figuring out what nobody this side of old Earth knew how to do. Once the Filly had fallen, a terrible spill, and Florian had been out for a few seconds, just absolutely limp; but he had gotten up swearing it was not the Filly, she had lost her footing, he had felt it—and he had staggered over and hugged the Filly and gotten back on while she and Catlin stood there with their hands clenched.

Now she took the Filly away from him, for the Filly's really public coming-out, and she knew Florian was sweating and suffering every step she took—knowing sera could be a fool; the way Catlin was probably doing the same, knowing if anything went wrong it was only Florian stood a chance of doing anything.

She was fourteen today; and she had too much audience to be a fool. She was amazingly sensible, she rode the Filly at a walk and kept her at a walk, anxious as the Filly started trying to move—no, Florian had said: if she tries to break and pick her own pace, don't let her do that, she's not supposed to, and she's bad about that.

Florian had told her every tiny move the Filly tended to make, and where she could lose her footing, and where she tried to get her own way.

So she just stopped that move the instant the Filly tried it, *not* easy, no, the Filly had a trick of stretching her neck against the rein and going like she was suddenly half-*G* for a few paces: she was glad she had not let the Filly run the first time she was up on her; but the Filly minded well enough when she made her.

It was not, of course, the show she wanted to make. She wanted to come racing up at a dead run and give everyone a real scare; but that was Florian's part, Florian got to do that: *she* got to be responsible.

She passed her audience, so self-conscious she could hardly stand it—she *hated* being responsible; and uncle Denys was probably still nervous. She came around to where Florian was standing by the rail, and stopped the Filly there, because he was walking out to talk to her.

"How am I?" she asked.

"Fine," he said. "Tap her once with your heels when she's walking, just a little. Keep the reins firm. That's the next pace. Don't let her get above it yet. Don't ever let her do it if you don't tell her.''

''Right,'' she said; and started the Filly up, one tap, then a second.

The Filly liked that. Her ears came up, and she hit a brisk pace that was harder to stay with, but Ari found it. Her body suddenly began to tape-remember what to do with faster moves, found its balance, found everything Florian had given her.

She wanted to cut free, O God, she wanted to go through the rest of it and so did the Filly, but she kept that pace which the Filly found satisfactory enough and pulled up to a very impressive stop right in front of Andy and Catlin. The Filly was sweating—excitement, that was all; and stamped and shifted after she had gotten down and Andy was holding her.

Everyone was impressed. Uncle Denys was positively pale, but he was doing awfully well, all the same.

Amy and the rest wanted to try too, but Andy said it was best not to have too many new riders all at once: the Filly would get out of sorts. Florian said they could come when he was exercising the Filly and they could do it one at a time, if they wanted to.

Besides, Florian said, the best way to learn about horses was to work with them. The Mare was going to birth again and they were doing two completely different genotypes in the tanks; which would be seven horses in all—no longer Experimentals, but officially Working Animals.

Of which the Filly was the first. Ari patted her—good and solid: the Filly liked to know you were touching her; and got horse smell all over her, but she loved it; she loved everything; she even gave uncle Denys a hug.

''You were very brave,'' she said to uncle Denys when she did it, and on impulse, kissed him on the cheek and gave him a wicked smile, getting horse smell on him too. ''Your favorite guinea pig *didn't* break her neck.''

Uncle Denys looked thoroughly off his balance. But she had whispered it.

''Even her inflections,'' he said, putting her off hers. ''God. Sometimes you're uncanny, young woman.''

_____ ix _____

"That's it," Justin said as the Cyteen election results flashed up on the screen, and: "Vid off," to the Minder. "Khalid."

Grant shook his head, and said nothing for a long while. Then: "Well, it's a crazy way to do business."

"Defense contractors in the Trade bureau, in Finance."

"Reseune has ties there too."

"It's still going to be interesting."

Grant bowed his head and passed a hand over his neck, just resting there a moment. Thinking, surely—that it was going to be a long while, a *long* while before either of them traveled again.

Or thinking worse thoughts. Like Jordan's safety.

"It's not like—" Justin said, "they could just ram things through and get that nationalization. The other Territories will come down on Reseune's side in this one. And watch Giraud change footing. He's damned good at it. He *is* Defense, for all practical purposes. I never saw a use for the man. But, God, we may have one."

_____ x _____

It was one of the private, *private* parties, weekend, the gang off from school and homework, and the Rule was, no punch and no cake off the terrazzo areas, and if anybody wanted to do sex they went to the guest room or the sauna, and if they started getting silly-drunk they went to the sauna room and took cold showers until they sobered up.

So far the threat of showers had been enough.

They had Maddy, 'Stasi, Amy, Tommy, Sam, and a handful of new kids, 'Stasi's cousins Dan and Mischa Peterson, only Dan was Peterson-Nye and Mischa was Peterson—which was one brother set, whose maman would have *killed* them if she smelled alcohol on them, but that just made them careful; and two sets of cousins, which was Amy and Tommy Carnath; and 'Stasi and Dan and Mischa. Dan and Mischa were fifteen and fourteen, but that was all right, they got along, and they did everything else but drink.

In any case they were even, boys and girls, and Amy and

Sam were a set, and Dan and Mischa both got off with Maddy, and 'Stasi and Tommy Carnath were a set; which worked out all right.

Mostly they were real polite, very quiet parties. They had a little punch or a little wine, the rowdiest they ever got was watching E-tapes, mostly the ones the kids' mothers would kill them for, and when they got a little drunk they sat around in the half-dark while the tapes were running and did whatever came to mind until they had to make a choice between the Rule and finishing the tape.

"Oh, hell," Ari said finally, this time when Maddy asked, "do it on the landing, who cares?"

She was a little drunk herself. A lot tranked. She had her blouse open, she felt the draft and finally she settled against Florian to watch the tape. Sam and Amy came back, very prim and sober, and gawked at what was going on next to the bar. While 'Stasi and Tommy were still in the sauna room.

Mostly she just watched—the tapes or what the other kids were doing; which kept Florian and Catlin out of it.

"*You have a message,*" the Minder said over the tape soundtrack and the music.

"Oh, hell." She got up again, shrugged the blouse back together and walked up the steps barefooted, down the hall rug and into her office as steadily as she could.

"Base One," she said, when she had the door shut and proof against the noise outside in the den. "Message."

"*Message from Denys Nye: Khalid won election. Meet with me tomorrow first thing in my office.*"

Oh, shit.

She leaned against the back of the chair.

"Message for Denys Nye," she said. "I'll be there."

The Minder took it. "Log-off," she said, and walked back outside and into her party.

"What was it?" Catlin asked.

"Tell you later," she said, and settled down again, leaning back in Florian's lap.

She showed up in Denys' office, 0900 sharp, no frills and no nonsense, took a cup of Denys' coffee, with cream, no sugar, and listened to Denys tell her what she had already figured out, with the Silencer jarring the roots of her teeth.

"Khalid is assuming office this afternoon," Denys said. "Naturally—since he's Cyteen based, there's no such thing as a grace period. He moves in with all his baggage. And his secret files."

Uncle Denys had already explained to her—what Khalid was. What the situation could be.

"Don't you think I'd better have vid access?" she asked. "Uncle Denys, I don't care *what* you think I'm not ready to find out. Ignorant is no help at all, is it?"

Uncle Denys rested his chins on his hand and looked at her a long time as if he was considering that. "Eventually. Eventually you'll have to. You're going to get a current events condensation, daily, the same as I get. You'd better keep up with it. It looks very much as if we're going to get a challenge before this session is out. They'll probably release some things on your predecessor—as damaging as they can find. This is going to be dirty politics, Ari. Real dirty. I want you to start studying up on things. Additionally—I want you to be damned careful. I know you've been doing a lot of—" He gave a little cough. "—entertaining. Of kids none of whom is over fifteen, at hours that tell me you're *not* playing Starchase. Housekeeping says my suspicions are—" Another clearing of the throat. "—probably well-founded."

"God. You're stooping, uncle Denys."

"Security investigates all sources. And my clearance still outranks yours. But let's not quibble. That's not my point. My point is—*ordinary* fourteen- and fifteen-year-olds don't have your—independence, your maturity, or your budget; and Novgorod in particular isn't going to understand your— mmmn, parties, your language—in short, we're all being very circumspect. You know that word?"

"I'm up on *circumspect*, uncle Denys, right along with *security risk*. I don't have any. If their mothers know, they're not going to object, because they want their offspring to have careers when *I'm* running Reseune. There are probably a lot of mothers who'd like to shove their kids right *into* my apartment. And my bed."

"God. *Don't* say that in Novgorod."

"Am I going?"

"Not right now. Not anytime soon. Khalid is just in. Let him make a move."

"Oh, that's a *wonderful* idea."

"Don't get smart, sera. Let him draw the line, I say. While you, young sera, do some catch-up studying. You'd better learn what an average fourteen-year-old is like."

"I know. I know real well. I might know better, if my friends hadn't Disappeared to Fargone, mightn't I?"

"Don't do this for the cameras. You think you're playing a game. I'm telling you you can really lose everything. I've explained nationalization—"

"I do fine with big words."

"Let's see how you do with little ones. You're not sweet little Ari for the cameras anymore, you're more and more like the Ari certain people remember—enough to make it a lot more likely you'll get harder and harder questions, and you don't know where the mines are, young sera. We're going to stall this as long as we can, and if we can get you another year, it's very likely you'll have to apply for your majority status. That's the point at which some interest will get an injunction to stop the Science Bureau granting it; and you'll be in court again . . . with a good chance of winning it: the first Ari did at sixteen. But that *won't* solve the problem, it'll only put the opposition in a bad light, taking on a fifteen-year-old who *has* to handle herself with more finesse than you presently have, young sera."

"I learn."

"You'd better. Age is catching up with us. Your predecessor's friend Catherine Lao, who's helped you more than you know—is a hundred thirty-eight. Giraud is pushing a hundred thirty. Your presence—your *resemblance* to your predecessor—is like a shot of adrenaline where certain Councillors are concerned, but you have to have more than presence this time. If you make a mistake—you can see Reseune sucked up by the national government, and Defense declaring it a military zone, right fast. They'll have a pretext before the ink is dry. You'll spend your days working on whatever they tell you to do. Or you'll find yourself in some little enclave with no access to Novgorod, no access to Council or the Science Bureau."

She looked at Denys straight on, thinking: *You haven't done that well. Or how else are we in this mess?*

But she didn't say it. She said: "Base One only lets me go so fast, uncle Denys."

"Let me try you on another big word," Denys said. "Psychogenesis."

That *was* a new one. "Mind-originate," she said, remembering her Greek roots.

"Mind-origination. Mind-cloning. Now do you understand me?"

She felt cold inside. "What has that got to do with anything?"

"The resemblance between you and Ari. Let me give you a few more words to try on your Base. Bok. Endocrinology. Gehenna. Worm."

"What are you talking about? *What do you mean, the resemblance—*"

The sound-shielding hurt her teeth.

"Don't shout," Denys said. "You'll deafen us. I mean just what I've always told you. You *are* Ari. Let me tell you something else. Ari didn't die of natural causes. She was murdered."

She took in a breath. "By who?"

"Whom, dear."

"Dammit, uncle Denys—"

"Watch your language. You'd better clean it up. Ari was killed by someone no longer at Reseune."

"She died *here*?"

"That's all I'm going to tell you. The rest is your problem."